The Undercover Secretary

BOOKS BY ELLIE MIDWOOD

ELLIE MIDWOOD

The Undercover Secretary

bookouture

PROLOGUE

LYON, FRANCE. JULY 1942

The blindfold was finally taken off my eyes. I rubbed them against the blinding light of the lamp—the only source of illumination in the dark, moldy cellar I'd been taken to. Slowly, feature by stern, unforgiving feature, a man's face came into focus. Dark, unshaven, full of shadows and ruthlessness, he regarded me for a very long time while I sat, dizzy and disoriented, in the rickety chair across the table from him.

"How did you find us?" he finally asked.

A Frenchman; local, not a capital import.

"I was looking." My voice sounded like a crow's, hoarse and alien. I hadn't drunk in what seemed like days, avoiding forest streams, due to the doubtful water, and village wells, out of fear of someone spotting and reporting me. Towns and cities were out of the question altogether. Not with my German accent and the absence of any identification papers, at any rate.

"A smart mouth, aren't you? Do you know what we do with smart little Nazis like you?" The Frenchman produced a long hunting knife and turned it deliberately in his great paws. Its blade glistened menacingly in the light of the lamp, but I was too exhausted, both mentally and physically, to be intimidated by such trifles as death.

"You can kill me right this instant. Honestly, it makes no difference to me. I've already lost all I had to lose and my life at this point matters little. All I'm here for is revenge. So, you can give me that glass of water, a cigarette, and listen to my story, or just get it over with right away if you truly believe I'm a German spy. Frankly, it's all the same to me."

He rose from his chair and lingered over me for an interminably long moment, the knife still in his hand. I let him examine me with his penetrating gaze. I had nothing to hide and, like I said, nothing to lose.

I still haven't the faintest idea what it was precisely that he saw in my eyes. All I know is that he turned on his heel, left the cellar and returned soon after with an aluminum mug filled with water. I downed it in one go.

"Now, speak."

"What about my cigarette?"

"They're rationed. You haven't earned one yet."

I almost felt like laughing. I was beginning to like this *Resistant*.

"Where do you want me to begin?"

"From the beginning."

I pondered the request and nodded slowly.

"In that case, I'll start with the beginning of the end."

The end of life as I'd known it, before it had been ripped away from me.

I wetted my lips and took a deep breath.

"I lived in Berlin back then. It was the winter of 1933. Hitler had been in power for almost a year. I worked as a sales-girl and just the manner in which the customer..."

ONE

BERLIN. FEBRUARY 1933

...Just the manner in which the customer marched toward my counter spelled trouble. Built like an outhouse, square and squat, she bore through the aisles of clothes like a great warship, all guns trained on me, a nameless salesgirl. Smoothing my uniform—a blue robe with the store's name embroidered over my heart—I pulled my face into a mask of servitude. This, too, was the uniform I wore. The customer is always right and all that rot.

"Good afternoon. How may I be of service to you to—"

"Just look at what you sold me!" She opened fire without allowing me as much as to finish my greeting. Her face a picture of indignation, she unraveled the bundle she'd brought with her and hurled a fur coat, with its silk lining undone, onto the counter.

I hadn't sold her anything—Wally, who worked the Tuesday and Thursday shifts, must have done—but I had long ago grown used to customers instantly forgetting the face of the salesperson who had assisted them with their purchase before they'd even set foot outside the store.

With the customer's pale blue eyes boring into me, I examined the coat from top to bottom. It was a handsome affair, one of our most expensive ones, silver blue mink with a standing collar and buttons made of Czech rhinestones. Sometimes, just before closing, Wally and I took turns trying them on in a fitting room in the back while the other stood watch. We would never be able to afford these coats with our meager earnings, but no one could stop us from wrapping ourselves in these unimaginable luxuries and pretending, just for five minutes, that the world belonged to us. These coats produce such an effect as one drapes them over their shoulders; passes their hand through the silky hairs; buries one's cheek in a collar and feels as though a hundred baby minks curl into them with their warm bodies.

Aside from the undone lining, the coat was immaculate. Divine.

I looked at the woman in front of me. "I would love to help you, but I don't understand what seems to be the problem. The lining couldn't have been undone when you purchased it. Our manager inspects each garment personally and he'd never allow anything of this sort into the showroom."

"Naturally, it wasn't undone, you daft girl!"

I thought this was coming. With my head patiently inclined to one side, I waited for further explanation. Or insults. Most likely a mix of both.

"I undid it because I heard from a friend of mine how a Jewish sales assistant swindled her and tried the same trick on her! She told me what to look out for and, boy, am I glad I did!" She narrowed her eyes, inspecting me closely. "What is your name?"

"Dora," I replied evenly.

"Your *last* name, girl."

This hadn't come as a surprise either.

"Davidsohn."

"Aha!" the woman shrieked, pointing a finger at me as though she'd just uncovered a wanted criminal. "I *knew* it! All you Jews are liars and swindlers! Take that coat back and return me my money before I call the police on you!"

"*Gnädige Frau*," I began, trying to ignore her wildly rolling eyes and the huffs and puffs coming from her flaring nostrils, "I will gladly process your return, but I need a reason for it. What seems to be the trouble with it?"

"The blasted cheek on you, asking me what the trouble is!"

The calmer I remained, the madder she was growing, as if her inability to rattle me was a personal insult of sorts.

A couple wandered into the store; heard the screams and hesitated. Over the fuming customer's shoulder, I offered the man an apologetic smile. He appeared much more uncomfortable than his wife, or lady friend, who was presently craning her long white neck, her eyes sparkling brilliantly at the prospect of free entertainment.

"I demand you return my money this instant, you swindling Jew!"

"I'm afraid I can't process your refund if you don't give me a reason."

"Look at her!" She swung round in search of support. To her great satisfaction, she had at least a two-person audience. "She refuses to give me my money back; that's theft. I'm calling the police!"

"If you need a phone, the payphone is located on the corner of the street," I said, pointing a helpful hand in the direction.

That last remark sent her entirely over the edge. She began screaming something frightful, hurling every possible insult at me that she could conceive—or borrow from the speeches of the Nazi Party leaders. Not even a couple of months ago, Berlin's left-wing Red Front, as the German Communist party was called among the population, had booed them out of beer halls, but after that fellow with an odd mustache—Hitler—had won the elections last January, the communists had sewn their Party membership cards into their mattresses. Social Democrats had grown quiet too after quite a few of their prominent leaders had been arrested. Now, all that was pouring from the radio speakers was nationalistic speeches and propaganda, and people like this woman were only too glad to lap it up.

Alerted by her screams, no doubt, Herr Lafler, our immediate supervisor, came out to investigate. His small office was all the way in the back, tucked in between a vast storage room and a cleaner's closet that doubled as our break room; ordinarily, he spent his days there doing accounting and placing new orders in perfect peace and quiet. The woman's shrieks must have been loud indeed if even he had heard her from his cozy little hideout.

Pudgy and pleasant-looking, with a harmless round face and soft mustache, he paused near the counter, squinting at us through the thick lenses of his horn-rimmed glasses. A terrifyingly efficient manager, he scarcely ever dealt with customers, preferring the company of catalogues and balance sheets to people. That task he left entirely to us, his salesgirls. After all, we were all well-trained and professional, graduates of the commercially oriented *Handelsschule*—business schools. The store owners' standards were high. They wouldn't just hire anyone from the street. We'd been trained to deal with any sort of customer relations and conflicts, Wally and Trudi—here in Berlin; I—back in my native Essen. We'd never faced issues we couldn't resolve on our own. Therefore, Herr Lafler's confusion at the present situation was very much justified.

"Is there anything I may assist you with?" he asked the woman after greeting her.

"Yes. This Jew"—another annihilating look in my direction —"won't give me my money back for the defective coat she sold me."

"Defective?" Herr Lafler pulled back as though she'd just slapped him. I didn't lie; he truly took pride in personally inspecting all of the new arrivals and could swear by their impeccable quality. "What do you mean, defective?" This time, the question was aimed at me.

"This was Wally's sale," I said, pulling the thick ledger from under the counter with all the sales and their dates written down. "*Gnädige Frau* won't kindly tell me what the defect is, though."

The woman gasped in indignation. "Do you see the insolence on her?" She turned to Herr Lafler, who only blinked at her like an owl once again. "Look at it. Look at the coat closely."

Wary of her frame that was towering over him, Herr Lafler still obliged.

"The lining couldn't have been undone at the point of sale —" he began, only to be interrupted by a wave of angry spluttering.

"The issue is not with the lining! Look under it. Do you see? That Jew sold me a coat made out of some pelt cuts, some... rejects!" The woman screamed, her entire body trembling. "I want a coat made out of a good cut of fur, with seams only along the sleeves and neck, as they ought to be. I'm not wearing something made out of some... rat tails!"

As the realization dawned on me, I bit into my bottom lip in order not to burst out laughing. "*Gnädige Frau*," I began, "all of the mink coats are made this way. You shall never find a mink coat made out of a whole piece because minks are very small animals. Their pelts are put together to create an impression of a seamless cut, but they're still small pelts and—"

"Do you think I'm an idiot, you impudent Jew?" She'd gone beet-red in the face.

I said nothing in response.

"I demand my money back," she said, addressing Herr Lafler this time, "and I want her fired immediately."

This time, Herr Lafler pulled himself up visibly. He might have had the appearance of a harmless accountant, with his thick lenses, a small pouch and soft white hands, but, whenever it came to us salesgirls, he was a protective mother hen who would peck any attacker to death before they got to his little chicks.

"*Gnädige Frau*, I can't process your return on the grounds of the reason for your claim. The coat is not defective, as Fräulein Davidsohn, my sales representative, has just explained to you. And I certainly won't terminate her employment solely because you aren't satisfied with the perfectly good product. Now, is there anything else I can help you with?"

The woman went so very pale and still, I began to worry that an explosion would follow and this time it would be Herr Lafler who would find himself on the receiving end of her magisterial wrath.

Instead, the woman swept the coat from the counter, made an about-face and marched toward the exit.

Just as I was about to release a breath of relief, she swung round on her heel and gave me a last withering glare. "You shall hear from me again."

"Thank you kindly for your business," I responded with a professional smile. "Have a wonderful day."

Herr Lafler regarded me with an expression of a proud father, nodded and disappeared back into his office, leaving the store once again in my hands.

I had all but forgotten about the couple who were lingering in between the clothes racks, until the husband materialized in front of my counter with a cashmere scarf in his hands.

"Did she really just say that she wanted a mink coat made out of a whole piece?"

His wife, too, broke into conspiratorial giggles as she deposited silk stockings and a few narrow neck scarves of different colors on the counter. "Do you often get such complaints?"

"You'd be amazed," I confessed and rang them in, quietly smiling to myself.

TWO

Later that evening, I opened the door to the room I was renting with Ashley and Amory, fully expecting to find them dressing to go out. Strikingly handsome—or beautiful?—the two men had made their name in certain circles of bohemian Berlin by performing their famous duets switching genders for each number with such stunning ease, the public was going mad for them. They had the looks for it, too: Ashley, with his glossy raven pageboy cut that he slicked back whenever he performed in a tuxedo, and Amory, with his golden locks and angelic blue eyes, slightly wide-set and bearing a look of youthful purity and innocence in contrast to the dark, smoldering gaze of his counterpart. But despite their stark differences in coloring, they shared the same fluidity, the same wonderfully androgynous manner that permitted them to be whoever they wished whenever they wished and had earned them such wild success with the public.

When I had first arrived in Berlin and discovered their advertisement for a room for rent in one of the newspapers, I, myself, had initially mistaken Ashley for a woman and, rather to

my embarrassment, addressed him as a *gnädige Frau*. It was an
honest mistake on my part; he'd opened the door to me, an innocent Jewish girl from Essen who hadn't seen anyone remotely
like him in my very traditional hometown. He was dressed in a
pale lavender Japanese kimono and leaning against the door-
frame with his long, beautiful arms folded over his chest, very
tall, half-starved just as fashion had it, with traces of mascara
still visible under his beautiful, smoldering eyes that assessed
me from head to toe like only women can, with a slightly catty
look about them. He had stood in the same pose while I was
stumbling over my explanations about the ad and wondering to
myself whether this Ashley was a model or an actress or some
such, until Amory had pushed Ashley out of the way and
hustled me inside.

"Don't pay heed to him. He's hungover and still half-asleep
and it's best not to disturb him until midday. Your rent shall be
thirty marks, if you decide to stay." I was wondering why
anyone would even consider not staying here for such a steal,
and in the center of Berlin, no less, at the very heart of Kurfürs-
tendamm, when Amory had smiled at me and announced,
causing me to blink in astonishment momentarily, "Ashley and
Amory are our stage names. We're actually Dolf and Heinrich.
But English names are all the rage now and, besides, they fit
both genders. And we perform as women as often as men. So, if
you're uncomfortable with that, we fully understand. And
please, forgive us for wasting your time in making you come
over here, but we can't just announce it in a newspaper, as you
can very well imagine."

Uncomfortable was the furthest thing from my mind at that
point. I was fresh out of school, new in Berlin, and it all was so
perfectly exotic, so perfectly delightful to me that I had handed
Amory the money for three months in advance, and I hadn't
regretted my decision once.

It had been Ashley who had taught me how to apply makeup just the right way; how to style my hair and transform myself into someone who I always wished to be. A professional and polished salesgirl during the day; a red-lipped and half-undressed flapper at night. A bare-faced someone-in-between on my days off, with my nose in a book in the Tiergarten or the zoo, or someone sophisticated, who knew how to hold a cigarette just right and how to nod gravely as I discussed international affairs with a progressive Berliner who supported Women's Lib.

It had been Amory who had accompanied me to art galleries and introduced me to van Gogh and Picasso, and dragged me to some very suspicious affair calling itself a theater to see Brecht's *Rise and Fall of the City of Mahagonny*, which had been banned as soon as the Nazis took power. It was thanks to Amory and his exceptional taste in literature and art that I discovered Mann and attended Dadaist performances in the short span of a few months, before it had all been purged, banned, announced amoral and contrary to German traditions and utterly disgusting... much like Ashley and Amory themselves.

I thought it was a miracle that their act hadn't been banned but merely booed by the few rare Brownshirts in the audience. I thought it was a miracle that nothing had changed much after Hitler had come to power. Their schedule was still fully booked and we still scarcely saw each other on the nights they worked at their cabaret. I came home when they were about to leave and left when they were still sleeping.

So, tonight, I opened the door fully expecting to find Ashley and Amory dressing to go out. Instead, I discovered my room-mates half-draped in their silk kimonos, surprisingly unshaved and with hair still bearing grease from last night's performance, drinking something straight out of the bottle they were passing each other. The room itself bore a faint smell of smoke, but perhaps the overflowing ashtray in front of them was the reason for that.

"Aren't you going to be late for work?" I asked by way of greeting.

A dark suspicion that something was terribly wrong was already churning inside my stomach, contracting its walls, squeezing my throat with its vise-like grip. But out of sheer fear to give in to it, I still teased them in the same tone we had adopted toward each other a long time ago, still smiled as I kicked my shoes off and dropped onto the carpet next to them and demanded the bottle for myself.

"Is that the brandy your admirer gave you for Christmas?" I nudged Amory's foot with mine. "Unseemly to pop it open without your roommate, you know."

He handed it to me, staring drunkenly into nothing.

I took a swig—liquid courage, which burned my insides but dulled the anxiety beating drums in my ears, sending blood pounding to my temples.

"Aren't you going to shave?"

No answer.

"Aren't you going to work?" I nudged Ashley's ankle with my foot this time.

He always held his liquor much better than Amory. Despite his lithe frame, he could easily drink his regular customers, invariably pot-bellied, with fat gold chains stretched over their extending stomachs, under the table.

He was silent and his silence screamed volumes.

"There is no more work," he said at last, in a voice cold and dead. He took the bottle from me and threw his head back. I watched his throat constrict as he gulped the liquor he needed more than I did. I'd only been cursed out at work; he had just lost his, it seemed.

"They fired you, Ash?"

I immediately regretted asking, for Amory drew his breath in sharply, hiccupped and broke into such pitiful sobs, it nearly tore my heart to pieces.

"No." Moving as though in a dream—or a nightmare— Ashley produced a handkerchief and handed it to Amory. "They burned it down."

"Burned down what?" I asked, feeling incredibly idiotic, but the announcement was much too dumbfounding to process in an instant.

"The entire affair," Ashley explained in his emotionless voice. "The SA. They waited outside for the show to be over, for the general public to leave, and ambushed us all—the performers, the manager, even the waiting staff. There was a panic after they hurled a few Molotov cocktails inside. As we rushed outside, they began grabbing us and beating us up. Amory and I should consider ourselves fortunate, I suppose." With those words, Ashley pulled the kimono off his shoulder; an ugly bruise marred his pale, finely sculpted forearm. "We only received a couple of baton smacks before we made ourselves scarce. I don't know how the others fared. It's not like we could call the police to aid us. They'd only hurl us away for disturbing the peace and provoking the good Aryan men with our immoral behavior," he finished darkly, his voice dripping with sarcasm.

His face buried in an embroidered white cloth, Amory wept harder.

"How was your day?" Ashley asked.

"Uneventful. I was called a filthy, swindling Jew, but that's all." I shrugged.

He snorted softly and raised an almost empty bottle in a mock toast. "Welcome to Hitler's Germany, sister."

"I don't feel all that welcome."

"Yes, well, better get used to it. Because I don't see this ending anytime soon."

I grimaced after taking a swig after him, but not due to the brandy stinging my mouth. The future stank worse than their hair, of singed flesh and bloodied dreams. I wasn't so sure I wanted to get used to it.

THREE

Perhaps it was the influence of recent events, but I dreaded going to work the next morning. From the moment I groped for my ringing alarm in the apartment that was still dark, I stalled and took my time getting dressed, brewing coffee and generally prolonging the inevitable. What it was precisely that was bothering me, I couldn't quite put my finger on, but the feeling of some inexplicable foreboding persisted.

To add insult to my metaphorical injury, it appeared as though the entire neighborhood had suddenly conspired to decorate their windows with *Hakenkreuz* flags overnight and now they snapped at me in the wet wind, their offensive black spiders moving threateningly. I couldn't quite tell why all of a sudden I began to notice them or why they bothered me so much. They were just flags, really; harmless pieces of cloth, but, all at once, they seemed to be insults directed at me personally. At me, and Ashley and Amory, and everyone else who didn't fit into their new "great Germany" narrative. Harmless just yesterday, that morning they snapped and mocked and jeered, silently but powerfully nevertheless, letting me know that I was an alien among the chosen ones, an enemy of their new empire.

A filthy, swindling Jew.

I dove into a U-Bahn station, pulled out a dog-eared paperback of Kafka's *Metamorphosis*—Amory's latest recommendation—and had all but forgotten about the flags and the burned cabaret and the general angst that had been plaguing me for a few months now, when someone remarked right above my ear, "That book is banned, you know."

Pointedly, I licked my finger and turned the page. The wellmeaning commuter with a Nazi Party pin on the lapel of his coat moved away from me to the other end of the train car, mumbling something to himself.

Kafka's world was profound, bizarre and slightly mad. I was still pondering the allegory of traveling salesman Gregor Samsa's transformation into vermin; was still far too deep in my head to notice anything around me as my legs, trained by months of regular routine, carried me to the doors of Herr Perelman's store, where I bought my lunch each morning: a prepacked rye bread sandwich made with boiled cow tongue and mustard with a side of a pickle Frau Perelman made herself and a few sweets also baked by her hands. There were several such stores on my way to work, but I'd been loyal to the Perelmans for my own reasons: when I had just arrived in Berlin, while I was desperately trying to stretch my meager savings before my first salary arrived, it was Herr Perelman who had offered to open a credit in my name, waving my concerns off with the smile of a kindly grandfather. He had fed me when I was at my most vulnerable, but, what was even more important, he had become a friendly face in a city of indifferent strangers. Sometimes, such spiritual nourishment, just knowing that there's someone who would notice if you failed to appear one day, is far more essential than any physical foodstuffs.

A bucket appeared in front of me as though out of thin air. I stumbled into it and cursed when the white paint spilled all around me, splattering my only winter half-boots with speckles of white.

"Watch where you're going, you clumsy cow!" a voice bellowed right next to me.

It belonged to an SA man in his long overcoat, his square paramilitary hat, just as square as his brains under it, according to Ashley and his sharp-as-a-whip tongue.

I stared at him, too stunned to reply; at the brush, dripping white, in his right hand.

"Did you do it on purpose?"

The second officer materialized from behind the first one's back. He was much shorter, much younger looking. But apparently he made up for his lack of height and experience with a big mouth and frightening grimaces—the kind that such men summon to their faces, when they have nothing else to impress others with.

"Well? Did you?" he repeated. "Sabotaging the government-sanctioned efforts..."

Only then did I notice the sign this pair of SA muttons had been painting before I upset their earnest efforts:

Filthy, swindling Jew.

Don't buy from filthy—

The message ended abruptly there. From the other side of the glass, Herr Perelman's ashen face was staring back at me. He looked as if he'd aged twenty years.

"I'm sorry, I didn't see you," I told the SA men and walked around them and their spilled bucket, wiping my feet before entering Herr Perelman's store. I was the only customer there. "Good morning, Herr Perelman," I greeted him with a smile. "My usual, if you could be so kind."

He set to the task in a silence that hung heavy and stifling over the room. With grave movements, he sliced the tongue, arranged it on the bread, smeared it with mustard and wrapped it slowly and deliberately. When I handed him the money, I saw his face stricken with tears. He cried without moving a single muscle on his face.

I couldn't bring myself to thank him. I was afraid my voice would break as well.

"Bitch," the younger SA called after me as I walked out of the store, not so loud as to offend the public with the comment, but loudly enough for me to hear.

"I am," I replied in the same tone.

A bitch and a swindling Jew and a parasite like Kafka's Samsa and whatever else they liked to call me nowadays in this glorious, flag-draped new Germany.

Wally's face fell as soon as she saw me walking into the store and shaking the winter morning off my coat.

"What?" was all I asked.

"Herr Weber is expecting you in his office."

"Herr Weber himself?"

She made no reply; only lowered her gaze mournfully to the shelf she was presently polishing.

Anyone who has ever worked for someone else knows that whenever the boss himself wishes to talk, the talk is usually not about a promotion. Taking a deep breath, I readied myself for whatever was coming and walked the last few steps along the corridor, past the storage room, like the condemned ascending the gallows.

"Enter!" Herr Weber called from behind the door before I had a chance to finish rapping on it.

I pushed it open and paused where I stood, for there wasn't much space for me in what usually constituted Herr Lafler's office. Herr Lafler himself stared out of a small window as though the company inside was making him nauseous. In his chair, Herr Weber was reading through a paper bearing an official eagle with a swastika—I could see its black outline even through the paper, even from where I stood. Next to Herr Lafler's desk, an SA man was standing. His leather boots creaked when he turned to assess me with his eyes, up and down, an insolent stare meant to be insulting.

"Fräulein Davidsohn, I have been made aware that there was an issue with a customer yesterday," Herr Weber began, his eyes still trained on the paper. In the rare days that he appeared in the store, he'd always been friendly with us girls. Last Christmas, he even shook our hands and thanked us for our great work as Frau Weber handed us presents. Now, he looked cold, distant and so very uncomfortable, I almost felt sorry for him and the predicament he found himself in.

"There wasn't any issue," I countered calmly but firmly. I already knew where this was heading, but I'd be damned if I went down silently and meekly. "She demanded a refund based on a wrong assumption concerning the nature of fur and the fur-coat manufacturing process. Herr Lafler and I explained why we couldn't process it."

I expected anything but the explosion that followed. The Brownshirt's face had grown beet-red in a matter of seconds; he gathered himself and lashed out at me like a python. "You insulted an Aryan woman! I ought to arrest you where you stand, you conceited Jew! You think you're better than everyone else. It's been too long that you lot have been acting as though you own the world. Our Führer shall put a swift stop to it. You'll see how fast he will!" He shook a fist in my face.

Herr Lafler turned his back on the room entirely, all but pressing his forehead into the glass as if he wished to hurl himself out of here and into the street. In the yellow light of the room, his shadow loomed over us, the biggest of all three.

"I think it goes without saying that your employment with

our store has been terminated immediately," Herr Weber mumbled, resembling a bad actor reading a poorly written script.

"Yes, Herr Weber. I understand. Goodbye."

I swung round on my heels and walked out of the office and out of the store, without stopping, without hugging Wally goodbye, without leaving an address for her to write to. At that moment, after the events of the past twenty-four hours, it had become crystal clear to me that I was no longer welcome here, in this country. Neither was I planning to stay.

"Dora! Dora, wait, please!"

The wind tore into my exposed skin as I turned to face Herr Lafler, running around the corner, out of the back of the store where trucks with goods pulled up every other week. Dressed only in his woolen pants, shirt and a knit vest, he was simultaneously gasping for air and shivering—from the wind or the nerves, I couldn't quite tell.

"Your money," he said, pushing a wad of bills into my hand. "For the past three weeks. That SA swine insisted that we keep it or, better yet, offer it to that woman," he spat out the word in disgust, "as compensation for the insult. But..." He nudged my hand with his again.

I took the money before he hid his hands in his pockets, pulling his shoulders up to his ears.

"Thank you, Herr Lafler."

"I'm sorry, Dora. I tried to—"

"I know."

"There's nothing I can do. I'm only a manager. I don't own the store. If I did..."

"I know," I repeated.

"If you need recommendations or anything," he began, but I only shook my head.

"Thank you kindly, but I don't think I'll be staying."

"In Berlin?"

"In Germany."

"Ach." He pondered something. "Well, perhaps, it's for the best."

For some reason, I was growing progressively more and more aware of the tongue sandwich in my bag. Its smell, hanging between us in such a grave moment, seemed inappropriate somehow, oddly out of place.

Herr Lafler was still considering something when I opened my bag and took out the lunch I'd bought for my job that I no longer had. "Here. From the Perelmans' store. They have the best meat cuts in the city. If you like it," I said, holding out the sandwich to him, "perhaps you could decide to shop there on occasion. They certainly could use customers..."

I let the meaningful silence fill the pause. Herr Lafler looked gravely at the brown paper tied with a string and took it into his hands as though it wasn't a simple sandwich but an artifact of some ancient, crumbling empire.

"I shall only shop at their store from now on," he promised, uttering the words like an oath.

I shook his free hand and smiled at him, sure that he would keep his promise.

FOUR

ESSEN, GERMANY. TWO WEEKS LATER

Coming back to one's hometown from a big metropolis is very much like coming home from a big party. It's nice and cozy and quiet, and each corner is inevitably familiar, but a faint melancholy follows you like a shadow. It paints the familiar quaint streets with paler strokes and makes reunions taste bittersweet on one's tongue.

I allowed myself to melt into my mother's and grandmother's warm embraces, but Berlin's pull was already tugging at my heart, calling me back with a voice of a siren, flashing its lights in my memory's snapshots, beckoning, luring me like a lousy lover promising to change after a fight that had left me battered.

It hadn't been a full day since Amory and Ashley had taken turns holding me tightly at Berlin's Alexanderplatz station, and I was already missing their sharp wit, graceful arms in which I felt safer than I would in steel armor, and warm lips on my temple whispering promises to keep my room empty until I decided to come back. Traces of their rice facial powder mixed with expensive cologne still clung to me, refusing to let go, just like my roommates themselves had refused to release me from their embrace, as if sensing that it would be our very last one.

As I stood there, in the middle of our familial home, my mother and grandmother fussed and chattered all around me— "Leave that suitcase in the hallway, Dora"; "You'll unpack later, after we eat"; "You should have sent us a telegram so we'd know you were coming, but such a pleasant surprise, nevertheless"; "Sit, sit"; "A shame you've just missed your father, he was just here for lunch and must have left for the store not ten minutes ago"; "We'll arrange something to eat in a jiffy"—and didn't notice, in their excitement, that I was much too silent, filled with longing for something I had left behind.

Not just the city, but freedom. The apartment that was my own, friends no one would judge because they knew nothing of them, a life that was all mine, with its missteps and disappointments and Saturday nights spent in drunk half-oblivion and hungover Sundays, cigarettes for which no one would scold me, dresses much too short, lovers for one night...

Now, sitting in the same rickety chair I remembered from my schooldays, in the same corner of the kitchen where our dining table stood, I felt like a small child once again, robbed of something, back to the coop I'd flown from with such excitement just a year ago, infinitely disappointed with myself for something that wasn't my fault.

"I'm so glad that you're back," Grandmother said without turning away from the stove, where the food was already sizzling and smoking and spitting oil—three dishes at once, all under control of my grandmother's watchful eye. With her thick braid that I always envied wrapped into a knot at the back of her head, and her body small and wiry, she danced her way between the sink, the counter and the stove with the effortlessness of a prima ballerina, only in place of a layered skirt was a pale olive apron embroidered with white flowers that hugged her girlishly thin waist. She saved it for special occasions only and took particular pride in having never gotten it dirty, no matter what culinary masterpieces she created in her small kitchen kingdom. "We missed having you home," she continued. "It just wasn't the same without you. Do you remember Stella, Heinrich's daughter? She works in a kindergarten now. She can put a good word in for you, so you can get a placement there as well. The kindergarten is right around the corner from Herr Klein's butchery, so it'll only take you fifteen minutes to get there by foot every morning. It'll be a nice change from Berlin for you," she said, chuckling good-naturedly. "I remember you complaining about all those U-Bahns and buses you had to take to get to work every day—"

"I wasn't complaining, Oma," I muttered, wrapping and unwrapping the tablecloth's fringe around my index finger—a childish habit that had suddenly reappeared after being all but forgotten.

"No, naturally you weren't." The nudge my mother gave Grandmother while reaching for the good silverware in the cabinet next to the stove didn't escape my attention.

Softly-spoken and possessing neither Oma's willfulness nor her forthright manner, my mother had always been the mediator between Oma and me. When I had first announced my desire to move to Berlin, Oma had raised hell on earth, somehow conveniently forgetting that she, too, had left home at my age. The only difference was that she'd left it to get married, instead of heading alone, unprotected, to that Gomorrah of a city, according to Oma's logic. I had long abandoned all hope of winning that argument. Both of us were too obstinate to acknowledge the other's point of view.

"Oma was just saying that it must have been tough for you, wasting so much time on your commute," Mutti said with a smile, laying out knives and forks atop napkins that were used also only for special occasions. "And besides, I remember you telling us how dirty it was and how you saw rats there and how all kinds of criminals and..." she paused before lowering her voice to whisper, "prostitutes prowled it in the evenings."

"It was all right." I shrugged, realizing just how much I missed the dirt and the insolent Berlin rats and even the prostitutes soliciting the customers right on the trains. "I got used to it. I didn't mind. And besides, I don't have qualifications to work with children. I finished business school, not kindergarten teacher training."

"So what?" Oma waved me off, unimpressed. "Only the senior staff have actual teaching qualifications; the rest are just young girls and all young girls—"

"—Are somehow supposed to know how to work with children and love them," I finished, rubbing the last few days off my face. All at once, I felt terribly warm in that small kitchen with its smells of childhood and innocence; all at once, its walls turned much too narrow, the air much too stifling. "I don't like children, Oma. I never did."

For the first time, she swung round and regarded me as though I was a patient from the asylum. "How can you know that? You haven't worked with them yet."

"I know because the very sound of a child's crying used to make me change train cars back in Berlin."

Oma was just about to counter this argument when Mutti gave her a stare—something that she applied hardly ever, but which both Oma and Vati took seriously for that very reason.

"She doesn't have to work there if she doesn't want to," Mutti asserted.

"Nobody says that she has to; it's just something to consider while she's looking for a different job that is more to her liking."

"Let her rest a few days first."

"I wasn't saying that she ought to start right this instant."

"Mother, really. She hasn't even unpacked yet and here you are—"

"She's sitting right here." I interrupted their bickering with an overly bright smile. "And I am not unpacking anything. I'm only staying for a couple of days. My train leaves on Tuesday."

I hadn't planned to drop the announcement on them like a bomb; to be frank, even after having my visa stamped at the embassy of the Netherlands and purchasing a train ticket to Amsterdam at the same time I'd bought a ticket to Essen, I wasn't certain myself if I would go through with the entire enterprise. But now, in my childhood kitchen, in my hometown, each crevice of which I knew like the back of my hand, I suddenly realized that I couldn't stay here any more than I could stay in Berlin. To be sure, there weren't any Brownshirts around and I had only seen two swastika flags in the entire town —one at the train station and another one mounted on the front of the bus that took me to the street where my parents' house stood—but the Nazi plague would spread here as well. It was a matter of time, but it would.

"What train?" Oma asked, holding a spatula like a weapon, suddenly on guard.

Mutti only threw me a quick wistful gaze from her cutting board—already resigned, already missing her daughter-the-gypsy, but far too used to her wandering ways to be surprised.

"A train to Holland," I said.

"Holland?" Oma cried as if I'd said the Arctic and not a neighboring European country. "Whatever are you talking about now?"

"I didn't leave Berlin because I got tired of it. I was fired from my job because I'm Jewish." I hadn't planned to say it; I just did. "With those muttonheads in power, it'll only get worse for us. They're already boycotting Jewish businesses, harassing people for nothing."

"Not here." Oma suddenly remembered her stove and turned her attention back to it. "Here, everything is as it was."

"And shall always be," I said, making a point.

"Precisely." Oma chose to misinterpret me. "Essen prides itself on tradition."

"Stagnation."

"Our ways don't change."

"How is that a good thing?"

"What's bad about it? It's stability."

"Stability leads to decline; never to progress."

"What leads to progress then? Black plague? Wars? That recent market crash we're still recovering from?"

I shook my head, resigning myself to the fact that the argument was heading nowhere. "I'm leaving, Oma."

"Leaving your poor mother all alone," Oma grumbled under her breath.

"Mutti has Vati and you, Oma."

"And when I die?"

"Oma, you'll outlive me with your spirit," I mumbled back and set Mutti off laughing.

"Let her be, Mother," Mutti said, still chuckling, waving my feisty grandmother off with a dish towel. "Do you honestly expect Dora to hold onto our skirts for the rest of her life? Let her travel, see the world, make a better life for herself—"

"...Get involved with some *goy* foreigner," Oma grumbled and Mutti exploded once again, apparently delighted with the idea of me dating a non-Jew instead of being appalled by it as Grandmother had intended.

I loved Mutti's laughter. I loved making her laugh and I would miss it dearly, like I would miss Oma and those obstinate ways of hers, and Vati, even though he'd always been at work at our family shop selling radios and phonographs for as long as I could remember, just like he was now, always the provider, always the protector, just like my grandfather who had died when I was much too young, leaving behind fond memories and the incredible drawings that now graced the walls of our small familial dwelling. But no matter how much I'd miss them, I just couldn't stay. Essen lulled them into an illusion of safety with its static life, but the change was already coming, whether they liked it or not; one of those changes that gave birth to progress, but the birth would certainly be bloody and painful, and it was anyone's guess if this new Germany would survive it.

"You're not a Jew; you're a gypsy if I've ever seen one," Oma grumbled in the meantime, heaving the contents of a tremendous iron skillet into the deep porcelain dish Mutti had set out before her. "Why can't you just sit in one place as you ought to?"

"Because I'm too much like you," I countered calmly and smiled at her with all the affection I felt for her. "I'll send for you once I'm settled in Amsterdam. Because we're not staying in this damned country that has lost its damned mind."

"Amsterdam!" Oma made a gesture of desperation with her hands as much as the weighty skillet allowed. "I'm not going to any Amsterdam." As though to accentuate her point, she deposited the pan into the sink with as much noise as she could summon. "My parents are buried here. Their parents are buried here. I'm planning to be buried here as well, if you don't mind, not in some Amsterdam."

"Whatever do you have against Amsterdam?" I broke into laughter in spite of myself.

"I don't like it."

"How do you know that you don't like it if you have never visited it?" I arched a brow, reminding her of the argument she'd used on me just minutes ago.

She pretended not to hear it.

That night, as I lay in my childhood bed, I was hoping that it was indeed my "gypsy" blood that was driving me out of the country; that Essen would indeed remain the same; and that when my grandmother's time came, she would indeed be laid to rest where she wished, among the many generations of her ancestors who'd called Essen their home...

FIVE

The days leading up to my departure were steeped in unreality. A one-way train ticket lay on my dresser as a stark reminder of the inevitable and yet I moved about as though in a dream, going through the motions of packing additional necessities that were supposed to see me through the next few weeks in an entirely foreign country, and not quite believing that I would go through with it.

After tearful goodbyes and Oma's reassurances—"You shall always have a home here, Dora; you hear me? Come back as soon as you've had enough of this adventurous nonsense; you have nothing to prove to anyone"—Mutti helped me take my suitcases to the taxicab Vati had arranged before leaving for work as a means of his own silent blessing.

The trip to the station was mostly silent. I was too tense, too preoccupied with my own thoughts, to give Mutti anything to remember me by except for monosyllabic answers to questions I scarcely even processed, and so she contented herself with holding my hand in hers throughout our much-too-short journey. Through the fog in my mind, I was painfully aware of the faint trembling of her palm. I squeezed it as tightly as I could, reminding me of my childhood, only this time the roles were reversed and it was me reassuring her that everything surely would be all right and that I should always be there for her, just one letter, one international phone call away, until we met again.

On the platform, it was worse still: she was on the verge of tears and I had to be strong for the both of us and so I joked and smiled until my cheeks hurt from the effort and promised her that I would write or call or both and that she'd see me before long, of course she would, it wasn't like I was leaving for Canada or some such...

"Promise to be careful, Dora."

"Of course."

"Send a telegram if you need anything... money—"

"I have enough saved, Mutti, but thank you all the same."

"I love you, Dora; you know that, right?"

"I love you too, Mutti. Chin up. We'll meet again very soon!" I spoke brightly and cut our last embrace short, because if I didn't, she would see the tears gathering in my own eyes and this would most certainly not do.

Despite all promises, I didn't know when we would see each other again; *if* we would see each other again, and I wanted her to remember me just so, smiling and excited, her fearless girl setting off on an adventure; not someone hunted, persecuted, who'd already seen what she was yet to see.

AMSTERDAM

It was difficult to believe that only a few hours had passed since I'd boarded the train in Germany. It felt more like years ago when I descended in Holland, with everything utterly foreign around me; alien and slightly frightening, as though in some parallel universe where the pale winter sun was the same, but somehow different. Surely, it couldn't have been the same day of my departure.

With the suitcase's handle squeezed tightly in my gloved palm, I glanced around, alien to myself, as well as older somehow...

The customs officer regarded me in frank wonder when I returned the filled-out form to him with an address line left blank.

"I don't know anyone in Amsterdam and I was hoping to find a room through a newspaper," I explained with a smile. "There's no rule against not having an address upon arrival, is there? If there is, I truly am sorry, but the embassy didn't warn me."

His eyes widened even further. He cleared his throat and asked me, as politely as it was possible given the situation, if I realized just how dangerous it was, renting lodgings from a stranger in a foreign city.

I only shrugged and offered him yet another disarming smile from my salesgirl arsenal. Certainly, I was aware of incidents when young girls had been taken advantage of, robbed of their money or even murdered by men who made it their business to prey on the most defenseless ones, but somehow, I couldn't see it happening to me. After all, I had rented a room in the same exact manner upon arrival in Berlin and doesn't fortune always favor the brave?

"I'll be fine," I promised, seeing him hesitate. "If you do need an address, I'll be glad to use one of the cheapest hotels you have, if you would be so kind and would recommend me one."

This seemed to reassure him somewhat. With a look of relief, he wrote down a name and address for me on a page he'd torn out of his personal notepad.

"This one is right next to the station, just across the street. You'll have no trouble finding it. This way, the police will have a means of contacting you in case something happens. You will have to provide them with your permanent address once you're settled. You know that, correct?" Once again, he looked suspicious.

"Oh, yes," I replied, sweeping the note off the counter and gathering my bags—a typical émigré, one of the many more to arrive in the next few months and years. "That, the embassy told me all about."

I made it out of the station but not across the street where the hotel was beckoning new arrivals with a bright neon sign, promising rooms and even free breakfast. Noticing a small crowd of my fellow travelers weighed down with luggage that suggested permanent immigration instead of a holiday trip, I headed straight in their direction—a herd instinct honed by millions of years of evolution.

Indifferent to the subzero temperatures and wet wind blowing from the river, the human flock shifted but pushed relentlessly forward, closer and closer to a tall newspaper board doubling as a private ad board. As I prodded my way forward, all the while mindful of my multiple suitcases, I saw a great number of handwritten advertisements on the board, with a fringe of addresses and sometimes phone numbers. From each side, hands reached and grabbed for them—room, board, work— they ripped off several at the same time, fighting for lodgings and scraps of labor the same way their ancestors fought each other for water and food.

I was about to grab a few myself, but soon realized that the only furnished rooms that were left either had exorbitant prices or were outside city limits, in villages with only one bus heading to the capital and back each day, no doubt. It was at that point, when I was all but resigned to overpaying for the customs clerk's recommended hotel, that a half-sheet of paper, faded but typewritten, caught my eye. "Furnished room and full board in exchange for services of a typist," it read—the words were too good to be true. In a few places, the ink was smudged with rain-water; it had been here for some time and yet no one had torn a single piece of the fringe with an address on it. With something feral possessing me for an instant, I tore the entire affair off the board and made off with it clutched firmly in my hand before anyone else noticed it and beat me to it.

Only when I paused by a city map, and slapped the ad on it in search of the address, did the caveat that must have stopped my fellow émigrés from taking it catch my eye. In small enough font not to attract any unwanted attention and yet distinctive enough for the trained eye, Cmr. Veidt was typed neatly right under the street name—an abbreviation for Comrade instead of Dhr, Mr.

All at once, it became clear: a red German émigré in hiding was looking for a secretary who didn't mind printing communist leaflets. I hadn't the slightest idea just how illegal the entire Red business was in the Netherlands, but for the furnished room east of the center of the city and full board, I was willing to find out.

"*Ja?*" Comrade Veidt—at least I assumed it was him—looked me over with suspicion through the narrow opening in the still-latched door.

I greeted him in German and explained that I was here for the room and secretarial job that went with it.

The lines on his forehead relaxed a tad. He even unlatched the door, but stopped short of inviting me in. "Can you type?"

"Yes, and very fast. I graduated from the business school."

This earned me an impressed arch of a brow.

"Criminal record?"

I pulled back, half-stunned and half-insulted. "No!"

"Are you a member of the KPD?"

The Communist Party of Germany. Was that imperative? I

quickly searched his face for clues, thought of lying, but then realized that I would be caught immediately for I knew not the first thing about communism besides the fact that their flag was red and they actively despised the Nazis.

"No, I'm not. I'm not a member of any party, I'm afraid."

"So, you're Jewish then."

"How did you—" I shut my mouth in defiance, not wishing to give him the satisfaction of catching me off guard.

"The only reason for Germans to leave Germany right now is persecution—religious or political. If you're not a communist and since you're too young to be any kind of a prominent journalist, writer, or dissident, I'm assuming you're Jewish." For the first time, a faint knowing smile tugged at his lips, instantly warming his features that were previously rather stern, rough even, as though hatched from a stone, all angles and uneven edges.

He was a man in his mid- or late thirties from the look of him, with inquisitive pale gray eyes and light brown hair he wore short and smoothed with water. When he stepped away to allow me in, I saw that it was already streaked with gray over his forehead and temples.

"Heinrich Veidt." He offered me his hand.

"Dora Davidsohn." I shook it.

"Are you here legally? I don't care one way or the other if you came here on a trip and overstayed your visa—makes no difference to me," he rushed to reassure me before I had a chance to answer. "I won't report you, don't fret. I'm only asking if you are—"

"I am."

He nodded. "...In case you have to report to the police with your new address. Don't tell them about our little arrangement, will you?"

"No, of course not."

"I won't make you type anything illegal, have no fear. No

Red Front leaflets or anything of that kind. Only boring meeting notes and certain quarterly budgets, terribly dull stuff." He grinned again, a smile of a conspirator that reached his eyes.

"I'm sure that you're a very honest man and wouldn't compromise my fragile position," I responded in the same conspiratorial tone.

Veidt regarded me appreciatively, not in that uncomfortable, ogling manner one grows accustomed to in a big city full of types who catcall and grope without any reservations, but with comradely respect. "I feel we'll make a good team, Fräulein Davidsohn."

"I feel the same way, Comrade Veidt."

We shook on that, two hunted Germans in a foreign land. I didn't know back that that it was that very handshake that would change the course of my entire life and turn me from vulnerable prey into a relentless hunter, feared by the Gestapo themselves.

SIX

Before long, routine settled in. The evenings were Veidt's, spent in a cavernous study of his in front of an ancient typewriter that smudged Cs into Os and lacked ß entirely, but the days were all mine, where I lost myself in a spiral of streets, crossroads and canals I was slowly unraveling day by day. Each morning, I ventured further and further from our building with its colorful shutters; from the pharmacy on the corner with its green snake wrapped around the chalice blinking its neon sign at passersby; from the safety of a linden alley framed by curved lampposts invariably surrounded with yellow snow and pawprints.

By the time the snow melted, I could easily orient myself in the city without a map. By the time apple trees burst into bridal blossoms, I biked along Amsterdam's bridges with the confidence of a local, swerving around cars and the occasional horse-drawn carriage—mostly carrying milk with a trail of its sweetish scent following it along the damp streets.

It was that dampness that required some growing accustomed to. For the first few nights in my new room, rather spacious but sparsely decorated (a single bed with a metal frame that creaked mercilessly each time I turned; an old oak dresser with a handle missing off its bottom drawer; an intricately carved stool in place of a night table and a small table in a corner with a porcelain bowl and a pitcher—whatever it was kept there for I could never tell, for the apartment had its own facilities on the premises), I awoke trembling and stiff with cold despite the temperature outside being virtually the same as in my native Germany.

"It's that blasted wet wind," Veidt had explained with a sympathetic shake of the head when I had asked him for a second blanket. "Picks up moisture from the canals and spreads it everywhere. Mold grows on walls like mushrooms; doors get stuck all the time in their frames, swollen with that moisture. Don't be surprised if you wake up to dew on the floors."

I'd already woken up to sheets that felt wet, as though just out of the washtub, so I had no reason to doubt Veidt's words, just like his apologetic explanation that the radiator was already working full force.

"But as soon as it dries, the night falls or the rain starts and in comes the blasted mist, wandering through the entire apartment." He'd shrugged and added after a pause, "I'd still take mold and stuck doors over the Gestapo beatings, to be frank with you."

He didn't elaborate further and neither did I pry. All of us expats had our own memories that we hid from others like ugly scars. Pedestrian curiosity was not just impolite but almost criminal.

By the time Veidt's comrades had gathered for a celebratory meeting on May Day, I had already learned the code from him and the mysterious men that visited him on certain nights and spoke in hushed tones and left parcels I pretended not to notice.

AMSTERDAM. JANUARY 1934

I shall never forget the day when I met him—another man who turned my life upside down and left me with nothing but ashes in my still-smoldering heart. It was a blinding, snow-crusted afternoon that made my breath catch in my throat as I pedaled toward a former theater that had been condemned but not demolished yet, with a dilapidated façade and a roof that had caved in just above the balcony, exposing it to sunlight and elements. Since last autumn, it had been serving as the local communists' meeting hall, for it was free of charge and, more importantly, free of police. For the past eleven months, I'd been coming to these meetings more and more often, first just as a stenographer on Veidt's request and, later, out of growing curiosity for the ideas I'd been writing down in my thick, lined stenographer's pads.

They were utopian and much too idealistic, and the weighty tome by Marx that Veidt had dropped in my lap one afternoon after I kept pestering him with questions didn't really help me one bit, except to serve as a sleeping aid on nights when sleep refused to come and the wind howled outside like a mad dog. I didn't understand much and cared even less until a certain guest speaker, Alfred Benjamin, ascended the stairs to the former stage and looked at the crowd in front of him with a clear, passionate gaze before posing a question after a very long pause during which we held our collective breath:

"Comrades. What can we do, physically do, now, to help people live better? I have just come from a very long trip that took me from Berlin to Moscow, Paris, Ankara, and London. I have attended countless meetings; I have heard countless speeches, all very elaborate and inspired, no doubt about it. But they all lack one thing, the thing that people need the most: concrete plans and means of achieving them. So, I have come here to ask you today: what can we, as an Amsterdam faction of the international KP, do to aid our fellow persecuted minorities? Because throwing leaflets in their faces is all well and good, but they can't quite spread those leaflets in place of butter on their bread every morning. So, the question is, what can we do to physically help? So many leave Germany every day—"

"What about the Party line?" someone called out from the front row.

Comrade Benjamin only raised his hand; somehow, that silent gesture and the sheer presence of his personality on the stage was enough to hush the crowd. "For those of you who worry about the Party line, ask yourself this: when you're on board a ship and see a person drowning, do you go to the captain first and ask for his permission to throw the drowning man a lifeline?" Even from the depths of the unlit rows of seats where I was hiding, I could see him arch a lively black brow and smile at the obvious. "No. We save a person first and sort out the details with the authorities later. Because if we do otherwise we're nothing but a bunch of petite bourgeoisie who differ not a shade from the oppressive classes we're hoping to eliminate. So, my suggestion is this: it's the beginning of a new year and we have a full budget. Let's invest a major part of that budget into physically aiding our fellow German expats. Let's provide them with financial aid and housing. Let's organize community drives to gather clothes and toys and—"

"Surely, you mean members of the Party only?" the same voice called out, interrupting once again.

Once again, Alfred Benjamin gave him a look of an adult indulging a child who couldn't grasp the simplest concept.

"No, comrade. I mean, every single expat—communist, Social-Democrat, Jehovah's Witness, a journalist, a Jew, a woman, a man, a child. The Party's goal is to drive as many masses into its fold; fine. Let's do just that, but let's lead by example. Let's show them that the Communist Party is not just empty words but actions. Let's prove to them that we are the creators of a fair future, of a just future, where everyone is equal and everyone is worthy of aid. Not just members of the Party," he said in a lower voice and I could swear I recognized a shade of disgust in it, "but every single constituent for whom our Party is responsible. Because we are the people. People elect us to serve them, not to govern them. So, comrades, let me ask you once again: are you ready to serve absolutely everyone who needs our help? A communist or not? Without reservations or conditions?"

A veritable uproar drowned out the last of his words. All at once, men and women were on their feet, clapping their hands as though enthralled, pumping fists in the air charged with sudden new energy that ignited the crowd, propelled it in the direction it so desperately lacked. It was at that moment that I understood what communism was all about and, all at once, I was a convert – all because of one man who actually cared— Alfred Benjamin.

My future husband.

My fellow comrade-in-arms.

The man who wasn't afraid to pay the ultimate price for the freedom of others.

THREE WEEKS LATER

"Don't touch me, you Bolshevist scum!"

The elderly man was about to reach for his cane to ward Alfred off, but his wife swiftly grabbed it out of his reach.

"Don't be daft, Helmut," she hissed at him, pointing an accusatory cane at its owner. "Herr Benjamin is here to help you."

"I'd rather lose my leg than let a Red touch it!"

The bickering went on for some time, during which I observed Alfred go about his business without paying the slightest attention to his patient's protests and insults. With the practiced motions of a trained medic, he was cleaning out a foul-smelling wound on the man's thigh inflicted by the Brown-shirts with the sharp tip of one of their banners. The "brave" SA were celebrating the anniversary of their Führer coming to power and, apparently, putting a spike through a Jewish tailor's thigh in front of his terrified family members was a grand finale of their celebration. To the family's misfortune, the assault happened in the overcrowded Alexanderplatz station, just as they were about to board a train heading to Holland. Over the few days that they spent traveling, searching for lodgings and moving from shelter to shelter, the man's unattended leg had gradually turned from red to purple to painfully swollen, driving his temperature to the point of him becoming delirious and bathed in sweat. Ironically enough, on the day that Alfred arrived with his small medical kit to aid him, the man was lucid enough to categorically reject any help from "the Bolshevist scum" and refused to see reason even when his wife threatened him with losing his leg to gangrene entirely.

"I fear that's the best outcome," Alfred commented in a perfectly unperturbed tone as he worked on the leg. "The poison from the wound is already in your blood, Herr Mendel-baum. So far, your body had fought it off but, if left untreated, the infection shall soon poison your liver and kidneys, and as soon as they are out of the picture, there's nothing that even the best surgeons in the world can do for you. Surely you don't plan on abandoning your wife, daughters and grandchildren to fend for themselves in a foreign country?"

Herr Mendelbaum grumbled something but stilled himself a little, though never taking his beady eyes full of suspicion off his makeshift physician.

"Where did you get your medical training, if you don't mind me asking?" one of Herr Mendelbaum's sons-in-law inquired from the corner, where he was bouncing a baby on his knee.

Despite the small quarters teeming with émigrés, the family

and neighbors cleared the room almost entirely, allowing as much freedom and light for kind Doctor Benjamin as possible.

"Back in Germany. I haven't graduated, though. My father was a war invalid with a pension that lasted exactly one day, with the inflation soaring and all that business, and my mother, our sole provider, died in '26 after fighting consumption for years. I only had another year to go, but I had to quit. Don't worry, I know what I'm doing. I tended to many wounded men when I volunteered in a hospital in Leningrad."

Greedily, selfishly, I was picking up bits about Alfred's life that he dropped like breadcrumbs. In the past few weeks, we'd been too busy with volunteer work to have any semblance of a conversation, no matter how much I craved one. I don't think he even wanted me there, with him; he had scowled dubiously when Veidt praised my stenographer's skills. He needed a nurse, not a stenographer, I'd all but read in Alfred's eyes, but there were no qualified nurses among our circles—there were very few women to begin with—and there was nothing else for it but for him to let me tag along.

"I learn very fast."

He had acknowledged my attempt at reassurance with a grunt and nod and hadn't exchanged another word with me, aside from work-related remarks and half-official hellos and goodbyes.

I'd taken him for a born orator and he'd turned out to be a silent type, terrifyingly efficient and wasting no time on empty jawing. He'd mapped out our route every morning and refused to reschedule any appointments he had for the next day even if work stretched well into the night. There were too many of them now, masses fleeing east, and only a small fraction of them arrived in Amsterdam legally and had at least some sort of means to see them through. The rest had no one to rely on except for the Red Cross, already overworked and overstretched in its resources, and us, the "Other Red Cross," as Veidt jokingly called us, with Alfred being the only one with some sort of medical training.

It was through the expat grapevine that one of Herr Mendelbaum's daughters had discovered us and pleaded for us to help her father before it was too late. It was supposed to be our first half-day off in several weeks of ceaseless work, but Alfred had gathered his medical bag without any hesitation and come to collect me when I'd just dropped down on top of my bed covers craving the rest for my aching, swollen feet.

"I wouldn't have bothered you if it was something simple," he'd said by way of apology as we made our way over the bridge, its water frozen stiff and sliced into circles by children's skates. "But in case I need to operate, I could really use your help..."

"It's no bother at all, really," I had replied in the brightest voice I could summon. "I'll be happy to help."

"I know you're tired."

"Not at all."

Another nod and another grunt was all I got, but I was glad just to be near him, this selfless man who gave his all to the people who cursed at him and called him all sorts of names without complaining once. No wonder I was so fascinated with him, with his enigmatic, thoroughly guarded personality that he appeared he wouldn't reveal even under torture, with the skillful hands of a healer and a heart too good for this world.

Now, watching Alfred pacify the elderly Jewish tailor with the patience of a saint, I once again felt my heart swell with admiration for him.

"You lived in Leningrad?" Herr Mendelbaum's son-in-law pulled forward, suddenly interested.

"In Leningrad and Moscow and Paris and London and even Argentina."

"Argentina?" This time, it was Frau Mendelbaum who voiced her amazement.

Herr Mendelbaum only narrowed his eyes further. "You're

not converting any of my family members into your religion, young man."

"I'm an atheist, Herr Mendelbaum," Alfred replied, perfectly undisturbed.

"You know what I mean, you weasel. You come here, spread your tales and lure people into your Bolshevist sect."

"I'm here solely as a physician, Herr Mendelbaum, I assure you."

"Don't let him give you any pamphlets, Lisl, you hear me?" Herr Mendelbaum shook a trembling finger at his wife.

"Please, do not excite yourself, Herr Mendelbaum," Alfred said, stitching up the wound he'd cleaned to the best of his abilities. "Any sort of nervous excitement shall slow your healing process. All you need now is plenty of rest and sleep and you shall be like new in a couple of weeks, you have my word." He raised a hand, stopping Herr Mendelbaum in his tracks before he could utter another word: "And I promise you, I have no pamphlets on me and neither has my assistant."

I felt my heart skip a bit at the glance he threw my way.

"We'll be on our way now. I'll check on you in a couple of days, but if you feel worse, do not hesitate to contact us." These last words he directed at Frau Mendelbaum, who nodded dutifully.

In the hallway, stacked almost to the ceiling with children's prams, pillowcases stuffed with clothes, shoes and suitcases of all shapes and colors, Frau Mendelbaum began counting the few local bills she had managed to exchange from some crook for an extortion-like rate, no doubt.

"How much do we owe you, Herr Doktor?" It was amazing that despite Alfred emphatically stating to all of his patients that he was not a doctor in any professional sense of the word, they insisted on addressing him as such. "We don't have much, I'm afraid, but whatever we have—"

"You owe me nothing, Frau Mendelbaum," Alfred said with

a smile, gently pushing the woman's hand, with the money enclosed in it, away.

"But let me pay you at least for your supplies... you have to buy them with something, don't you?"

"We have a budget for it, Frau Mendelbaum, don't worry."

"Truly, Herr Doktor..." Frau Mendelbaum's voice trailed off, suddenly choked with tears that were already pooling in her deep brown eyes.

But Alfred only smiled at her again, full of such infinite kindness, I could swear the dingy narrow space brightened somehow, getting just a bit warmer.

"If you want to repay me, Frau Mendelbaum, just spread the word among your friends and neighbors. Seeing people like your husband getting well is the best payment one can ask for."

SEVEN

AMSTERDAM. SPRING 1934

With spring came fresh quarterly reports, which Veidt dictated to me in a voice slightly altered with astonishment. The Party membership requests, just like the number of donations, suddenly skyrocketed to heights previously unimaginable, resulting in someone anonymous and attired in a black leather coat descending on Amsterdam Communist Party headquarters to—no doubt in my eyes—inquire on the methods of the local Party leaders.

What reduced me to stunned silence, though, was not the Soviet political commissar himself, but Alfred's disinterest in his visit. When I, trying to match my steps to his long strides on our way to yet another émigré needing the help of a medic, mentioned a dinner Veidt was planning for our esteemed guest that night and to which Alfred was invited, Alfred only tossed his head.

"Dinner," he mumbled with a shade of annoyance and came to an abrupt halt, causing me to nearly stumble into him. "Have you got iodine?"

"Yes."

"Good."

With that, he resumed his marching, his medic's leather bag swinging in time with his steps.

Once again, we were in the middle of a typical émigré tenement nightmare: run-down, with outhouses in the street smelling so sharply of human waste and refuse, it turned one's stomach just to walk past them, roofs caving over some of the condemned flats and vermin rummaging through garbage freely on the street corners. I hadn't the slightest clue whom we were about to visit here. I had long ago grown used to Doktor Benjamin testing me in such an unorthodox manner, exposing me to all sorts of experiences as if to see just how much blood and gore and sheer human misery it would take to make me quit. Only, I never as much as complained. First, just out of stubborn desire to prove him wrong, and then, out of the realization that no matter what inconveniences I was going through, they were nothing compared to the suffering of the people we tended to.

"What do you want me to say to Veidt?" I asked, following Alfred into the gloomy maw of the tenement and groping my way on the stairs, all but immersed in darkness. The only window that was supposed to shed at least some light had been painted dark blue and shut.

From somewhere above, a strangled scream of such a wild, animalistic quality stopped me in my tracks and raised the thinnest hairs on my neck.

Alfred also paused, only to resume his ascent almost immediately, this time taking two steps at a time.

"Will you come?" I called after him.

"What?" Alfred stumbled over something and issued a curse under his breath, kicking a child's beaten and half-deflated ball out of our way.

"To Veidt's dinner?"

"Ach, that..." He mumbled again under his breath and rapped on the door, behind which a child was wailing at the top of his lungs. It appeared that the dinner was the last thing he would be considering.

When a young girl with an ash-white, tear-stricken face opened the door, with her small brother holding onto her skirt and screaming in a voice that was already growing hoarse, I all but choked on my words, feeling guilty just for asking.

"Where is she, Gerti?" Alfred, a picture of composure as always, asked the girl, who must have come and fetched him in the first place.

"In the furthest room to the right, just before the kitchen," Gerti replied in a voice that was still shaky with tears, and pointed at the door that stood partially opened. "I thought of bringing her water, but she screamed so... I was afraid..." Her bottom lip trembled. Next to her, her little brother, who couldn't have been older than two, wiped his nose with the back of his hand, somewhat pacified by our appearance.

"You did good, Gerti," Alfred assured her. "It's best that she doesn't drink anything anyway. We'll take care of her and you two go and fetch me as many pine cones as you can. Can you do that?"

The girl nodded solemnly and pulled her brother after herself with a renewed sense of purpose about her.

It was when we made our way through the long row of rooms in the communal apartment to the kitchen to wash our hands that I came to the terrible realization that it was entirely devoid of any adults, spare the patient we were about to see.

As though on cue, out of the room came such an unbearable wail, my stomach somersaulted in spite of myself. I would have liked nothing better than to shrink against the wall with its peeling wallpaper stained with age and grease and stay in the safety of the corridor where the air was stale but untainted by the tinge of metal inside the room itself—Alfred had just pushed the door open and I could already smell it, taste its rust-like essence at the back of my throat.

Inside, the curtains—moth-eaten and threadbare, the color of red wine—were pulled over the window, tinting the room in crimson hues. It took some time for my eyes to adjust to that artificial twilight. Firstly, behind Alfred's frantically moving form, I made out a woman's shape, her bare, protruding stomach, at the bottom of which she was clawing with her hand; then, her legs moving restlessly in visible agony; and, just before Alfred called my name for the third time, sharply like a slap to bring me out of my paralyzed state, sheets that were soaked with blood to such an extent, I took it to be their original color.

"Dora! We need to operate. Alcohol, instruments—now!"

As I sprang to action, fumbling for the disinfectant, he was already leaning over the woman's face, pallid like melting wax, apart from broken blood vessels that stood out like a purplish cobweb around her nostrils and sunken eyes. In his voice reserved only for children, Alfred was cooing at her as he placed a gauze mask over her nose and mouth and told her to *Breathe, just breathe deeply and it'll be over before you know it, love; you'll wake up with your babe in your arms; you have my word, angel, just one more deep breath...*

I watched her eyelids flutter like the wings of an injured butterfly before closing at last in their ether-induced sleep.

Over his makeshift surgical mask, Alfred's eyes met mine. For a fraction of a second, his hand faltered over the gauze generously wetted with iodine I was holding for him. "I don't have much experience in this," he whispered in a surge of sudden candidness. "It's a breech; should I have tried to turn the baby? But she's asleep now at any rate, so it won't make any difference; it's much too late. She won't be able to deliver it herself. I'm not quite sure how deeply I should cut... What if I catch the baby with the scalpel by accident? Or damage any internal organs?"

I hadn't the faintest idea of the protocol in such cases. I had never seen a pregnant woman up close, let alone aided one in birth. I thought of saying just that, but clamped my mouth shut at the last moment. He didn't need my opinion. He needed reassurance; it came to me clear as day.

"You did a fabulous appendectomy the other day," I said, pushing the brown-colored gauze into his hand. "I suppose the depth of the cut in the abdominal wall should be the same; no? At any rate, you're excellent with the knife. If anyone can help this woman, it's you, Herr Doktor."

"It's not like this poor soul has much of a choice when it comes to doctors." Alfred's eyes crinkled in their corners—I believe he made an almost superhuman attempt at a smile under his mask—but he took the gauze from me all the same and suddenly was all composure once again, sanitizing the surgical site, putting his hand out, palm up, for a scalpel, making a resolute cut as if he wasn't searching my face helplessly just moments ago.

Before long, he was holding a small babe by her chest, rubbing at her back vigorously, clearing out her tiny nose and mouth with his finger, whispering curses or prayers to himself—I couldn't quite tell. And, at last, a loud wail penetrated the room full of stillness, a life-affirming one, hungry and protesting at being brought into the world in such a manner, at such a horrible time to be born.

It was when I was cleaning the baby in a small basin in the kitchen that Alfred exhaled the words I'd been fearing, but expecting, just over my shoulder, "The mother is dead," and dropped into the only chair by the wall.

"You did everything you could," I said, but, as I turned to face him, I saw him staring at his bloodied hands as though the mother's death was somehow his fault.

"Gerti told me the woman arrived all alone," he said at length, gazing ponderously at the squirming baby in my arms. "Either the husband is in jail or he's German. Divorced her on racial grounds and told her to get lost."

"Together with his baby she was carrying?"

For the first time, he looked at me. In his eyes, I saw the shattered image of the world that had gone to the devil. "It's very inconvenient now, to have a baby of a mixed racial status, Dora. You should know that much." He tried to grin, grimaced instead, and shook his head at the cynicism of this new Germany Hitler was making "great" again.

For a moment, silence hung over the kitchen, interrupted only by the pitiful meowing of the small fussing wrap in my arms. She was most certainly hungry and there was absolutely nothing we could give her.

"What shall we do with the baby?" I probed Alfred gently. He still bore the look of a man who'd just been stabbed in the gut—pale, shaken, unable to comprehend the senseless violence of an attack. "She needs milk..."

When Alfred made no reply, I probed further.

"The Mendelbaums. One of their daughters had a newborn; perhaps, she could—"

"No." Alfred was suddenly on his feet. "We're not condemning this poor mite to a life of misery. She's already lost her mother. That's enough suffering to last one a lifetime."

I watched him silently as he scrubbed his hands of the brownish crust until they were raw.

"We'll take her to the children's home," he said with grim resolution. "Pin a note on her with a Dutch name. Pass her off as a gentile abandoned baby. They'll register her as such and raise her as a Dutch citizen. She's a precious little thing," he said softly, turning the corner of the towel to take a better look at the newborn's face. "It is my profound conviction that a good childless family will adopt her in no time. This way, she'll have a future. She'll have a good life ahead of her."

. . .

In the evening, as we stood under the amber light of a lamppost and watched the door of the orphanage open and a nurse on duty reach for a wicker basket with the little "Dutch" newborn in it, Alfred's hand suddenly grasped mine and pressed it with great emotion.

"You're a great comrade, Dora," I heard him say before the spring wind picked up his words and scattered them with the white petals of the apple trees. "I would have been lost without you."

"You?" I asked with mock surprise, unable to look at him for the same reason he refused to look at me. "You're the definition of composure. You're a portrait of self-possession. You're a Teutonic Knight who could put any SS man to shame with your mind of purest ice and hands of gold, Herr Doktor."

Alfred beamed, shook his head at the joke, but didn't let go of my hand. Something was already shifting between us, something that could forever alter our working relationship into something I was too afraid to imagine, but, while we were looking straight ahead and not at one another, while we could joke about it, it was still safe somehow, just two comrades holding hands.

"You would do just fine without me, Alfred. You're just humoring me by taking me along because I'm a pest and wouldn't leave off, no matter how much you tried to make me," I continued, glad to hear soft chuckles emerge from his throat, too often choked with the grief he had to deal with daily.

"You're not a pest, Dora."

"No?" I raised my brow in theatrical confusion, turned to search his face and regretted it at once: in the light mist rolling off the water, his profile had such a noble and dreamy quality to it, I found him to be a creature from another planet just then.

"No," he whispered and added, after a pause during which I held my breath and didn't notice that I did, "you're the strongest woman I've ever met."

"We're missing dinner at Veidt's, you know," I said, because nothing else occurred to me to say at that moment of highest gravity.

"Do you think they'll take our Party membership cards for snubbing a Soviet commissar in such a manner?"

"I think we should go and apologize, at least." I didn't think so in the slightest. Nothing was further from my mind than the blasted commissar and his idiotic dinner, but it was not only my fate I had to concern myself with. Alfred's entire life was connected with the Party. It was because of that that I pulled my hand gently out of his and turned away from the orphanage and everything that didn't happen between us that evening.

EIGHT

AMSTERDAM. SUMMER 1934

"How's work?"

Hearing my mother's voice, even if distorted by the static of the international phone line, instantly brought me back to Essen and filled my nostrils with the smell of her signature apple strudel she was presently baking; made my chest swell with memories of childhood's innocence when I was utterly and blissfully oblivious to all the evil man was capable of.

"Work is good," I reported brightly, wrapping and unwrapping the tight black cord around my index finger—a nervous habit I could never get rid of. If it wasn't the cord, it would have been a lock of my hair, the cloth belt on my dress—anything really that translated the nervous energy of my mind into physical tics.

It was never my intention to lie to her in such a blatant manner, but how was I supposed to explain to my poor mother that instead of working as a salesgirl I was volunteering for a local communist Party section and all my pay came from them, which was enough only to cover necessities—the rest went to those who needed it more than I did? How was I to explain it to her that I was in the Party myself? Vati, a hardworking bourgeois man descending from generations of similar middle-class bourgeois, would have had a right fit. Oma, with her pride in Jewish tradition and devotion to the Temple, would have likely renounced me altogether for my "wayward, godless Bolshevist ways."

But the entire Party business was only one of the reasons why I'd been avoiding making this call for so long, resorting to colorful postcards with a few short lines here and there and some parcels stuffed with hand-painted clogs, licorice, a porcelain salt and pepper set shaped as windmills, chocolate bonbons and even local Dutch beer for Vati—my pitiful substitution for the real Amsterdam I'd promised to bring them to. Despite all of Alfred's assurances to the contrary—"You've been here only for a year; surely, they don't expect you to have made enough in such a short time to support you all?"—I was a failure in my own eyes.

"I haven't been able to save much because..." I released a breath and leaned against a hard wooden wall of the phone booth, my finger growing numb in the phone cord noose I'd been strangling it with. "There are so many immigrants here now, mostly from Germany, and it's not that easy—"

"Dora, little one, you don't have to explain." Somehow, my mother's soft voice made me feel even worse about myself. "Don't you fret about us. We're doing just fine here. Do you need money?"

"No, I don't need money." I closed my eyes against the shame.

A pause. My mother, trying to read between the lines of my silence. "Dora, do you want to come home?"

"What? No!"

"Are you quite certain?"

"Yes, Mutti. I'm needed here."

"You're needed here too. We miss you."

I smiled at the black mouthpiece tenderly. "I miss you too. But I'm not needed in Germany."

"I'm not talking about Germany. I'm talking about our family."

This time, it was me who pricked my ears, picking the bits of information from whatever was left unsaid, implied, hinted at. Long distances do that to a person. One learns to read minds over the phone, over the letters with lines smudged with tears.

"They've come to Essen, haven't they?" I didn't have to spell out the Nazis for her to understand who exactly I was talking about.

"We just had local elections not that long ago, yes." Another evasive reply. Another silence full of meaning. "There are a few new laws that have been passed."

"Is Vati still working?"

"He... has his own clients, yes."

Other Jews.

Behind the thin wall, in the neighboring booth, someone laughed loudly. The phone cord was now twisted around a fist I hadn't realized I'd made.

"What about you?" I asked Mutti.

"Ach, I've been thinking of quitting for a long time, so I finally did." Her voice was just as bright as mine had been when I was lying about how well I was doing here mere minutes ago.

Inside my summer sandals, my toes were curling with silent fury. I'd heard enough stories from the new arrivals about more and more discriminatory laws that had forced them out of their apartments, businesses, and official positions and into nowhere —a forced immigration policy of a new nationalistic government purging itself of "enemy elements." Heard, and discarded them as something that was happening in Munich and Berlin but not on the outskirts, not just yet; and the parcels that my family sent to me were just as brimming with goods as the ones I sent them, assuring me that everything was peachy, that there was absolutely nothing for me to worry about... God only knew how much of their severely depleted savings had gone into supporting such a pretty illusion. Lies that we tell each other out of love...

I exhaled and rubbed my temple, my mouth, my neck; began scratching at it with my nails. "I'll get you out of there, Mutti, all right? Just give me a couple of months. I'll figure something out. I have very good comrades here. They'll think of something."

"No, Dora—"

"Mutti, I promise—"

A voice cut into our conversation, informing me that if I wished to continue the conversation, I needed to pay in advance at the front desk.

"Mutti, I have to go now, but I'll call as soon as I can—"

"No, Dora, don't call—"

The hissing of the static.

"Mutti? Mutti!" I shouted into the mouthpiece.

The same voice from the booth next to me that had laughed loudly before now advised me to shut my trap.

"—down. Dora?"

"Mutti?"

"I said write to us instead. They're taking our phone down next—"

The same emotionless female voice announced that my funds had expired.

I hung up the phone and felt like hanging myself next to it.

Hands jammed in the pockets of my summer dress, I wandered through the streets, numb and sightless with worry. By the riverbanks, square on the concrete, people were enjoying the sun, bicycles leaning against the embankments, discarded clothing hanging off the handlebars. I nearly walked into such a bicycle rider, mumbled an apology; tangled myself in a dog's leash I didn't notice until I nearly planted myself face first onto the sidewalk; got cursed out by a bus driver who had to jam the brakes to avoid running me over.

In the end, I dropped onto the grassy patch across from the photo shop and stared stupidly into nothing until a solicitous Dutch policeman on patrol bent over me to inquire if everything was all right and whether I needed assistance of any sort.

"*Ja,* could you kill Hitler?" I asked him in a dead voice and forced a smile in response to his kind and sympathetic one. "I'm not drunk, I promise," I said, taking his proffered hand to rise. "I'm just an immigrant."

"I figured that much," he replied and wished me the best of luck before tipping his head and moving off in the direction of the fishermen lined up by the waterfront. Most of them released the fish they caught after measuring them diligently and exchanged bragging remarks in Dutch. But two of them fished silently, with great purpose, and kept all the fish they caught. They were immigrants, too. To them, fishing wasn't sport; it was their dinner.

I stumbled through the next few weeks in the same manner, too preoccupied with thoughts of my family to notice anything else. Of course, I still helped Alfred and did my work for Veidt, but all my work was mechanical now, overshadowed by the German newspapers I kept buying from street vendors and the local advertisements for those with work experience and immigration papers, the last word underlined and in bold font.

I went to a couple of interviews, received a couple of promises to get in touch soon that came to nothing. I missed a couple of Party meetings and squirreled away a membership fee instead of leaving it on Veidt's kitchen table, under a potbellied teapot with a chipped nose. Veidt chose to politely ignore it. Alfred didn't.

He ambushed me in my room; well, not ambushed per se, but I'd just returned from yet another interview I could have sworn I failed because of my bad Dutch (one could well imagine that speaking mostly to German émigrés and communists didn't do wonders for its improvement). I had guilt written all over my face and there he was, standing by the window looking at me with those concerned, searching eyes I couldn't stand just then.

"Veidt let me in," he said by way of greeting. "I hope you don't mind?"

I stood in the door, making no motion to go into my own room. "Is it something urgent?"

He made a step forward, peered at me closer. "Is everything all right with you?"

I didn't budge. "Yes."

A very long pause. "I've been worried about you. It's not like you to miss the meetings—"

"I'm fine. I've just been busy lately."

Another pause, longer than the previous. I could hear the alarm clock ticking in Veidt's bedroom.

"Have you met someone?"

That caught me off guard. "What?"

"I thought, maybe you'd met someone and that was the reason why—"

"Alfred—"

"I know it's none of my business and I haven't the right to ask—"

"It's not that."

He was studying me, with his head tilted to one side, emotions shifting his expression several times. "No, it's not that," he repeated after me, nodding mildly to himself. "You would have been all glowing, smiling, walking on air, and you look..."

"Pale and tired?" I offered him a lopsided grin. "Why, thank you. One can always count on you when it comes to compliments."

"What can I say? I'm a regular ladies' man when I'm not busy fighting the Nazis on the home front."

Something shifted inside of me at the familiar jesting; some block of ice that had hardened inside was beginning to thaw out.

"Talk to me, Dora."

"Make me a drink."

He did, opening Veidt's prized cognac he had left from the commissar's visit, and before long I poured out my entire life story in one uninterrupted stream of consciousness: my school in Essen, Berlin's nightlife, Ashley and Amory and the Brownshirts drawing swastikas on Jewish stores; the man I lost my virginity to, who had disappeared into thin air as soon as he'd discovered a golden Star of David in my nightstand's drawer; the job I was fired from and the year during which I'd done so much to help others and nothing whatsoever to help my own family... The rest Alfred knew already, for he'd been a part of my life, whether he wanted it or not.

He listened to me closely, without judgment, nodding in all the right places and refilling my glass until my head began to swim with alcohol I had long lost the habit for since my Berlin days.

"Be honest now: have you lost all respect for me?" I asked him, only half in jest, terrified to hear the answer but drunk just enough to handle it.

He blinked at me as though awakened from a dream. "Lost all respect for you? Why?"

"For being selfish. For thinking of leaving the Party to earn money for my family."

"You're the least selfish person I've ever come across, Dora."

"What is it then? Now you look..."

"Pale and tired?"

I smiled at him, thankful for a timely jest. "Preoccupied."

He was considering something; I could tell by how relentlessly he was chewing on his lip. Somehow, driven to half-insanity, we'd become a nation of neurotics without a land, unmoored and traumatized for life and having absolutely no one to rely on.

"Talk to me, Alfred," I uttered the same words he'd lured me into conversation with.

His eyes turned a shade darker at the recognition of it. "Make me a drink."

I pushed mine toward him. He drank it in one shot, pressing the side with my lipstick on it to his mouth.

"I have just received an assignment from Moscow. They want me to relocate to Paris for... more imperative Party business; you understand?"

I understood very vaguely but nodded all the same.

"I wanted to ask you to come with me, Dora."

My eyes widened in spite of myself.

"But there go those plans, I suppose." The tragic smile on his face nearly choked me with emotion. "I wasn't preoccupied. Just... It's a bit of a blow to my best-laid plans, but it's all right. You do what you have to do, Dora. Quit the Party, go find a well-paid job, provide for your family—"

"What do you have to do in Paris?" I asked him, sobering up at will. It was one of my talents Ashley had admired a very long time ago, in some other life of mine I could scarcely remember.

Alfred was silent. In his eyes, I saw his mind at war with itself: to tell or not to tell. He opened and closed his mouth a few times as though searching for a good place to start.

"Have you read Hitler's manifesto, *Mein Kampf*?" he asked eventually.

"I would chop my right hand off with an ax before I shell out my hard-earned money for that garbage," I admitted honestly.

Alfred nodded, as if he'd expected that much. "Soviet intel-ligence people have. They'd been following Hitler's ascent to power closely through their German agents. They'd been watching him even closer after he and his cronies had staged the burning of the Reichstag, which they'd pinned on the first communist scapegoat they could get their hands on."

I nodded. I remembered the event clear as day. Closed stores, police and SA pouring out of tarpaulined trucks on every other intersection, entire streets cordoned off, paper checks inside U-Bahn train cars, and then, all at once, the palpable collapse of a Weimar democracy that my roommates and I mourned in cigarette-smoke-wreathed silence to the sound of Minister Goebbels screeching about the Bolshevist threat from the East, Wall Street Jewry from the West, and the Nazi Party and the Führer at its helm being the sole savior of the world.

Everyone knew that the entire Reichstag fire affair had been staged, just like the trial that had come after; we all whispered about it, but it was much too late by then. The newspapers that dared to question the official narrative had suddenly discovered their offices ransacked and padlocked and editors arrested; former communist leaders began to disappear in droves, just like their Social Democrat counterparts, and, all at once, even whispering any thoughts of dissent was a crime against the Fatherland. Denunciations, arrests, re-education, forced labor, prison terms soon became a new reality for the country whose people had collectively lost their minds.

"He might be a first-rate public speaker," Alfred continued in the meantime, "but he's not too bright when it comes to concealing his plans for world domination. In fact, he'd laid them out in plain sight for everyone to see in the little book he wrote in jail. In it, Hitler says loud and clear that it is Germany's mission to rid the world of the Bolshevist threat and the West's decadent influence. He took some half-baked racial theories, mixed them up with some Nietzsche, and voilà: now the people of Germany will have 'justified' reasons for the holy war. Holy in his eyes, that is. For the rest of the world, it shall be pure genocide of everything non-Germanic, but for Hitler's supporters it's just what the doctor has ordered. Even the ones in doubt shall be eventually convinced. There is no more independent media. All of the information the Germans are presently receiving is coming directly out of Goebbels' lying gob. All of the dissenting professors, scientists, artists, writers and what have you have been jailed, murdered or forced to flee. Teachers in schools compete in whose class can create a better swastika formation. Women compete in who can pop out more blond-haired children for the Reich. Men shove their pinstriped suits into the back of the closet and don lederhosen instead..." Annoyed with himself, Alfred tossed his head impatiently. "Forgive me, please. I get carried away when I talk about these things."

"It's all right."

"You must wonder what this all has to do with the Paris assignment?"

"I think I might be starting to see where this is going. The Soviets think Hitler shall start a war at one point or another?"

Alfred pulled back, visibly impressed. "Now you see why I wanted you to go with me. You're born for this."

"For what?"

"Intelligence work."

I rolled my eyes. "Men in Berlin dives used to say similar things to get me into bed."

Alfred chuckled. It was amazing to see the person he could be without the black cloud of injustice and death constantly hanging over him. "Did it ever work?"

I shrugged. "Sometimes. When I was drunk and they were handsome."

He threw his head back. I swiped at a tear in the corner of

my eye as well. I had forgotten when I had last laughed in such an uninhibited manner.

I still don't know how it happened, but all of a sudden we were upon each other, all searching hands and hungry mouths. In the blurred afternoon, we made love first in the kitchen and then in my room with some animalistic urgency, like the two last people on Earth devouring one another at the dawn of the apocalypse. By the time Veidt returned home, we were dressed and formal with each other, bed made, cognac glasses washed and put away on the shelf, just like our feelings for one another. We shook hands and bid each other good evening, pretending as if it didn't matter all that much, our first time together.

Only, at night, with Veidt snoring softly behind the wall, I realized that I was crying silently, without a single muscle moving, just because my pillow smelled of his aftershave, but the scent, just like Alfred himself, was already fading.

NINE

AMSTERDAM. SEPTEMBER 1934

I biked to my new job past the old cemetery, still and serene in the early hours of Friday. The mornings came later now, grayer, and the shadows thrown by the ancient oaks grew longer with each passing day. The leaves hadn't yet turned, but there was a new chill in the air and the mist had returned with a vengeance, rolling in waves every morning along the cobbled streets and turning the water in the canals the color of spilled milk.

Most of the city still slept, but I cycled forward in a state of greatest excitement: today was pay day and since Veidt still provided me with free board in exchange for my typist's services, most of this pay would go into a hiding place under one of the floor planks I had arranged precisely for this reason. If I received as much as Herr Biese, the photo studio owner, had promised to pay for my services as his assistant, in a year's time I'd save enough to rent an apartment for my family.

It was a fortunate thing, to be so pigheaded, as my oma loved to call it. She had never missed a chance to chastise me for being like a dog with a bone whenever I would get something into "that obstinate head of mine": "There's a difference between determination and stubbornness, Dora. Determination keeps you focused. Stubbornness, in contrast, blinds you. All you see is your end goal and no matter how dangerous or even illegal the path to it is, you take it because you refuse to back down. You won't get everything you want in life, child. It's important to recognize when to back down."

Wise words, perhaps, but I was a pigheaded little thing who never listened, wasn't I? I needed money and got sick and tired of the countless rejections I kept receiving and so, yes, no matter how dangerous or illegal, I had marched one August afternoon into Herr Biese's photo studio and given him a hearty Heil Hitler salute before announcing that I was there for a job. The poor old nationalist (I'd been certain of that much after spotting a portrait of Hitler and a few other high-ranking dignitaries in his display before plotting my further steps) had leapt to his feet from the little velvet chair behind the counter, waved his arms at me, all the while herding me behind the green velvet curtain. There, in a brightly lit room where the portraits were taken, bright patches on his cheeks shone even redder.

"My good woman, whatever are you doing? *Herrgott,* you must be new in Amsterdam."

I had promptly lied that, yes, I was from Alsace but couldn't stand those French harassing us, poor Germans.

Herr Biese had tutted sympathetically. I had laid it on even thicker: not only had they taken our native German land after that humiliating Versailles Treaty, but all but banned us from speaking German, reading German.

"It is as though they're set on erasing our very identity!" I'd lamented my fate, wringing my hands in front of the old Nazi sympathizer. "I'll make a very good worker. I graduated business school with honors"—that much was true—"and have tons of work experience with customers." Also, true.

He was already nodding eagerly, holding his hand out for my passport, which I, naturally, couldn't show him due to the very Jewish last name in it. But as Oma had said, I was a pigheaded one and just refused to admit defeat even when it was staring me in the face.

"I have to confess to you, because I feel that you're a good man and will understand: I came here as a tourist and never left. I know your sign outside says that the assistant must have papers, but is there any chance you could..." I'd feigned further distress, a trembling waif suffering from the world's persecution with only him, Herr Biese, to rely on. "I'd agree for half the pay if it's in cash and not in any books... If I don't get this job, I'll have to go back to Alsace and those French—half of them are bloody Bolshevists; one can't go into the street at night; they pluck the girls and violate them and, if you're German, you can't even report it to the police because they're all Stalinists as well and will never take a German's side..."

He'd enclosed me in a fatherly embrace before I had chance to dissolve into the best theatrical tears I could summon.

Dangerous and illegal? To be sure, but I got the job and that was all that mattered.

And today, I'd get paid for that illegally obtained job and to the devil with social conventions. I could live with myself just fine by being a liar and a cheat as long as it meant my family's survival.

I hummed to myself as I pushed my bicycle through the delivery door. I cherished those early-morning hours, when I had the store all to myself; when the silvery shadows crept along the hand-painted photographic backgrounds breathing life into their still forms and turning canvas gardens and woods into a magical world of its own. I loved its silence interrupted only by the slight creaking of the boards under my feet and the faint chemical, almost citrusy smell lingering near the door of the printing room.

But most of all I was fascinated by the faces—hundreds of them—gracing the entirety of the reception area: neat, organized rows of them lining the walls, and the mosaic of bigger and smaller ones assembled on the green velvet inside the glass counter and on top of it as well, in oval frames and square ones, in stained oak and intricate silver. It was a favorite pastime of mine, studying the couples frozen in time as I polished the counter's glass and wondering which adventures life had taken them on; whether they were still in Amsterdam or perhaps in Argentina or South Africa, or maybe even the Orient, having their next portrait taken in traditional Japanese dress... Or whether they were émigrés like me, taking one last still together while running from something that was spreading over Europe faster than the black plague, and wondering if it would be their last one.

The bell's chiming startled me momentarily, tearing me from my reverie, which was taking on much too dark an overtone. I swung round, my lips already curling into my signature salesgirl smile, welcoming as can be and almost sincerely sorrowful at the same time.

"Good morning," I greeted the tall man in the door in my best Dutch. He was just a dark outline of a silhouette against the bright light pouring from the outside. Inside the store, it was twilight still; only a fan was turning unhurriedly above our heads with its bulb unlit. "I'm so sorry, but we're still closed."

The shadowy man, his hat pressed against his chest, gestured over his shoulder apologetically. "The door was open," he half-asked and I thought I recognized an accent similar to mine.

"Fire-safety regulations," I explained and wondered, once again, if he was a local. Locals knew to look at the "open" or "closed" sign on the door. It was mostly tourists who probed the door instead.

He scrutinized me with his head slightly cocked. "Forgive me, but... do you happen to speak German by any chance?" he asked in German.

I hesitated for a few moments, taking in his finely tailored

suit, the black valise he held in his hand, the dull sheen of gold
on his wrist, and decided that he wasn't a policeman. Neither
was he a fellow refugee. All the new arrivals had a bit of a lost,
frightened look about them. The stranger, in contrast, carried
himself with the confidence of a man who had a right to be
where he wanted to be. A traveling man of means, of quiet
power that lay about him just like the faint cloud of his expensive cologne.

"Yes," I admitted, but didn't offer further information.

He stepped into a single column of light, in which tiny brilliant particles of dust swirled, and broke into a smile of most
extraordinary charm. He had a strange face, as though assembled of different parts sketched by art students drawing Greek
sculptures. Separately everything was perfectly *korrekt*—a
straight nose, a good chin, the angle of his cheeks, the brows, the
eyes—but put together it all represented the most nondescript
face I'd ever come across. There was absolutely nothing about
this man that stood out, that would make me identify him from
the crowd or even remember him. It suddenly occurred to me
that if he turned out to be a serial killer and a police detective
asked me to give a description to a sketch artist, I'd be
completely and utterly at a loss.

"What a marvelous coincidence," the potential serial killer
said, regarding me closely with eyes that could have been gray
or pale blue or hazel even. "I, myself, happen to be from
Germany too."

"I'm not from Germany," something prompted me to say.

"No?"

"No." When the pause began to stretch to uncomfortable
lengths, I finally volunteered, "I'm from Alsace."

"Ach! I should have guessed."

Before he had a chance to continue this conversation, I
dived under the counter and produced a thick appointment
book. "Herr Biese will be delighted to assist you today. He's a

German like yourself. What time would you like to come in? We have a few wedding couples scheduled after twelve, but before that—"

"Pardon me, but what is your name?"

Ordinarily, I offered my name as soon as a customer walked in. However, there had been something about this particular gentleman that had made me clam up in spite of my best intentions, but now he had asked me outright.

"Dora," I said at length.

"Dora?" he prompted with an innocent grin.

"Dora Hess," I lied. The last name slipped off my lips just as easily as when I'd offered it to Herr Biese together with my just-as-fake sob story.

"Hess," the man drawled, as if finding the name positively delightful. "Not a relative of Deputy Hess; no?" He was all playfulness now.

Only nationalists like Biese called Hitler's henchmen by their respective titles. To them, Rudolf Hess was a deputy. To us, he was a bastard and a raving lunatic.

"I wish." I played along, all smiles and charm, and tapped my pencil on the lined paper. "Is eleven all right with you? Will it be a formal portrait with a background or do you need it for paperwork—"

"Just a portrait," he said. "As I am now. It's for me. To mark the occasion."

"May I ask what is the occasion?" I gave him my best playful look.

"My first day in Amsterdam," he said and something in his voice sent another wave of goosebumps down my back. I wondered if that was what dogs felt when their heckles rose at the sight of a predator.

"Eleven it is, Herr...?" I waited for the name.

"Wildgrube."

Even when he was long gone, the air remained thick with

unease, as if he had somehow tarnished it with his very presence.

He did return at eleven precisely; pumped Herr Biese's hand with great emotion and chatted to the old man with the easy charm of a long-lost son. My employer not only covered the undercurrents of the city's immigrant society and the locals' attitude to it, but even my own story, half-whispering and shielding his mouth as he recounted my tales of Gallic Stalinists harassing innocent German maidens.

I listened with my ears pricked from behind the velvet curtain, all the while searching the valise Wildgrube had left next to the umbrella and cane stand right in the open, risking being exposed by the first client wandering in. It went against my very nature, rummaging through a stranger's personal belongings in such a shameless manner, and yet, some ancient instinct in my Jewish blood, honed by the thousands of years of persecution my people had had to endure, alerted me to something predatory and alien in the German's nature. No harm would come of my little search. I wasn't here to steal, after all; just to assure myself that he was indeed a harmless businessman and not a Nazi spy sent to the heart of the nation his bosses were plotting to invade. Was it simple paranoia? It could have been. And yet...

"Better safe than sorry," I whispered to myself as I dug deeper.

In it, there was suspiciously little, given Wildgrube's story of being a German traveling salesman. All of his personal documents must have been either carefully stuffed in the inner pockets of his elegant double-breasted jacket or left in the hotel's safe. I was about to abandon my search empty-handed, when a silver mechanical pencil lost in the folds of the valise attracted my attention. I turned it upside down in search of initials and nearly dropped it on the tiled floor as, instead of two letters, an infamous double lightning bolt presented itself to my eyes.

"That poor child... Such suffering, at such a tender age..."

Hushed voices murmured behind the curtain.

"She won't suffer long. Alsace shall be a Reich's territory very soon and then all of the German nationals shall be avenged, and those dirty Bolshevists and Jews purged like the vermin they are. The Führer shall see to it."

Riveted to my haunches, I sat with the dreaded SS-marked pencil in my hand, images of annihilation unraveling before my eyes as though in some demented nightmare. Inside my chest, my heart lay heavy as stone as a grim realization was gradually dawning on me that no matter where we ran, no matter how long we tried to hold out for, there was no escape from this black plague. It was already here, it was already spreading; the first harbinger of it was already sitting in the room next to me and it was only a matter of time until his entire army would march in and slaughter us all in cold blood.

As silently as possible, I placed the pencil back into the folds of the leather valise and closed the buckle. I slowly gathered myself and whatever was left of my shattered illusions and went about my day as though nothing had happened, as though my entire life hadn't just gone to pieces. I gathered my first pay, felt the bills burn through my hand with a bittersweet emotion, stopped at the local bar instead of going straight home and tried to drown my sorrows in four glasses of cognac I would have never splurged on before. And at quarter to eleven, still half-drunk and mad at the entire world, I rang Alfred's bell until he ran out and physically took my finger off the bell, wrapped in a bath towel, dripping with water and impossibly handsome.

"What is it, Dora? What happened? Is something the matter?"

"Something certainly is," I muttered, stumbled inside and began searching my pockets.

"Are you drunk?"

I made no reply; only slammed the photo I finally found on his mail table so hard, the keys in the small crystal vase that stood on top of it rang faintly.

"I stole this from Biese. Goes by the name of Wildgrube. An SS man, likely from their foreign intelligence department. Passes himself off as a traveling salesman. Got anyone to pass it to?"

Alfred picked up the photo and studied it closely for some time.

"Anything else?" he asked, looking up at me from under his wet bangs.

"Yes." I leaned against the door because my legs just didn't want to hold me any longer. I almost physically felt the ground going from under me and it wasn't due to the alcohol; not at all. It was a sense of freefall, a point of no return, a passing of a threshold that would change one's life for all eternity, and I'd just made that first step into nothing. "I'm going to Paris with you."

TEN

"Are you absolutely certain?"

The doubt in the barber's eyes reflected twofold through the mirror. For the umpteenth time, he brushed a fine-toothed comb through the ropes of my wheat-colored hair—my most prized possession, which scissors hadn't touched ever since I was a little girl. Released from its bounds at the nape of my neck, it cascaded down my back, over the barber's chair, covering my shoulders like a cape of pale gold.

I eyed the money he'd laid down on the counter in front of me and clenched my jaws together.

"Just get it over with," I said through gritted teeth and watched with masochistic fascination as the shiny steel sliced into my hair just under my earlobes.

It was a strange separation, completely painless on the outside, but one that left me with a phantom-limb pain deep in my aching soul for weeks and even months to follow.

"It would make a fine wig for some rich but aging Parisian lady," the barber muttered before chopping it off. All I cared about was the money that would see Alfred and me through winter. Hopefully. Because, frankly, aside from the hair I had nothing else to sell. Myself only, and who'd want a German émigré's skin and bones when Parisian prostitutes were so well-dressed and good-looking?

"I would," Alfred announced later that night, lovingly tucking the short strand of my hair behind my naked ear. My earrings had been sold a long time ago as well, just like his silver cufflinks and a watch with a golden face—his late grandfather's present, just before he'd passed away. Trapped in the maze of the French capital's streets, we were slowly selling pieces of ourselves until there would be nothing left of us but memory.

As I lay in bed, tormented with insomnia in addition to being cold, I sifted through pages of my most recent memories, wondering just how exactly we'd gotten here, in this dingy room in the outskirts of the city where we knew no one.

The excitement of our arrival had worn off faster than the scent of a cheap Chanel perfume imitation. For the first couple of weeks, we'd been on a Paris honeymoon of sorts, drunk with the city lights, golden and diffused by the mist rolling from the Seine; kissing under the Arc de Triomphe lit up by searchlights and wreathed in flowers for the Armistice anniversary; giddy with anticipation of the mission to be carried out, of the clandestine work to be done in the secrecy of the night, fully believing in our ability to save the world with the naiveté of children left alone to their own devices for the first time.

Everything was mysterious and impossibly exciting—the plot of a spy thriller in which we were suddenly the main characters. Even our hostel room in the Fifth Arrondissement, as seedy as they come, had somehow transformed in front of our eyes from a former prostitute's abode into our personal headquarters, perfectly inconspicuous and all ours—a place from which the fate of Europe would be decided. A communal kitchen was rodent- and roach-infested; the mattress in our bed had to be turned upside down (which didn't really help things as it was just as stained on the bottom as it was on the top);

entering the communal bathroom was only possible with one's nose held closed—and yet, we paid no heed to such trifles. Undocumented and existing on five francs a day from the International Red Aid organization, it was us against the formidable Nazi machine. Never before had I slept so soundly in my lover's arms, content with my role in this invisible war we were about to wage. Never before had hunger tasted so good to me, with a subtle hint of noble sacrifice to it.

But, before long, winter descended upon us and the first blast of its freezing temperatures sobered us up at once. Blinded by a noble cause, we'd set out on adventure in a foreign country just to realize that we were cold, hungry, undocumented and, it appeared, thoroughly unneeded by our Moscow bosses. The losses wouldn't be so deep and personal if there was a tangible reason for them, something to justify our misery with. But months had passed and not a word from Moscow, no directions whatsoever, apart from "sit tight, you'll hear from us when the time comes."

At last, Alfred couldn't tolerate this torture any longer. One frostbitten February morning, he threw up his hands, grabbed his coat from the nail by the door and walked out with his mouth full of hidden curses, only to return almost at night, frozen to the bone and covered with coal dust but beaming with delight as he arranged a few wrinkled bills atop the windowsill doubling as our dining table, or writing desk when the occasion called for it.

"Helped to unload coal from a barge," he announced with a smile that appeared almost feral in contrast with his smudged-with-gray face. "The fellow in charge gave me another fellow's name, some fishing boat affair. They need hands too."

"Undocumented?"

"They don't care, as long as one doesn't fear hard work. Pay in cash right on the spot, too. Can't get a better deal in our situation!"

Refusing to be upstaged, I went out the very next day and declined to return home until some Turkish fellow took pity on me and agreed to take me on—on a trial basis, he emphasized, looking over my skinny frame with obvious doubt—as a dishwasher in his coffee house, which doubled as a hookah bar for the local Turks and Parisian artists frequenting such dives.

The work was merciless and poorly paid; my hands were scrubbed raw and my back would feel like that of an ancient woman by the end of each shift. A few times, I cried silently into the gray dishwater as I scrubbed grease from enormous pots and skillets. A few times, the cook shoved me for being a useless broad with two left feet for hands when a cup slid out of my numb fingers and shattered with a thunderous explosion I was certain could be audible in the café's main room, or when the pot I washed at the end of the exhausting twelve-hour day was not clean enough for his liking.

"Look here!" he said, grasping me by the nape of my neck with his great, hairy paw. "Do you see your silly mug reflected here? Neither can I. Which means it's still dirty. Wash it again."

"Can I have more soap?" I had dared to ask.

"No, you can't have more soap; what do you think this is, a soap factory? Use your hands, girl! That's how my mother did it, and her mother before her."

And so, I stayed late, and scrubbed, and swallowed down my tears and pain and all the injustice in the world because after the shift was over, I got my own few wrinkled bills to lay out in front of Alfred and smiled smugly at him before he'd cover me in kisses and promise me that he'd outwork me the very next day.

We'd turned misery into competition, despair into success. And, as though they'd been watching us this entire time just to see if we were the right material, if we swam instead of drowning or retreating back to the safety of Amsterdam, one of our invisible bosses suddenly materialized as though from thin air, quite literally in our hostel room, and announced that there was a job for us.

He had the perfectly inconspicuous appearance of a Russian émigré, one of the former White Russians turned taxicab drivers, in a tweed cap he'd thrown casually onto our sill/dining table, in rolled-up shirt-sleeves under a faded coat he'd also thrown without much care over the back of our only chair, with dark stubble on a square chin untouched by a razor at least for a couple of days and fingers stained with tobacco. It was his eyes that betrayed his profession, steely and steady and sharp as a whip, observing everything from under the heavy lids with the watchfulness of a spider spreading his net for his victims to fall into, motionless and yet deadly alert, ready to pounce at a moment's notice.

"The name's Sergey. Sit, sit," he said, gesturing us to the bed with the confidence of someone who had all the right to be there. "Make yourselves comfortable. This will take a while."

He observed us for a time as we sat before him like two schoolchildren, hands folded neatly on our laps, and, for the life of me, I couldn't shake the feeling of those watchful eyes penetrating into me, reaching deep inside the folds of my innermost thoughts, reading them with ease as if from the open pages of a book.

"Dora Davidsohn," he said. His heavy accent made him sound as if he was turning stones in his mouth. "Good work with that Wildgrube fellow. Valuable information." That, and a small appreciative nod, put an end to the compliment. Despite the stingy manner in which it was presented to me, I felt my cheeks warm with pleasure. "You don't mind going through strangers' personal affairs, do you?"

A blush of pleasure turned into the stinging heat of shame.

The Spider—he would always be the Spider to me, for I was quite certain that Sergey was just a random name his bosses from GRU, the Soviet Intelligence Service, had put into his passport along with an equally fake last name—raised his hand, anticipating my protest. "No, no, there's no reason to justify yourself, particularly to me. It's a highly appreciated ability in our profession, abandoning one's principles for the cause."

Something about the way he put it made me wince inside, but he was already talking over my doubts before they had a chance to set in.

"You'll have to do this a lot where I shall be sending you to. Sometimes, several times a day. Will this be a problem?" he asked pointedly and fixed me with those razor-sharp eyes.

"Not at all." The cool resolve in my voice surprised even me.

Another nod; heavy lids dimmed the gleam of the metal in his eyes momentarily. "Here's an address."

My eyes widened at the name of the street lined with mansions and high-fashion boutiques.

"You'll need to become a maid to this Mademoiselle Charlotte. She's the mistress of a Spanish nationalist who visits her each time he's in town, which is almost every other weekend. You'll have plenty of opportunity to go through his valise while he's busy with his little French lady friend. I don't need to add that he mustn't suspect anything, do I?" He arched a brow—the first semblance of emotion on his otherwise immobile face.

"No, but I do have a few questions."

"Memorize and report any paper you come across," he answered one of them before I had a chance to pose it. "We'll sort the important from unimportant later."

"All right." I nodded. I thought about asking why in the hell I was to watch some Spanish sod if the threat was coming from Germany, but then didn't. Something about the Spider advised against asking too many questions. "How do I become her maid? It's a very exclusive area and I don't even have any papers..."

The Spider smiled like a snake. "Mademoiselle Davidsohn,

with all due respect, I suspect you rather underestimate yourself. Didn't you figure out how to become a photographer's assistant in Amsterdam without presenting him with any papers as well?"

I blinked in silent astonishment. For an instant, I wondered if Alfred had informed someone from our cell about my illegal job, but, judging by the manner in which he stiffened next to me just now, I assumed that this was very much not the case.

"We don't delegate tasks just to anyone, Mademoiselle Davidsohn. You've been selected because you have an ability to find your way out of dead-end scenarios." He paused and lightly cocked his head to one side. "Or am I mistaken?"

"No." I swallowed nothing. My throat was suddenly dry.

"Good. It's settled then." He turned to Alfred. "As for you, Monsieur Benjamin, you'll need to drop all that fooling around with barges and fishing boats and apply your best to getting yourself a position here."

Another scrap of paper with an address on it—in an area much seedier than mine, a typical immigrant exchange not too far from the Turkish café where I worked. *Had* worked, I supposed. The Spider quickly put an end to that career.

"It's a dive frequented by Italian soldiers on leave who are looking for cheap whores and French champagne. Get yourself the position of a waiter, or, better yet, a barman, and keep your ears open. They talk a lot when they drink and love to boast. Get whores on your payroll if you like. In short, use your imagination and report everything you hear, just like Mademoiselle Davidsohn here. We'll sort it out ourselves."

"What sort of information should I listen to?" Alfred inquired. "I mean, they're Italians. What do we have to do with Italians?"

"You'll find that out soon enough," the Spider promised darkly. "Listen to everything they say: where they're stationed, where they're going, who Mussolini's screwing—everything. Understood?"

Alfred nodded stiffly just like I had done a few minutes ago.

"Good." The Spider slapped his knees and was suddenly on his feet. "Now that's sorted, I'll be on my way. And don't drag your assignment out too much, hear me? Time is of the essence. Get to it sooner rather than later."

"Wait, Monsieur—" Alfred called after the Spider's retreating back; stumbled over the name he didn't know—"how do we find you... well... to make our reports?"

From the Soviet agent, another grin. "You don't find me. I find you."

ELEVEN

PARIS. FEBRUARY 1935

I shed my old self like a lizard sheds its skin and wrapped myself in a new one with ease. Dora-the-dishwasher had been killed and buried, and out of a foggy Parisian night emerged Dora-the-spider, knitting her own web of deception all around the Champs-Élysées. I stalked my prey and studied her habits. I followed her like a shadow and set out my trap. Market days on Tuesdays and Saturdays—Mademoiselle Charlotte preferred her groceries fresh. Laundry day was Monday—that was when all parties were over and the bedsheets changed. Mademoiselle's shopping day was Friday, twelve to three like clockwork; and there she was, my unsuspecting victim, Mademoiselle's maid weighed down by her mistress's round hat boxes and small paper lingerie bags—for the Spanish Colonel, no doubt, together with scarves and dresses and stockings and small vials of perfume of which those bedsheets smelled on Monday. I'd learned that much by now too: I'd befriended the laundry owner, just like I did the doorman and the flower girl selling roses near the Arc de Triomphe that the Colonel's driver bought each Friday evening without fail. There was a flower shop right there, with the fitting name Blumenthal's Blossoms, but the Colonel never sent his driver there and it was this little detail from which my entire plan had been hatched: just like her Spanish lover, Mademoiselle Charlotte thoroughly despised everything Jewish. All of her groceries only came from French stores. All of her jewelry was overpaid for but purchased from French shops.

From time to time, a faint pang of conscience disturbed my concentration, but when the moment came, I struck out without hesitation because there was one thing the Spider was right about: I did possess a very "valuable" ability to abandon my principles for the cause. As long as the end justified the means, I'd readily pay for my guilty conscience with sleepless nights— later, after the work was done.

It was a sunny Friday afternoon. Mademoiselle Charlotte had just finished her daily rounds and was ready for her oblig-atory bath and hairdresser. Holding onto her intricate green hat with an ostrich feather descending from it onto her chestnut locks, she exited the taxicab and gave a smile of an extraordinary charm to the doorman who'd raced to open the car door for her.

I hastened my steps. I thought I had timed everything just right, but Mademoiselle Charlotte appeared to be in a rush today and was walking towards the building's entrance faster than usual. For an instant, the elderly doorman looked help-lessly from her maid struggling with Mademoiselle's shopping bags to Mademoiselle herself and back, until his sense of duty triumphed and he hurried over to the door to get it.

One more second and she'd disappear inside and it would all be lost for me. Another week wasted.

"Sophie! Sophie, it's me, Gudrun Schulz from Alsace!" I shouted, waving manically at the maid as I ran towards her.

The girl would have ignored me entirely—Sophie was just as much her name as Gudrun was mine—but I was making such

an obvious spectacle out of myself, even Mademoiselle Charlotte paused at the door, suddenly interested.

"Don't just stand there like a Carmelite monk on leave, give
me a hug!"

Before the maid could protest, I wrapped myself around her
like a python. Weighed down by the shopping bags, she didn't
have much power to push me off, so she just protested weakly,
still too stunned to speak. And I was already placing resounding
kisses on her cheeks and inquiring of the non-existent Uncle
Moishe of hers and Aunt Frieda and her parents, the wonderful
Madame and Monsieur Grossman and lamenting how Ostwald,
our small Alsace town, just wasn't the same ever since she'd left.

"But what do you know? I decided to follow your steps and
here I am! We're both Parisians now; what do you say to that?"

"Sophie Grossman?"

With my back turned to her, I hadn't realized that Mademoiselle Charlotte was standing next to us now, her thin nostrils
twitching lightly with scantly contained anger. Even though it
had been my plan all along, I'd figured she'd overhear the
conversation, mull it over for a while, consult the Colonel
perhaps... However, Mademoiselle Charlotte must have been a
much more rabid nationalist than I'd originally given her credit
for if she was upon us the moment the possibility arose of her
maid's supposed "Jewishness."

"Why, yes!" I snapped my eyes even wider, with all the
enthusiasm of a newly reunited best friend plastered over my
face. "We used to be so tight growing up, like sisters!"

"I don't know you!" The maid stared at me, white as ash.
Her hand, still clasped firmly in mine, preventing any escape,
was beginning to tremble.

"Would you look at her? She doesn't know me!" I laughed,
making a grab for the colorful ropes of a few hat boxes. "Here,
let me help you with your bags. My, but you've gotten yourself
up swell! Do you live here? You must be a big fish now," I

carried on, drowning all of her protests, which were growing progressively more frantic, in my overpowering chatter. "Did you get a tutor to get rid of the accent? You sound just like a native Parisian now! I need one too; will you give me his number for old friendship's sake?" I gave her a conspiratorial wink as she struggled to pull the bags out of my hand.

"My name is not Sophie! I have never known any Sophie in my life! I've never even been to Alsace!"

"Sophie Grossman from Ostwald," Mademoiselle Charlotte drawled with such ice in her voice, it felt as though the temperature outside dropped even further.

"Mademoiselle Fournier, I swear to you—" the maid pleaded.

However, her mistress had already yanked the bags out of her shaking hands. "I should have known. I thought that nose of yours was just an unfortunate incident, but now it's all clear to me. A Jew and a liar. To think that I allowed you into my house! I ought to report you to the authorities." She turned to the doorman. "Get rid of her and ensure that she never sets foot inside again! And order someone to fumigate the rooms. To imagine that she lived here, with me!"

The maid was on the verge of tears now. Wringing her hands, she begged her mistress to listen as I stood between the two, my hand over my mouth, guilt transforming my expression at will.

"Oh, no!" I slapped myself on the forehead and laughed unconvincingly. "Forgive me, Mademoiselle. I made a mistake. You look just like my best friend from Alsace. Madame," I turned to Mademoiselle Charlotte imploringly, "I have never met this woman in my life before. Please, don't dismiss her. I didn't mean to—"

"You oughtn't apologize or beg on that Jew's behalf," Mademoiselle quipped. "She did it to herself. She ought to have known that, sooner or later, the truth always triumphs."

She was talking about the maid who had served her faithfully for several years as though she was a distant and unpleasant memory; not someone who stood opposite her, tearful and wrongfully accused.

For a fraction of a second, a white-hot rod of guilt pierced me square through my chest as I watched the girl's life crumbling in front of her eyes—all because of me. For a fraction of a second, I almost pulled at Mademoiselle's sleeve, confessed to the whole scheme, but then I remembered the injured Jewish tailor with a leg almost lost to gangrene, the dead woman in the Amsterdam slums who never got to hold her newborn, the ignorant, racist broad who had got me fired from my job, the scores and scores of lives ruined or lost, and bit back the words ready to escape my mouth. The Spider was right. Sometimes, one had to abandon one's principles for a bigger cause and so, instead of mending the situation, I reached for the hat boxes in Mademoiselle Charlotte's gloved hand.

"Allow me to help with your bags, at least, Madame."

Graciously, she released her hold on them and didn't object when I followed her into a warm marble lobby, the elevator and even her very apartment on the top floor.

"Allow me to apologize once again, Madame," I said, placing the boxes on a velvet settee she'd indicated precisely for that purpose. "That big mouth of mine..."

"What did you say your name was?" she asked, removing her tight suede gloves finger by finger.

"Gudrun Schulz, Madame."

"Are you an Alsatian German then?"

"As German as they come, Madame."

She smiled at my short blond hair, contemplating something.

"Are you currently employed, Mademoiselle Schulz?"

"No, Madame. I just arrived in Paris a few days ago. Was

wandering around, taking in the sights when I stumbled into Sophie."

Mademoiselle Charlotte's eyes sparkled. "Well, since you're partly at fault in my losing my maid," she said, suddenly all playfulness, "how would you like to replace her? I pay generously. You can ask Sophie next time you see her."

The poison in her words splashed fresh acid on my wounds, but I merely beamed at her as brightly as was possible and thanked her and God for not burdening this particular specimen with intellect, making her trade a loyal servant for a veritable snake.

I felt like one, cold and unfeeling and full of venom, as I threw off my shoes in our small room later that day as Alfred watched on.

"You got the job, I take it?"

"Why? Do I look triumphant to you?"

"No. You look like my sister when she first went out late at night and returned with money a few hours later. For our sick mother's medicine and to pay for my final two years in medical school."

I looked at him for a very long time, not quite knowing what I felt, what there was to say.

"I didn't know you had a sister."

"She died soon after that. Her pimp got her addicted to morphine. One day she simply took too much—it is my profound conviction, on purpose."

"I'm sorry."

"I don't really like talking about it."

"I understand."

There was a silence that stretched years, ripped through the thin shroud of memories, raising them from the dead in all their foul glory. I saw it all reflect on his tortured face in the bright neon light from the cabaret on the opposite street.

"If it goes against your conscience, Dora—"

"It doesn't."

"—It's all right to stop. No one will hold you accountable."

"This is a job that needs to be done," I said. "If not me, someone else will do it instead and it shall be on their unclean conscience. And just how shall I be a better person for delegating it to some poor devil instead of doing it myself? No, Alfred. It's better this way. And don't fret. I won't get addicted to anything. Can't afford it," I finished with a grim grin that reflected on his thin face, sickly green in the light pouring from the window.

Something broke inside me that night. But just like a broken bone, something calcified, grew stronger in its place, preparing me for the battles that lay ahead. That they would come—in months or years—I had no doubt.

TWELVE

I put on an apron over my new uniform and regarded myself in the small mirror. It used to be Mademoiselle Charlotte's maid's room—a tiny closet-like space with a window looking out onto a brick wall, and a narrow cot in the corner. The uniform also used to be the maid's; Mademoiselle Charlotte hadn't bothered buying a new one for the occasion, and so, I was sentenced to bathe in guilt all day long as I smelled the maid's sweat and the lavender soap masking it on my first day at work.

I had let myself in with the key the doorman had given me while the sun rising over the Champs-Élysées was still a mere blush against the indigo sky. The list of instructions Mademoiselle Charlotte had left me was as pedantic as it was aggravatingly long. Everything had to be just so before she and the Colonel finally arose: the breakfast china with the golden rim was to be used and the breakfast itself was to be served on the terrace and not in the main dining room. The coffee had to be scalding hot and the vanilla ice cream had to be served alongside it for Mademoiselle Charlotte, and goat's milk—cow milk was too heavy for his sensitive stomach—was to be served room temperature for the Colonel. As for the breakfast itself, I had not the faintest idea of how to even begin to approach the preparation of deviled eggs and buckwheat crepes my new employer had requested.

Thankfully, the old maid had left the cookbook bookmarked on the recipes Mademoiselle Charlotte demanded the most and, miraculously enough, though sweating and cursing all the way throughout the preparation process, I managed to create something resembling the illustration and serve it just in time, before Mademoiselle Charlotte emerged from her bedroom wearing a pale lavender silk gown and soft matching slippers that sank into the Aubusson rugs lining the floors.

While I stood by the terrace's door with my hands folded primly over my apron, gaze downcast, she wrinkled her nose at the breakfast table arrangement and moved the fresh flowers, freshly cut baguette and butter around until it was to her satisfaction.

The Colonel had all but passed me by, with the typical arrogance of a man who considered it below him to notice the help, but came to an abrupt halt at the last moment.

"Who's that?" he demanded from his mistress instead of addressing me directly.

He wasn't tall in stature and his robe concealed a certain roundness, but it was the roundness of muscle gone to fat. His pale lips were a thin bloodless line under a moustache he undoubtedly took great pride in, as it was pomaded and curled at the sides despite the morning hour. Above his suspicious, narrowed gray eyes, bushy eyebrows were knitted together.

"Oh, that's Gudrun," Mademoiselle Charlotte replied airily, pouring the Colonel coffee from the silver coffee pot. I was convinced she would have made me do it, had the terrace not been far too narrow to accommodate the table and the maid as well. "She's my new maid."

"Whatever happened to the old one?" The Colonel still hadn't budged from his position by the door.

"She turned out to be Jewish! Imagine that?"

"What?" He finally quit boring into me with his eyes and stared at his mistress instead.

"Mm." Mademoiselle Charlotte nodded, scooping the egg filling with a dainty silver spoon. "It was Gudrun who uncovered that deceitful rat by sheer chance. It turned out they're both from Alsace. Gudrun knows her entire family and they're all yids of the first order."

"And Gudrun... that's German, I presume?"

Once again, the question was directed not at me.

"She is, yes. Such luck I came across her! I always wanted a German maid. German maids are the best. So very clean and don't put their noses where they don't belong, like that little rat always did." Mademoiselle Charlotte stretched her shapely leg under the table to push the Colonel's chair away. "Come, eat. Your crepes are getting cold."

With great reluctance, the Colonel released the terrace door handle he'd been holding and took his place opposite his mistress.

As discreetly as possible, I emitted a breath of relief once they busied themselves with conversation that had nothing to do with me. Moving stealthily and silently, I made my way into the depths of the living room so as not to remind them of my existence. The feast I had slaved over in excess of an hour should keep them busy for the next thirty minutes at least, I surmised—which gave me five minutes to make the bed and twenty to try to go through the Colonel's pockets and valise, and copy whatever Spanish documents I came across into a small black notebook I carried in my pocket specifically for this purpose.

Arranging the pillows into their pristine state, I located the black leather valise with a golden buckle in the corner, right by Mademoiselle Charlotte's dressing table overflowing with perfume bottles, brushes and an assortment of creams, powders and makeup that would put any department store's cosmetics section to shame. The Colonel's civilian jacket was thrown casually over the dressing table's chair as well. I inched closer and closer to it as I was straightening the heavy embroidered duvet over the silk sheets, thinking that it was a damned shame that I didn't speak the language; how much easier it would be for me to just memorize everything instead of copying unfamiliar words—

"I suppose Charlotte didn't tell you."

I nearly jumped out of my skin at the sound of the Spanish accent.

Swinging round on my heel, I managed a smile at the Colonel as he stood in the door, forbidding and stern like a statue of an ancient god. Aubusson rugs; damned Aubusson rugs and the manner in which they muffled every sound, I cursed inwardly as my heart pounded wildly in my chest. How fortunate I was that he had entered when he did, while I was still smoothing the edges of the duvet diligently instead of rummaging through whatever top-secret documents he carried in his valise.

"You don't enter the bedroom until I leave," he said, softening his voice a tad, as if taking certain satisfaction in the fact that he had frightened me so. "In fact, the less we see of you, the better. Go busy yourself in the kitchen or wherever else. Charlotte will ring for you if we need you."

And just like that, I was banished to the old maid's room for the duration of that day and much of the following one. When Mademoiselle Charlotte finally dismissed me on Sunday evening, the Colonel and his valise were long gone.

THIRTEEN

AUGUST 1935

Ordinarily, I waited for Alfred at the back door of his Italian dive, but tonight it was he who was waiting for me, pensively smoking his thin brown Italian cigars for which he'd recently acquired a taste, wrapped in wreaths of smoke and silence.

"You're out early." I kissed him on his mouth.

He only grumbled something unintelligible in response to my searching looks and threw an unfinished cigar on the ground as if it suddenly tasted foul.

We set off in the direction of our hostel, stepping over the waste hurled out of back doors of closing businesses, past working girls smoking languidly on street corners, street vendors wrapping up their goods, no longer appetizing but stale and smelling of old grease. The air was muggy and charged, heavy with the promise of a storm in it. My hand was clammy and hot in Alfred's, but I refused to pull it out of his grip. He was still in his barman's attire—a white shirt with sleeves rolled up and black slacks; only the black apron, smelling faintly of orange liquor and lime, was thrown over his shoulder, instead of embracing his waist. In the street emptied by the night, our steps appeared to be amplified, echoing off the walls as though an army marched through Paris and not just a couple with a lot on their minds.

A taxicab pulled up alongside us. Alfred was about to wave it off, but a voice that was clearly used to giving orders commanded us to get in. In the unshaven face under his usual cap, I recognized the Spider.

"And here we thought you had abandoned us entirely," Alfred said by way of greeting, clambering inside after me.

The Spider only snorted softly and angled his rearview mirror to better see Alfred's face. "Any news?"

"Hardly." Alfred shrugged. "Hardly anyone to get such news from either. You ought to get a new dive for your reconnaissance. The Italians don't favor this one all that much any longer."

"Is that what you think?" In the mirror, the Spider's eyes crinkled with what could be taken for mischief.

Alfred mumbled that he didn't know what to think anymore.

Somewhere in the distance, the first echo of thunder rolled.

The Spider kept on driving unhurriedly, one wrist atop the wheel, the other arm's elbow hanging out of the rolled-down window.

"Anything to report, comrade?"

This was addressed to me.

I shrugged, just like Alfred did a moment ago. "Nothing, really. The Colonel never leaves his valise unattended. Takes it with him to the bedroom even. And aside from regular gossip, he doesn't say much to her. The other night, as they were in bed and I listened on the other side of the door, he bragged about some tailor who makes the best silk shirts, cursed at Marxists some more, indulged in some juicy gossip about someone high-ranking in the Italian army being suspected of being 'a fairy,' as he called it, talked about the end of his career... Either he doesn't trust his mistress or he simply isn't dumb enough to tell her anything. Either way—"

"What I don't understand is why we're wasting our time with Italian soldiers on leave and with that Spanish sod and his French broad when it's the Nazis who ought to be watched!" Alfred, who had been squirming in his seat this entire time, exploded at long last. "Just a few months ago, they announced— out in the open—that they spit on the Treaty of Versailles and that they're officially beginning the program of rearmament."

The Spider only moved his shoulder lazily. It appeared he had no interest in the Nazis and their rearmament threats whatsoever.

"The war is about to break out and you—"

"So, the Italians are gone then, eh?" the Spider asked, cutting Alfred off mid-word.

"That's just what I said," Alfred replied through gritted teeth. "It's just local immigrants now. No soldiers."

"No soldiers at all?"

"No."

"As if they suddenly stopped giving them leave, eh?" The Spider's tone was outright teasing.

Alfred had already opened his mouth to give the Soviet agent a piece of his mind, but drew back all of a sudden, overcome with some revelation that hadn't occurred to him before.

In the driver's seat, the Spider was chuckling quietly.

"Italians are going to war?" I asked what Alfred didn't. "But with whom? Spain? Certainly not Spain; the Colonel wouldn't have been here, vacationing on the verge of the invasion."

"No, not Spain," the Spider agreed readily.

"Not with France either," I continued, raking my mind for possibilities. "Not after we'd just signed the Franco-Soviet Treaty." It was strange thinking of myself as French but, somehow, France had become my temporary harbor in very hostile waters, and that "we" slipped only too naturally from my lips.

"It's one thing to deal just with France, but with France and the Soviet Union..." I shook my head doubtfully. "Mussolini might be a right ass, but even he isn't that stupid."

"No, they aren't interested in France; not quite yet and not with the Soviets backing it. You're right about that, little comrade," the Spider said, suppressing a yawn as the car pulled up to a broken curb in front of our hostel. "Made it just in time before the storm. Well, children, thank you kindly for your reports. You'd better hurry. This one looks like it'll be a nasty one."

The Spider left us out in the street with more questions than answers and disappeared into the night just as the first heavy drops of rain began to fall upon our faces. By the time we reached our room, the sky had split open and was pouring streaks of quicksilver over the glass, wiping the street from view, obscuring everything besides our little room.

Just a few weeks later, we woke up to the news that the Italians had marched into Africa, and in March of the next year Germany entered the Rhineland. The rest of Europe looked on and did nothing.

SUMMER 1936

Together with the heat, helplessness crept in and covered us both with a sticky film, impossible to wash off and physically nauseating. No matter how many times we pleaded with the Spider to send us someplace where we could actually be useful, he only half-closed his eyes, like a cat feigning disinterest in a mouse, and promised that the time to be useful would be here before we knew it.

"Send us to Spain!" Alfred had pleaded during our last meeting in March, just before the Nazis had effectively torn up and stomped their iron-lined boots on the Versailles Treaty. "Isn't it why you placed Dora in that French broad's household?

To spy on that Spanish Colonel who serves under Franco? The Nationalists are planning a coup against the Republicans, aren't they? Can you not send us there, so we can aid the Popular Front? Has not the Communist Party of Spain requested the Soviets' aid? So, why are we still here?"

"You're in the very right place, in the very right time," the Spider had promised. "The Party knows what it's doing."

It didn't seem like it did; else, why would it permit fascism to spread its ugly shadow over Europe without countering it with any significant moves? That was the question that kept Alfred and me awake during the stormy May evenings and suffocating June nights, talking ourselves into headaches and losing precious hours of sleep before setting off to our ridiculously unhelpful jobs to waste more time on nothing.

It injured Alfred more than me, the fact that he had to resort to polishing glasses and serving cheap wine to local crooks and bookies instead of helping émigrés invariably carrying luggage with that lost look about them that immediately set them apart from the crowd. With desperation he sighed and averted his eyes at the sight of the new arrivals—German Jews mostly, a fresh wave of outcasts that had lost all hope to exist in their Fatherland ever since the passing of the Nuremberg Laws —and grimly went about his business as if their fate didn't concern him any longer. Overcome with helpless fury, he broached the subject with the Spider; swallowed his pride and all but begged the Soviet agent to allow him to resume his Amsterdam work, at least in his own free time.

"It's not that there's any use in spying on Italians any longer," he argued, clasping and unclasping his hands atop his knee on the back seat of the Spider's taxicab.

"Do you not think that the Germans may have placed a few spies among them?" the Spider countered calmly.

"Whatever for?" Alfred stared at him.

From the Russian came a deep sigh and an expressive roll of

the eyes. *Did he truly need to explain?* his countenance read. "To uncover and report on communist agents like yourself. The risk is too great. The Party wouldn't approve."

Permission denied; case closed.

"I don't believe that the Party doesn't approve," Alfred would grumble when we were alone, pacing the room like a cage. "It's him who makes the decisions, most likely. Maybe, maybe someone on a regional level, but not the Soviet Party leadership. They would never... That's not what communism is about, Dora. Communism is about helping people, first and foremost. And what they're doing is turning it into capitalist spy games, a power struggle, I know not what else, but this... this is not what..." He groped for words that wouldn't come and ended up falling into a heap on the bed. "I'm a healer, Dora. Not some spymaster."

At least he knew what he was. I couldn't boast of even that much.

I sat on the edge of the bed, feeling the old bedsprings whine and sag even under my minuscule weight. We'd both been overworked and half-starved, but what was worse was the purposelessness of it all. I felt Alfred's agony deep inside my own chest, as though the same blood was flowing through our veins.

"There is something you can do that they won't forbid and which will allow you anonymity," I suggested, moving myself next to him, molding to his form.

He half-turned his head towards me, suddenly interested.

"You could publish a newssheet. Something aimed at the locals that would warn them of the dangers of fascism and turn them from indifferent onlookers into fellow antifascists."

Alfred sat up, holding his weight on one elbow. In the dim amber light of the lamp, his face was suddenly aglow with renewed purpose. I could see the old passion ignite in the depths of his eyes with every word I said.

"You don't have to sign your name under it. Just sign, French-German antifascist league or some such. We can get the paper from the local German Comintern office, can't we?"

As a beaming smile transformed his expression, Alfred took my face in his hands and exclaimed, before covering it in kisses, "You're a genius, Dora, do you know that? A regular genius!"

All at once, the night outside was not a well of dark desperation any longer.

"No, not the pearls; the diamonds for tonight," Mademoiselle Charlotte said, pointing at one of the many open velvet cases I had laid out in front of her.

Her eyes sparkled with a different emotion today. Since the morning, she had been all excitement, padding around her penthouse apartment as though walking on air, throwing the doors to the balcony open and closed again, requesting champagne to be served with her breakfast. I could tell she was itching to impart some terribly exciting news, but didn't, solely because she considered it below her to share anything personal with the help unless asked directly.

At last, I put her out of her misery. "A special occasion tonight?" I asked as nonchalantly as possible, picking up a heavy necklace from its velvet red bed. It caught the slanting rays of setting sun and instantly broke into a myriad of lights.

Mademoiselle Charlotte's eyes shone just as brightly as I closed the clasp on her white, swanlike neck. "The Colonel made a reservation at Maxim's. Which isn't a special occasion on its own," she rushed to clarify, in case her maid—me—would mistakenly assume that dining out in restaurants which were impossible to get into was something out of the ordinary for her, "but the Colonel has hinted that he had a surprise for me." She fixed the neckline of her long, emerald gown, feigning indifference and failing miserably. The girlish smile she desperately tried to suppress gave her away. "I'm suspecting he's going to propose."

"Mademoiselle Fournier!" I gasped in the best imitation of excitement I could muster. "Congratulations! You shall make the most beautiful bride Paris has ever seen. *Vogue* ought to feature you on its cover."

"Gudrun, you're too much!" She play-swatted me in mock protest, but the pleasure in her brilliant eyes was obvious. "*Vogue*. What an imagination you have."

As I watched her float around the dressing room like some magnificent butterfly, regarding herself closely from this side and that in several tall, gilded mirrors, it suddenly occurred to me that she indeed loved something about this Colonel. With the face of a Greek goddess and a body to match, she could have any man she laid her eyes on; however, it was the Colonel for whom she waited with the patience of a saint every Friday. It was for the Colonel for whom she bought all these dresses and hats and did her hair just the way he liked it.

"He's a very good man, you know," she uttered quietly, as if reading my thoughts. She didn't look at me when she said it. "A man of great integrity; a most noble man. He isn't like our local cads who only know how to waste their ancestors' fortunes at the casinos and play politics when they grow bored of the Riviera life just so they have something to gossip about as they gather round for their brandy and cigars. And Victor"—that was the first time that I heard her call him by his first name—"he works tirelessly, for the good of the people."

I was about to arch my brow and caught myself just in time. A rabid nationalist working tirelessly for the good of the people, that was certainly news to me.

Fortunately, Mademoiselle Charlotte was too preoccupied with her fantasies about her lover to notice. "Why did you think he only comes to visit me on weekends? Did you imagine he had a family in Spain?" She laughed her silvery laugh. The idea itself was ridiculous to her.

I didn't think any such thing and cared even less but, for women like her, it was difficult to imagine how the world could revolve around anyone but them. The fact that I could have had my own family to worry about—the family from which I only received an occasional letter—didn't occur to her. She never even bothered to ask me about my fake Alsatian family, I realized just then.

"Victor has sacrificed his entire life for the people," she continued with a dreamy look about her. "First, as a soldier, and now, as someone who shall protect their very values from the Reds and socialists that have gnawed their way into the body of his nation he loves more than life. They call themselves the Popular Front, ha! There's nothing popular about their idiotic liberal policies. They wish to rid Spain of everything that makes it exceptional and turn it into an emasculated, disarmed, shameful version of itself. Poor Victor! Each time he talks about Spain's glorious past, when it ruled the land and the sea with its unconquerable Armada, when its armies instilled fear in their enemies just with the sheer sight of their might, his eyes grow moist with devastation. What the former glorious nation has been reduced to! Just like France, if you think of it. Just like Germany. Ah, thank God for Franco and Hitler and Mussolini and whoever picks up their banner to carry here, when the time comes. And it shall come, you mark my words, Gudrun."

I nodded along and bowed my head lower and lower, just so she wouldn't recognize the spark of hostility, growing into flames, in my eyes.

I was grateful to her just then. For the first time in my life, unwittingly, Charlotte Fournier showed me precisely what I was when I myself was at a loss for a definitive answer.

I was the enemy of everything she and her idols stood for.

I was a freedom fighter on the other side of the barricade.

I was a citizen of the world with a loathing of their rotting nationalism and longing for times past, when the inquisition was the law of the land and witches like me were burned at the stake.

I was a woman who would die so that others would live freely.

The Parisian headquarters of the German Communist Party in exile were squeezed in between a mechanic's garage and a tailor's shop facing the Seine. It was a poorly lit cellar office, suffering from floods more often than not, smelling sharply of mold and rotten water and, faintly, of the oil and gas seeping into its walls from the mechanic's shop next to it.

Early Sunday morning, there was only one orderly manning the desk above which the red banner was hanging crookedly, with portraits of Marx and Engels framing it—more to mask the peeling paint than to celebrate the survival of the pitiful handful of comrades was my guess. Everyone else, he had informed us, was gone for the day. He was a middle-aged man with close-set eyes and a high forehead, heavily lined. Wagner, he introduced himself, pulling at his frayed sleeves self-consciously.

I noticed Alfred's hopeful expression fall as he shifted his gaze from the permanently damp banner to the bare concrete floor and boxes by the wall that served as desks, judging by the presence of small stools next to them.

"We're a volunteer organization," Wagner explained with an apologetic smile. "There's no set office hours, for anyone. Can't quite afford it, so we rotate shifts. Whoever can come in, comes in. Sometimes we stay a few hours. Sometimes an entire day... But it's rare that one can devote the entire day to the office. There are families to be considered, too."

Alfred nodded slowly, solemnly.

"Were you interested in joining?" Wagner asked without much hope.

"No, we're actually..." Alfred cleared his throat. He was hunching his shoulders. The cellar's ceiling was much too low for his tall frame, the darkness in the middle of the morning too oppressive. "We're both members already."

"Just arrived?"

"No. No..." Alfred stole a glance at me. There is no paper to be had here, I read in his eyes. Only fungus and lung disease caused by it.

"Are you looking for work? I'm afraid we can't pay anything... As I said, we're a volunteer organization—"

Seeing that Alfred was ready to surrender and walk out of there, I stepped forward. "Are you producing any information sheets by any chance?" It didn't look like they were—there wasn't even an old typewriter on Wagner's desk, let alone a phone. But for the life of me I couldn't bear Alfred's anguished look, that grimace of pure agony one imagines a surgeon would have if someone tied his hands behind his back and left him staring at the patient writhing in pain right in front of him—so much skill and compassion and yet so very unable to help.

"Information sheets?" Wagner asked as if hearing the term for the first time.

"Yes. Leaflets, agitprop?" I probed, hoping to extract from the folds of his memory the image of Berlin with walls lined with red, of May Day parades and red ribbons in women's hair. The very first political party suing for suffrage. The very first movement of equality—back when it was still in its infancy, when people were ready to die for their ideas that still meant something.

Wagner only smiled at me tragically. "Oh, no," he said in his soft voice. "Nothing of that sort."

He didn't say anything further; it was the silence that spoke for him. It was too much work, too much *unpaid* work. Oh, the

irony of it!—a political party proclaiming their disdain of capi-
talism refusing to work for free. But as it had turned out, one
can only be political when one has citizenship and money.
Refugees couldn't afford such luxuries. They had families to
feed and gendarmes to avoid when performing illegal labor.
One eye on the merchandise, another on all four corners, one
foot always pointing toward the back door to dart through. For,
if one was caught, one would be deported, to Switzerland most
likely, which wouldn't have been half as bad if it wasn't for the
starving children left in Paris. And then came the trouble of
obtaining new papers from some crook the border villages were
swarming with, and then paying off another crook to get one
through the border and back to France, and so many days of
work already lost...

I nodded to show him that I understood. I was a refugee too;
it was all too familiar to me. "But could you obtain any paper
perhaps? You see, we don't mind producing information sheets
ourselves. We have a typewriter and Alfred here, he's a very
good writer. We only need the paper." I paused, choking down
the inappropriate laughter that was about to break free and
invade this sorrowful, silent space, mournful like a tomb. And
yet, one had to laugh. One beggar asking another for a favor.
"But we have no money to spare."

"Paper?" Wagner brightened. "We have plenty of that!" He
was suddenly on his feet, revived with a breath of a purpose. "It
might be a tad damp, but if you lay it out to dry..."

He was already disassembling makeshift desks, stacking
crates one upon another to reach into a shelf at the very top of
the ceiling—the driest place in the entire office, reserved for the
most treasured possessions, it occurred to me just then.

"You don't have a mimeograph, I imagine?" Alfred
breathed, looking up at Wagner, holding his arms out to him
like a child waiting for his birthday present.

"I'm afraid not. But you can use the one in the public

library. They charge a very small fee, just for the ink, if you bring your own paper. And nothing at all if you have a library card, but you aren't registered with the police, I suppose..."

Alfred laughed, weighed down by yellowish stacks Wagner had deposited into his outstretched arms. "We'd been registered with the police back in Germany and almost ended up in Dachau. Once was enough for us."

Wagner's shoulders were shaking with soundless laughter as well. "To be sure, comrade. To be sure."

On the same Sunday night, Mademoiselle Fournier was seeing her Colonel off to resume his fight against the Popular Front as we, those very Popular Front sympathizers, crept along the city streets and plastered the newly printed leaflets atop shaving cream advertisements—"New face of the twentieth century. Sponsored by Palmolive"—so that on Monday morning, as Parisians set off to work, instead of familiar smiling clean-shaved faces, the death masks of Gestapo victims would stare back at them from information columns, newspaper stands and even Metro car windows. Alfred had sketched them by hand, from memory. He had pondered the text for a few laborious hours, but then put only one single line under the horrifying visage: "New face of Hitler's Germany. Sponsored by the Gestapo."

He hadn't broken the Spider's orders. No one knew the author of the disturbing pamphlets. Only Alfred set off to work at his Italian dive on Montmartre with purposeful calmness and shoulders squared in quiet pride instead of curses hissed under his breath and a look of haunted desperation. And that was enough for me.

FOURTEEN

SUMMER 1936

I was on my way to the taxicab stand with my latest report. Despite his bragging that it would be him who found us instead of the other way round, I had long since discovered that the cab line-up by the Arc de Triomphe was the Spider's regular stomping ground. Here, as he waited in line together with the other drivers, he smoked, spat through his teeth to accentuate one elaborate French curse or the other, or, on a particularly fine day, played cards. Fine days were bad for taxi business. It was the rainy days that made money, just like it was the war that made the coin; never the peace. And that was the biggest irony of our generation.

I had spotted him from afar, long before he had noticed me, but perhaps that was because all his attention was directed at a tall, albeit rail-thin, young man with hair so blond it was almost white, who was screaming something frightful at the Spider, his accusatory finger never leaving the vicinity of the Soviet spy's face.

To his credit, the Spider remained largely unimpressed with the verbal assault in the language that was not familiar to me, but which I'd assumed to be Russian. With the languid smirk of a beast who was far too entertained by the man's attempts at threats to show any real concern, he was leaning against his taxi with both his arms and ankles crossed, as if the idea of having to protect himself never even crossed his mind. Though, I knew the posture to be misleading. It would be the young man's mistake not to notice the ropes of muscles bulging under the Spider's shirt-sleeves or to ignore the steel in his eyes—the eyes of the predator, half-closed at the moment but watchful as always.

There was something about the scene that prompted my legs to move of their own volition; conceal me from the Spider's eyes before he got the chance to notice me. Years of clandestine living under false names and with an invented life story had honed my instincts to the point where I relied on them more than I did on logic. Because logic is for civilized societies only; in those slowly crumbling to death, only survival instincts could be relied upon.

And so, instead of approaching the Spider as I'd initially planned, I waited for the altercation to be over and followed the blond foreigner instead. He walked at the pace of someone outraged to the utmost; nearly stumbled into a few passersby in the blinded state of his rage. By the time he'd run out of steam and slowed down a bit by the river, just to mutter unintelligible words under his breath and pat himself for the cigarettes he'd obviously run out of, the burning question of just what feud he had with the Spider was consuming me alive. Still, I remained unmoved on the outside. Paused by the railing, which was too hot to the touch, I quickly figured from which side the wind was blowing, took a strategic position by the young man's left shoulder and lit up the delicious, thin Italian cigar Alfred had supplied me with.

The young man's Adam's apple bobbed as he swallowed, teased by the smell, much like a dog with a juicy bone. I caught him looking at the thin brown cigar in my fingers and feigned a solicitous smile.

"Want one?"

"I'd kill for one, to be frank," he admitted in broken French that was even worse than mine when I'd just arrived in Paris.

"No need for such sacrifices." I grinned and offered him the pack.

He took a cigar quickly, saw that I wasn't pulling away the pack, and took another one, which quickly disappeared behind his ear. Just then, I noticed that a chunk of it was missing.

"The Bolshevists, devil take them all." He was staring at the river now, his eyes burning with such hatred, I nearly pulled back and particularly when he shifted the blazing gaze of those eyes back at me with sudden suspicion. "You're not one of them Reds, are you?"

"Me? No. I'm just a regular maid. From Alsace."

He nodded; relaxed his grip on the railing a bit. Just how he hadn't burned his palms on its black surface was a miracle. The sun was particularly merciless that day. Under my thin dress, I felt rivulets of sweat running down my spine and gathering just above my belt.

"I was just a regular farmer too. Fat lot of good it did me, being a member of the proletariat in the wrong republic."

I pulled on my cigarette and cocked my head slightly, inviting more information. An immigrant myself, I was familiar with his type: we don't like the questions, but look at us a certain way, with compassion, see a human being in us instead of a burden on society and we'll pour our entire life story on you as we would on a best friend—that one very special person we'd all left behind.

"I was born in the year of the October Revolution. My father was so proud! No more wealthy landowners making us slave for them for pitiful coins. No more clergy telling us that it's God's way, respecting our Tsar and suffering nobly so that he and his nobles could eat caviar. The dictatorship of the prole-tariat. The Party of the workers and peasants, at long last!" He broke into laughter that sounded more like sobbing.

"Isn't that how it is now in the Soviets?" I asked, genuinely curious. Alfred had gone to Moscow in the past and claimed that it was indeed a paradise for the former persecuted masses. I had no reason not to believe him.

"In Russia, perhaps," the young man said. "The trouble is, I'm from Ukraine."

In the distance, a dog plunged into water, prompting laughter from its owner. "Look at Rooster go!" The still air wavering with heat carried his words far over the river. "That four-legged sod is smarter than us!"

"Do you blame him?" One of his female companions joined in the laughter. "I wouldn't mind following him, to be frank."

"So, do!"

"I don't have a bathing suit on!"

"All the better!"

The young Ukrainian watched the scene with the longing of someone who had long ago lost the habit for all the inno-cence, all the joy of someone his age. "When I was a child, it was all right indeed. We worked for ourselves, gave our share to the collective farms but kept enough for ourselves. We had two cows, sheep, chickens, geese, even pigs. The piglets and a certain percentage of milk and eggs had to be given to the collective, but we had more than enough left. And the grain— my, you should have seen the fields! I loved playing there with my friends until the big..." He stumbled on the word. "*Kombainers?*" he probed in his native language. "I don't know what's the French word for those harvesting machines..."

"Combiners?" I supplied.

"Yes. That's the one. Combiners." He repeated it a few times to commit it to his memory. "When they came, we weren't allowed to play in the field any longer after an accident happened... A boy was playing hide-and-seek with his friends; not from our village but the neighboring one, but it was still our common tragedy. When those combiners work, the sound of their rotating blades is so loud, you can't hear yourself thinking. It's disorienting, and particularly when there's a whole fleet of them, combing through the field. Anyway, the boy couldn't figure out which way to run and must have run square into the machine's maw."

He was silent a beat, chewing on his pale lip as the past had veiled his eyes over.

"The local Party leader descended upon our village within days—but not to offer his condolences, as one would imagine, but to fine us for spoiling his grain production with the boy's blood and gore. It was unusable now, he said. The production numbers were ruined. The quota wouldn't be fulfilled." He smirked and shook his head. "We should have known that this was the beginning of the end. It was as if that boy's blood put a curse on the entire country."

"How so?" I probed as gently as possible.

"Did you not hear about the famine?" He regarded me as though I had just crawled from under a rock.

"The famine?" I repeated after him, frankly at a loss. The Soviets were the biggest exporters of grain. They were feeding the entire continent for years; what famine could there possibly be with such riches?

"You must think me mad, inventing stories about famine when the Soviets have more wheat than they know what to do with, eh?" The Ukrainian smiled at me—not with accusation, but with such great sorrow, I felt heat creeping up my cheeks for my ignorance.

"No, I don't think you mad at all. I think we all have stories that the rest of the world is unaware of."

He cocked his head, regarded me with curiosity. "What do you know about it? You're just a regular maid from Alsace."

"I'm a German Jew who was fleeing the Nazi persecution."

He looked at me with something akin to respect for the first time. Before that, I was only a random shoulder to cry on. Now, I was an accidental ally; someone who could relate, sympathize, share her own grief in exchange for his.

"A couple of years ago, Stalin decided that it was a good idea to starve most of the population of Ukraine to death. We were being insolent, you see. Ungrateful. Wanted to keep our language and customs and refused to give most of our grain to Moscow to profit off. Our leaders thought it would be only fair if the Ukrainians mostly profited off what they produced, but Stalin disagreed and that was the end of our local leaders. Some were executed, some shipped to the gulags or southern republics, or to the very north. No one knows what happened to them. And then they came for us, regular people. They took and took and took, and when our parents began to revolt and pleaded for them not to take any more, they..." He receded, pointed to his ear sliced in half, which told his story better than any words could, and lapsed into silence altogether, as if there was nothing else there was left to say.

"Are your parents—"

"Dead," he interrupted me with grim finality. The word dropped into the black water below us and didn't even leave ripples in its wake. "The entire village is dead. Half of Ukraine is dead. But there's plenty of grain now, which is harvested and sold by the Russians. So, no one would ever believe that there's any famine. Stalin is very cunning. He thought it all through."

A chilling thought occurred to me. Suddenly, I wasn't so certain that I was fighting on the right side. Suddenly, I felt mortally betrayed, as if I had walked inside my own bedroom and discovered my husband in bed with another woman.

"Do you have a place to stay?" I asked the only idiotic question there was to ask. I simply couldn't summon the strength to inquire any deeper. I was far too lightheaded, far too nauseous.

"Yes, I have."

"Do you have papers?"

"Do you?"

"No."

"But you fare just fine."

"Yes."

"So will I. We're survivors. It's in our blood, surviving against all odds."

I nodded and shook his hand with my limp one and watched him disappear into the wavering air—a ghost of the past and the future with no name but with a face I would never forget.

For it was the face of universal suffering.

I was wandering aimlessly around the city, my mind at war with itself. It happens to the best of us, this metaphorical punch to the gut, this sensation of freefall when everything we'd thought we knew comes crashing down in front of our eyes; the walls of our past life crumbling, churning, deteriorating and turning into ash, leaving nothing but shock and disappointment in its wake.

I inhaled the Parisian air in short, strangled breaths. Gasoline, warm buttered croissants and coffee in local bistros, brasseries and the sharp tang of cheese and fresh oysters—the very scents that I had grown to adore were suddenly nauseating and alien. Disoriented and lightheaded, I was an alien myself—alone among the locals with places to go to, with jobs to fret about at a time of recession, with bosses to loathe and badmouth, with warm dinners waiting at home and wives who nagged, or husbands and their affairs, and bratty children with music lessons to pay for. What I wouldn't give to trade places with them just to taste that long-forgotten normality once again instead of trying to untangle world intrigues I had no business to play with in the first place.

I wasn't ready to see Alfred yet. Instead, I made my way back to the Spider's usual haunt and made my report as though nothing had transpired as we drove without direction somewhere east.

"The Colonel is nowhere to be found and they were supposed to have their engagement party last night."

The Spider half closed his eyes, as was his habit whenever he was pleased. I watched him closely thought the rearview mirror, trying to see through the mask he had never quite parted with.

"He's mad about her, so I'm guessing something important is happening."

The Spider nodded, noted the time on his wristwatch. "The Nationalists must have finally made their move. Or are making it, as we speak."

Inside the car, the air was stale and suffocating despite the open windows. The upholstery smelled strongly of cheap cigarettes and sweat.

"What's the Party line on Spain, comrade?" I asked and at once caught the dissecting look of his eyes on me.

"Why?"

"Just curious. They don't have any formal agreement with Spain, unlike with France."

"No, they don't."

"So, there won't be any assistance then?"

He slowed down and came to a complete stop at the end of the street. It used to be a bohemian quarter with cheap studios for rent and the sharp tang of paint thinner hanging permanently in the air. Now, with all the painters dead or gone and their masterpieces going for unimaginable fortunes at auctions, it had a haunted look about it. Boarded windows stared blankly back at us like tombstones at the cemetery, overgrown with weeds and moss.

"Why the interrogation, comrade?" The Spider's voice was almost silky to the touch.

Alone with him, alone in this entire deserted street, I considered backtracking, playing a naïve fool, laughing the matter off, but then I saw his eyes fixed on mine through the mirror, a grin growing wider and wider on his face as he read me like an open book. I realized that with him, showing fear was no option.

"I want to know if the side that I'm fighting on is the right one."

"Thinking of swinging to the Nazis, eh?" he teased, all playfulness as he half-turned in his seat to see me better.

I pulled forward instead of leaning back. "You're just a regular comedian, aren't you?"

"And you're a regular thorn in my flesh, with all your incessant questions. Have you ever heard of minding your affairs and following orders without being a pest?"

"Didn't have the pleasure of formal army training, comrade."

"And it shows."

We both were silent for a very long moment. In the half-shadows of the old bohemian quarter, his nostrils twitched ever so slightly. My back was stiff as a board. I could smell my own sweat and wondered if he smelled it too and took it for fear. Just for that reason alone, I refused to avert my eyes as if my life depended on it.

But then again, perhaps it did. No one would stop him from wringing my neck with those great paws of his, finishing his shift with my corpse in his trunk and having his usual dinner and wine right after he'd hurled it over the railing and into the Seine under the cover of darkness. No one would investigate the death of an undocumented immigrant. We were nameless, faceless, inconsequential and disposable. According to local

Nazis—there were plenty of those in Paris too—France would be better off without us.

To my immense relief, it was the Spider who looked away first. Rather to my surprise, he laughed, too.

"You're something else, Dora Davidsohn."

"Thank you."

"It's not a compliment."

"Sounded like one."

He laughed again, baring all of his teeth this time. "That big mouth of yours shall either take you places or will be the death of you. At any rate, no, there shall not be any official assistance, not to" —he paused, made a vague gesture with his hand—"not to upset the present and very fragile world order, let's put it that way. But the Party won't stop volunteers from joining the international brigades fighting on the Popular Front's side. Sound good enough for you?"

He was about to start the engine when I reached out all the way forward and folded my arms on top of the front seat, resting my chin on them. "Just one more question. Say, Popular Front wins. Say, Spain decided to join the Soviets—"

"Wouldn't that be great?" Judging by his skeptical tone, he seriously doubted at least one of those outcomes.

"What would its position be?"

"A Soviet republic." He looked at me as if I'd just said something utterly moronic, started the car and pulled away from the curb.

I nodded. "Yes, but not all Soviet republics are equal."

His smile dropped, leaving only his teeth in its wake. "Whatever does that mean?"

I wasn't certain anymore whether it was the cobbled street that made me tremble or my nerves. And yet, with the best will in the world, I couldn't force myself to shut my trap.

"Someone still wields more power, even among Soviets. There's still someone at the head of the round table. Someone who makes decisions. Someone who's in charge of the communal wealth."

"Where are you heading with this, Mademoiselle Davidsohn?"

The purposeful form of address didn't escape my attention. All of a sudden, I wasn't a comrade any longer.

"If, let's say, Moscow decided that it would be beneficial for all of the Soviets to export most of Spain's olives, tangerines and wine, leaving Spain only a fraction of profits, and let's say Spain decided to revolt against this... what would the Party line be on its behavior?"

The car stopped so abruptly, I bit my tongue as I lurched forward.

"You saw me with that Ukrainian." It wasn't a question. "You saw me with him and you followed him and spoke with him, you little—"

He laughed once again, but there was a very different quality to it this time. I tasted blood in my mouth.

"Dora." He rubbed his face with both palms, suddenly looking very tired. When he looked at me again, there was such paternal compassion in his eyes, I momentarily felt almost disoriented. "He's an enemy agent, girl. Something the French call a *provocateur*. He's been sent here with one goal only: spread propaganda, just the kind you fell for. And he's very convincing, too. Look how fast you turned against your comrades just because of his lies."

"I haven't turned against anyone," I began to protest, suddenly ashamed, suddenly very cold inside, but he silenced me with a raised hand, all patience and benevolence.

"Even though the Soviet state has been working diligently to exterminate the last pockets of nationalists and White Russians in its former republics, there are still factions of them left. Many have escaped and are now operating from foreign grounds, many have gone underground in their own home states, but they're still there. They're Nazis as well, Dora. The same ones that have run you and Alfred off your native land. The Soviets, we don't persecute Jews. Hell, half of the Party is Jewish! That's why Hitler calls it a Judeo-Bolshevik threat. And who opposes Jews and Bolsheviks? That's right, nationalists. Nazis."

"But what about the famine?"

"Famine?" He regarded me like an innocent child who knows not that the Earth revolves around the sun rather than the other way round. "Dora, it's all lies and propaganda. A sob story, invented and rehearsed countless times and aimed at kind souls just like you and Alfred. I bet his good heart would break if he heard of children starving to death at their mother's dried-out breast. I bet his healer's soul couldn't bear to hear of entire villages dying, just because the vile Reds decided to kill them all. Dora, really? Do you believe that someone in Moscow had risen one day from his bed and said, hey, why don't we starve the entire country? Just for thrills and laughs. And then closed his eyes, rotated the USSR map in front of him, had his finger land on one of the republics and said, well, there's that for you, Ukraine. Rotten luck!"

I was desperately trying to say something, but there was such ironclad logic in the Spider's words, such conviction, that I was beginning to doubt—the second time in just one day—whatever I was just beginning to learn.

"Do you truly believe, Dora, that the Ukrainians could have been starved? That they had all this grain and farms and couldn't secure something for themselves, couldn't hide it from the bad, mean Soviet commissars? Blast it, I wonder just how many commissars would it take to search all of Ukraine! Comrade Stalin would have to send an entire army there!"

And I was chuckling with him, my mind full of fog, unsure of what to believe but chuckling nevertheless, full of loathing for myself and my ignorance, but still chuckling, like an idiot who couldn't tell right from left.

"It's all right, Dora. You were bound to meet one of them sooner or later. It's good that you told me about him. Now we'll know to watch him. Come, I'll take you home. Alfred must be worried silly about you, girl."

And I let him take me home and shake my hand, thanking me for my great service to the State and the Party.

FIFTEEN

TWO WEEKS LATER

Inside the communal bathhouse, the mosaic floor was heaven itself—a soothing balm for our burning feet. Here, having bathhouse slippers wasn't a requirement, unlike in fancy spas frequented by the likes of Mademoiselle Charlotte whenever she needed a break from... it was anyone's guess from what exactly, but while she was lounging somewhere in Vichy, I was making use of my unexpected holiday here in dusty, heat-strangled Paris.

To be fair, most of the bathhouse customers couldn't afford such frivolities as bath slippers. Most of them only passed through—through the bathhouse, through Paris, through France to the very end of the Earth, where they hopefully would be left alone and in peace—and showered just like they lived: on the run and in a great rush, in between trains and ferries and whatever else could carry them and their sorry belongings.

Alfred and I observed them while waiting in line for our allotted thirty minutes in a separate bath—a luxury we could only indulge in once every two weeks—and wondered if we'd had the same look about us when we'd just arrived in Paris. Glassy eyes staring sightlessly into the void, a permanent scowl that wouldn't smooth over even in sleep, and lips chewed to bits that had long ago lost the habit of smiling.

They exchanged their destinations like cards in a game of skat and compared their scars with the knowing look of soldiers who had survived the same battles.

"Mexico? Good, warm country."

"Cuba, that too. I'm planning to sell German vacuum cleaners there. My former neighbor from Bremen will ship them to me as soon as I have a permanent address."

"Can he be relied on?"

"We're splitting profits fifty-fifty, so if he doesn't hold up his end of the bargain, he's the one to lose."

"What if you don't hold it up?"

"My daughter and her husband are still in Germany." A silence full of darkness. "He knows I shall pay up."

A bearded Jew, dressed all in black and with his eyes trained strictly on the floor, chased three of his sons out one of the bathrooms. With a sigh of almost comical weariness, a bath-house attendant rose from the bench by the wall and waddled into the steamy room to perform a completely superficial job of washing it before admitting another family. It was mostly families now. Hardly anyone could afford lounging in a bath for an entire half an hour by themselves.

The conversation around us was mostly German, spiced up with Yiddish here and there and with just a smattering of Italian and Spanish. The big exodus of Europe had begun while the entire world was sleepwalking through its third decade, a mask of silk pulled over its eyes, thoroughly pretending that it wasn't teetering at the edge of a disaster.

At last, the attendant waved us through with his great meaty palm and handed us two off-white towels and one piece of soap.

"Thirty minutes," he called after us, pulling the door closed after himself.

It didn't have a lock on it. Not after an immigrant had locked himself inside and sliced his veins open with his shaving razor. By the time the gendarmes had broken the door open, he'd bled out to death. According to the same bath attendant who was on duty today, he'd never seen such serenity on anyone's face. That's the curse of our generation: some of us only find freedom in death.

"Madame."

Alfred's velvet voice pulled me out of my musings. I regarded his gallantly proffered hand, realized that I'd already undressed like an automaton, without noticing, and grinned at him as he helped me into the bath. He climbed in after me and sat with his legs splayed so that I could nestle in between them with my back to him and offer him my hair that he loved to lather with soap, and massage my temples and the back of my skull until I dissolved into a puddle of whipped cream in his attentive hands.

As long as I kept my eyes closed, I could almost imagine us someplace warm and distant, in Mexico or Brazil, where ripe fruit grew on trees and where the ocean was our bathtub, free and endless and warm, salty due to its nature and not because so many émigrés' tears had fallen into its water.

"Alfred?"

"Mm?"

"Why don't we leave too?" I looked at him over my shoulder. Even in the harsh light of the overhead lightbulbs, his face was serene, lines of worry smoothed over with water and relaxation for a few precious moments.

"You know why." He didn't open his eyes. "Because there's work that needs to be done and someone has to do it."

"I don't feel we're making any difference whatsoever in the grand scheme of things. I feel as though we're trying to irrigate a desert with two drops of water."

"And just what do you think storms are made of?" He

finally looked at me, a trifle teasingly. "Many separate tiny drops, each of which think that they mean nothing while they obliterate entire cities."

"Do you honestly believe we can stop the war from happening?"

"No. I have no illusions on that front."

"Then why are we still here?"

"Because when the war comes and we can help at least one person, our presence here shall be justified. And that's good enough reason for me."

I didn't know if it was a good enough reason for me, but I said nothing because he was here and I didn't quite know how to live without him any longer. In the course of these years that we had lived together—not lived, but survived, in shabby rooms, in between scraps of food always shared, making love like animals, always on the go and with primal hunger—he had become a part of me, like a limb, and leaving him would be equal to chopping that limb off. That was a pain I wasn't quite prepared for, not for all the oceans and palm-lined paradises in the world.

By the time we had emerged from our private bathroom, dressed in a fresh set of clothes, our cheeks pink from steam and vigorous scrubbing, the line outside had grown even longer. We were almost at the end of it when Alfred heard something in the cacophony of the crowd's dialects and accents, and swung round so abruptly that I nearly stumbled into him.

"Vasilevsky, *ty*?" Alfred grabbed one of the men, the tallest one, raven-haired, with the ramrod stature of a career officer, into the embrace of a long-lost brother. *"Glazam svoim ne veru!"*

If the Vasilevsky fellow was caught off guard, he didn't let on. Unlike his comrade; I noticed at once. While the two men were exchanging back-claps and pumping one another's fists, he had made every effort to withdraw himself entirely from the situation, to blend in with the tiled wall. For some reason, such frank fear of Alfred, my good, kind Alfred, made me think of possums and their feigning death in front of a predator who is about to strike. Quite an odd reaction to a comrade of a comrade.

And Alfred was already pushing me forward, introducing me to his friend. "This is Dora, my wife"—it slipped so easily off his tongue, I almost didn't notice in my delight how Vasilevsky nodded to me far too stiffly, how cold his grip was despite the steam all but clouding the bathhouse, dampening everyone's clothes and moistening our skin.

After that, the exchange only grew odder by the minute. Alfred listed out a few names just to receive a negative shake of the head in response. He pushed, and inquired further, only to get a sudden snap from Vasilevsky's friend, who, after yelling something that sounded far too close to an obscenity even in a language I couldn't understand, stormed off, tearing his admittance ticket in the process.

The matter must have been serious indeed.

Vasilevsky said something softly, apologetically. Alfred tossed his head; as if he refused to believe what his friend was trying to explain. They argued. A few people in the line craned their necks, expecting a showdown. Only a couple didn't even blink an eye. It was this purposeful ignorance about them that betrayed them. These were the ones who understood the language; understood, and didn't wish to have any part of it.

Alfred was shaking his head like someone who had just received the news that their loved one was about to die any day now. It was the desperate dance of the very first wave of denial, accompanied by anger and a constantly repeated "*nyet*"—one of the few words he had taught me, together with the Spider.

I watched them both and understood it all without understanding their language. *No, no, no; you're wrong; it can't be; it's impossible, what you're saying—*

And in response, Vasilevsky's eyes fixed on Alfred, with a look so tragic, so utterly funereal, I felt my own heart growing into a lump in my throat despite not knowing the first thing of whatever it was they were on about.

They parted ways after a last mistrustful handshake. Alfred couldn't bear this torture any longer. His elbow in my hand for support—I didn't trust him to walk on his own—we staggered into the white-hot afternoon and stood there for a while as he mumbled to himself, blinking fast, all disoriented in the familiar city that was suddenly so strange to him.

"He has invented it all, the idiot," he stammered at long last, taking the first probing step in the direction of the Metro. "He must have gone mad. Yes. That's what happened. He must have lost it entirely, the poor sod."

"What did he say to you?"

Alfred looked at me, disbelief and frank shock still written plainly in his eyes, and regarded me as if he had just realized that I didn't speak their language.

"He said..." He swallowed hard, passed an unsteady hand over his forehead as though to get his thoughts in order. "He said, he and Lavrentiev had to make a run for it... Someone had tipped them off that they were next on the list."

"What list?"

"The NKVD list. The list of enemies of the state, subject to immediate arrest, interrogation and, in most cases, execution," he finished in a shaky, incredulous whisper as though he, himself, couldn't reconcile the possibility of the Soviet secret police acting very much like its Nazi Germany counterpart, the dreaded Gestapo.

"I thought you knew him? Isn't he a communist?"

"He is! Of the highest quality." Alfred looked at his palms, thoroughly at a loss. "We worked together, back in the early thirties. He's a Stalinist. He's not a Trotskyist. An army officer... loyal like a dog... why would they... No, it makes no sense, whatsoever."

"They put him on the list?"

"Yes. The enemy of the state list. There's... some sort of a purge going on against the army, he said. The NKVD are arresting officers right and left. Good, loyal officers who would die for Stalin and their motherland. I don't believe it. We would have heard of it; wouldn't we?"

We hadn't heard anything of the Ukrainian famine either; it suddenly occurred to me. It was only natural the Soviets wouldn't publicize their secret army purge either, but, just like out of a faulty faucet, the information trickled down, seeped through the cracks and, before long, those like me, the skeptical ones, the politically unreliable ones, would begin putting two and two together. Because that's how the consolidation of power worked in autocracies: first, gather capital and power, then eliminate all opposition. The capital came from starving Ukraine to death and selling their edible gold—the grain—for great profit, and the opposition... the real one had been eliminated a long time ago. Now, it appeared, Comrade Stalin had decided to dispatch half of his own loyal army officers, much like Hitler did with the SA, just to make sure that no one would get into their stupid heads to ever doubt who was in command.

All at once, the Spider was the spider once again, a cunning predator knitting his web of lies, and the Ukrainian was the victim, just like these two bathhouse Russians, and the world was upside down once again and we were on the wrong side of it.

But when I voiced my doubts to Alfred later that night, as I sat in the nook of his opened legs atop the windowsill, my back against his chest, my head wreathed in cigarette smoke and doubt, he only snorted softly somewhere in my hair, sending shivers of pleasure down my neck.

"And what is the right side, Dora? Fascism?" he asked—a rhetorical question, really—and passed his cigarette to me.

"No, of course not." I paused; blew the smoke out of the opened window. "But this is not what I want to support. The only reason why I became so enamored with communism was you. It's always been you and your ideas; not some manifestos I never bothered to read. With you, communism was about the commune, the community; we helped people and asked nothing in return. With them, it's about purges, intrigues and famine."

"But, unfortunately, as of now, communists are the only ones who are openly fighting against fascism, Dora. Sometimes, it's about choosing a lesser evil."

A lesser evil indeed. I swallowed that idea, together with the bitter smoke, and closed my eyes against the night, against everything I didn't wish to see, to keep carrying out the work we'd signed up for.

SIXTEEN

SUMMER 1938

"...And remind that daft man that I want lavender orchids. Not pink, not purple like the samples that he sent me—*lavender*. If needed, tell him that if he can't differentiate between their shades, we'll just have to order elsewhere. From that Jew who has the shop by the Arc de Triomphe, if it comes to that. Yes, tell him that. That should make him think twice before sending me the wrong samples next time."

My face blank as a wall, I was nodding to all of Mademoiselle Charlotte's requests like the good servant that I was, all the while wishing that the wrong shade of flowers at the wedding rehearsal was my biggest trouble in life. Ever since the Colonel had put that enormous emerald on her finger, all my employer concerned herself with was planning the most lavish and outrageous wedding one could throw. In the meantime, the Republican government in Spain was pleading for peace after suffering countless losses and Austria had ceased to exist altogether as an independent country after Hitler had annexed it without much ado, further expanding his empire of black uniforms and bloody banners. While some international papers wrote it off as sensationalism and debated about letting those countries sort it all out among themselves, I felt the growing threat of the entire continent plunging into a war of annihilation in the very marrow of my bones. It had already touched me personally, just this very morning, when the hostel's proprietress had handed me a letter and mumbled without bothering to take a cigarette out of her mouth, "from Germany. If you need another room, let me know."

I had opened it on my way to work and felt as though I'd been punched in the gut when the words, written by my mother's hand, stared back at me from the paper.

> We would never wish to impose on you and Alfred, but do you think you could lend us a few marks until we try to find the best price for your father's gold watch? Whatever they're offering us is ridiculous and Vati is thinking of going to Berlin to sell it. They say there are still Jewish shops in Berlin and they offer good prices for their own kind... On a good note, your oma is operating a private bakery of sorts out of our kitchen! She has to employ a local gentile boy to deliver the pastries to her customers, as it's illegal to buy from Jews, but she works ceaselessly and it's thanks to her that we still have a roof over our heads. It wouldn't have been so bad, had they not imposed new taxes on Jewish tenants and they're almost as high as our rent...

The meaning was blunt, like the business end of a cudgel: their life in Germany was reduced to survival. And not like Alfred's and mine, but *actual* survival, when one is hunted, robbed of all means to earn a living; when one's very life is hanging in the balance and the smallest whim of a government official can tip it in the wrong direction and then...

Dreadful scenarios, one more apocalyptic than the other, flashed before my eyes as I wrote down the changes to Mademoiselle Charlotte's wedding rehearsal's menu that she machinegunned me with. She wanted profiteroles instead of meringue and profiteroles with ice cream, not regular cream, vanilla flavor only, not that ordinary, regular business that has no taste whatsoever.

"I'll be damned before I serve it to my guests," she went on, pacing the living room as her toy poodle looked lazily on. "There will be high-ranking officers and their wives in attendance. Two German ministers, including Minister Ribbentrop; I was friends with his wife before he got into politics, back when he was still in the champagne business." She gave me a coy look meant to impress.

I looked at her silently. Out of nowhere, a wild desire emerged in me, the desire for her to look—*actually* look at me and see me—and ask me if anything was the matter, for I was as pale as death; I knew I was; I could see my reflection in her full-length, gilded mirror leaning against the opposite wall. I wanted to grab her by her luxurious chestnut mane, shove her into that mirror and ask her how she could look at herself every day and not feel all-consuming disgust at the fact that here she was, with all this influence in the world, with all this money to spend, throwing it away on lavish parties when Jewish refugees begged for food just outside her building's door, and throwing hissy fits over the wrong shade of flowers when my father was forced to sell his golden watch that was his grandfather's, the grandfather who had raised him when his own father had died and whom he loved to death and spoke of with such reverence. Vati always said that he'd part with a limb before he'd sell that watch, but apparently, in this new Germany, Jewish limbs didn't go for much and so he was selling his memories instead, hoping to get a good price for something utterly priceless.

When I didn't acknowledge her last remark with the obligatory impressed smile—I simply had no strength in me to feign something so difficult as a smile that day—Mademoiselle Charlotte studied me for a few moments with her green eyes. A hope twitched in me that perhaps not all was lost yet for her; that maybe she would care about my situation simply because I was her maid, somewhere below her poodle in social standing, but somewhat a member of the household, someone who drew her baths and bought antiviral cream for her from the pharmacist to treat genital herpes and listened to her shriek in apparent delight when her Colonel slapped her luscious thighs and call him a beast, while polishing silver in the next room.

"Well? Why are you just standing there?" she asked and I blinked. "The bakery is at the other end of the river and you'll have to rush to get there before they close."

The veil had fallen from my eyes, hardening something inside me even further. My entire heart was slowly turning into a knot of calluses.

And so, I crushed that tiny sliver of hope between my teeth, swallowed it, together with the tears that would no longer come, and left Mademoiselle Charlotte and her blasted vipers' nest.

I set off in the direction of the Arc de Triomphe, only not with the intention of putting the fear of God into her poor florist; I was seeking the Spider. He owed me for my services. The least he could do was bring my family here, help them with papers—whatever it took. It wouldn't be his first time.

Only, when I reached the familiar taxicab rank, a stranger looked up at me from the newspaper he was reading and asked me indifferently, "Where to?"

"I..." I made a step back, studied the car closely. Unquestionably, it was the same one. I wasn't mistaken. "Is Sergey sick?"

The stranger narrowed his eyes, scanned me quickly from head to toe, motioned for me to get in. Reluctantly, I did.

"Where's Sergey?" I repeated as he pulled out of the taxicab queue.

The stranger only grinned at me through the mirror. "Sergey and his boss Yezhov was yesterday. Today it's Comrade

Beria and yours truly, Maxim." He tipped his cap by way of introduction. Case closed and filed, somewhere in the depths of the NKVD prison, sentenced to life with men who'd fallen out of favor. The purge, of which we'd been first warned at the bathhouse by Alfred's former Soviet counterparts who'd been fortunate enough to escape with their lives, must have been truly at its peak... It was anyone's guess what happened to the field officers under Yezhov's command, including the Spider. One gulag or the other, if not a bullet in the back of the head...

However, I didn't have time to think it all over or figure out this new specimen. "I need to get my family out of Germany."

Maxim sucked air through his teeth. "How many?"

"Just three people."

"*Just three people*," he mocked. "Are they useful in any way?"

"They are my *family*."

"Dora, aren't you?"

Either I was their only female operative in Paris or the Spider had described me well enough in his reports for his successor to recognize me so easily. But just like their inner circle intrigues, the way he'd come by my personal information was the least of my troubles.

"I'll pay, if needed," I said. "For papers, for tickets, for any expenses—"

"Before he was... recalled, Sery—" he called the Spider by his Slavic nickname, the Gray one—"said you'd have a guest list for us, for the wedding. Did you happen to bring it?"

Silently, I tapped my temple with my finger.

"The entire list?"

"Once I see a list or a picture or a document, I can recall it in detail even months later."

"A useful quality."

"So Sergey said."

"Don't be shy then. Impress me."

For some time, it was a staring game between us.

From amused and condescending, Maxim's gaze turned into a steely glare. "Blackmail, eh?"

"I'd never. Just like my employers, I'm certain, would never do anything to compromise their employee's trust."

"No, of course not. We're big on trust."

In light of the last purge and whatever the hell else was going on behind the red curtain of the Soviets, the exchange took in a highly ironic tone.

"So, it's only natural that you will help me, and I shall continue to help you. Minister Ribbentrop will be attending with his wife. Surely, whatever he says while sharing a brandy with the Colonel at the reception will cost somewhere around three train tickets and three fake passports."

Maxim pulled the car over to the curb and looked at me again, this time with something akin to respect. "Sery wrote in his reports that you weren't politically reliable." A pause. "But he also wrote that your other qualities outweighed your unreliability. Recommended you higher than your boyfriend even."

"I'm nowhere as good as Alfred." He was a healer and a saint. I was a blackmailer and a nihilist, mad at the world and even more so at the people in it.

"In this profession, yes, little lady, you are."

SEVENTEEN

AUTUMN 1938

If Alfred and I didn't think that we could change the fate of the world singlehandedly, leaflets or not, someone else apparently had a different idea. In a matter of hours, the news engulfed Paris like wildfire: a Jewish teenager had walked into a German embassy and shot the ambassador dead.

"Not the ambassador, you daft cow; his secretary," the butcher argued with his wife as she was wrapping the finest cuts of meat for me. Well, not for me, of course; for Mademoiselle Charlotte's cook she'd hired specifically for tonight's dinner. I would have to satisfy myself with whatever leftovers I would be able to salvage after my employer's guests ate themselves into oblivion.

"It wasn't a Jew who shot him, but a Spanish communist," a seamstress shared her version of events as she handed me Mademoiselle Charlotte's altered dress for the evening. "I'm telling you this on the most reliable authority."

"The embassy fellow isn't even dead; he's only been wounded and is recovering in the hospital as we speak." The doorman waved off everyone's concerns with his white glove. "The Germans are getting themselves in an uproar for nothing.

He shall be back to work by the end of the week; mark my words."

I didn't share his blasé attitude, but there was nothing else for it but to busy myself with preparations for the big night, even if all I could think of was the worst possible timing of all this failed assassination business. Maxim had greeted me with great news only a few days ago: his connections in Germany had finally sorted my parents' and Oma's papers and even purchased the tickets for them that were presently held at the ticket seller's booth at the station.

"Everyone who can is leaving," he'd explained with a shrug. "The nearest date was November tenth. But they can risk waiting a few more days, can't they?"

I'd nodded stiffly. A few more days of starvation, for surely they'd run out of whatever meager money I'd sent them. I prayed that they would sustain themselves on the hope of all of this torture ending soon—I knew this from experience. *And once they're here, Alfred and I shall feed them silly; we'll go hungry ourselves if it comes to that, but my family shall feast on a baguette with salted butter that melts on it like clouds on a sunny day and tastes just as light and fluffy and have a hearty dinner at the bistro on the corner—the fanciest place we can afford, but it'll count all the same—and savor their cheese with wine.* I could almost see them shut their eyes with delight. The promise of having them near was so close, I could almost grasp it, and now this. I moaned inwardly as I polished the silver with a maid hired just for the evening.

Just three more days, I repeated like a mantra as we spread the pristine, snow-white tablecloth on top of the heavy velvet one.

Just three more days, the words drummed in my ears along with my frantic heartbeat when the Colonel arrived, removed his military cap with a somber look about him and declared,

"Well, that's that then. He's dead. The German embassy has announced a day of mourning in his memory."

Just three more days, I pleaded with whatever higher power there was as Mademoiselle Charlotte's guests spread their *foie gras* over toasted bread and mulled over the appropriate response for the German government to make.

"First off, our French government ought to publicly execute that Jew and his entire family to set an example," Mademoiselle Charlotte said, washing down the duck liver with pre-war Sauvignon Blanc, her eyes just as cold as the ice on which the oysters were sitting. "Dust off the guillotine and off with his head."

"The trouble is, his family is dead," the Colonel quipped, patting his moustache with a napkin. "I heard that was the reason for his outburst."

"I don't think they're dead," the Colonel's fellow officer said, chasing a grape that kept escaping his fork around his gold-rimmed plate. "They were beaten by the SS or some such. Or chased out of their house, supposedly—who the devil knows. The Jew boy was avenging them, or at least so he claimed during his interrogation."

"Well, better yet," Mademoiselle Charlotte said. "I say, bring them here and execute them all."

"Your socialist government run by the Jews, my love, shall never execute ones of their own kind," the Colonel said teasingly.

"It's not my government." Despite her fiancé's playful tone, Mademoiselle Charlotte still bristled like a cat. "You know I loathe it just as much as you do."

At these words, one of the guests who had been sitting silently the entire time cleared his throat, somehow instantly commanding attention from everyone present, including the Colonel himself, folded the napkin unhurriedly and placed it next to his plate. He fixed his hostess with the gaze of his pale blue eyes, even more vivid due to his hair being whiter than the tablecloth, betraying not just his age but in some inexplicable way his status. "You won't have to suffer from that government for long, dear child."

At once, I recognized the accent, not unlike my own. Only, I seriously doubted he was an Alsatian. Someone from Berlin, to be sure. Someone perhaps not as famous as Minister Ribbentrop, but even more influential in his inconspicuous, invisible mantle of a gray cardinal; someone who pulled all the strings behind the curtains with the long, knotted fingers of an experienced puppeteer.

"Today, things that had been debated, which could never be agreed upon by the Reichstag gentlemen, were unwittingly set in motion by that silly boy. The wheels of history are turning—faster, thanks to his action. The destiny of his kind, just like the destiny of those sympathizing with his plight, is now decided. From this day on, there shall be no turning back." He pushed his chair back with a deliberate motion, rose to his feet with the bearing of a monarch and lifted his crystal glass, in which burgundy wine was dark as blood. "And there's nothing else I'd like to toast more than this day. To the future!"

"To the future without those yids!"

"To the future without those Bolshevists!"

"To new Europe! Let it live for a thousand years!"

Three days, a sob nearly escaped my lips. *Three days too late...*

Along with the first winter frost, a cloud the color of lead had descended upon Paris, robbing it of light and warmth. I rather welcomed the change as my own world had lost all color. The darkness was befitting somehow. I bathed in it, sought out the shadows on purpose and drank the poison of despair and melancholy as if it was ambrosia itself. Together with every trace of my family, the only fear that was left in me had disappeared.

After the *Kristallnacht*—the infamous Night of Broken Glass during which German Jews all over the Reich had been beaten, killed in cold blood in front of the police, who stood and did nothing, or shipped off to God knew where—even Maxim's people couldn't find them or even what had happened to them. And if Soviet spies failed to locate you, you were well and truly gone. Dead, that is, not just arrested; erased from the memory of the country in which you had the misfortune to have been born, as though you had never existed at all.

Death was no longer my enemy but a release—from all the pain in the world that I suddenly could no longer carry.

As days got slashed in half and the grinning skull of the moon crept along the sky for most waking hours, I no longer avoided seedy alleyways, no longer took lengthier but safer routes, no longer flocked to crowds seeking safety in numbers. Instead, I let the sound of my heels echo off the walls next to which pimps and thieves smoked and met their gaze with my own, challenging, almost daring them to harm me in some way —any way they wished, to be frank—just to feel something other than this unbearable numbness. However, whatever they saw in my dead cold eyes made them avert their gazes first and even step out of my way. The creatures of the night, they smelled the aura of some ancient plague around me and scattered like rats before they could catch it. I didn't blame them one bit. It was a terrible burden to carry.

"I don't want you going through the park tonight," Alfred warned me one Tuesday morning as we were getting dressed for work. "The gendarmes issued a warning that there is some madman on the loose. Stakes women out and snatches them when they're all alone. Slashes their throats with a razor like Jack the Ripper."

I kissed him tenderly on his lips and promised to take the

Metro. But when the night came and my work at Mademoiselle Charlotte's was over, I went straight to the deserted, snow-shrouded square, dusted the bench with my bare hand, feeling no cold whatsoever as I did so, and sat with my arms spread like wings atop the bench's back. I leaned my head back and closed my eyes, a serene smile creasing my lips for the first time in ages.

I felt the planks of the bench creak lightly under someone else's weight. In spite of myself, my smile grew wider.

"Mademoiselle."

A voice, cold and probing, like a serpent's tongue.

I didn't budge. Didn't even bother to open my eyes for that matter.

"Mademoiselle?"

A hand on my shoulder; faint scent of leather gloves.

Perhaps he liked seeing his reflection in the eyes of the women he killed. I indulged him, hesitantly, not out of fear of him, but out of concern that he wouldn't see that fear he was seeking in my eyes and leave me like the walking corpse that I was. Trembling maidens are much more interesting to play with. Me, not so much.

His face was a shadow among the army of shadows around us. Dark overcoat, dark hat pulled down on his forehead.

"It's too a cold night to be enjoyable," he said.

"I like the cold."

His hand was still on my shoulder. I shut my eyes and dropped my head back once again.

"You're not local, are you?" he asked.

"No."

No one will be looking for me if I disappear and I so wish to disappear. No more small talk, I beg you. Just give me your mercy in one sharp slash and I shall die with your unspoken name on my lips, forever grateful... Poor Alfred will suffer for a while, but he'll find someone soon enough with that loving heart of his... Someone better; someone unbroken and undamaged;

someone who won't go out at night looking for death as the only way out.

"Do you have a place to go? A room?"

"I'm not a prostitute."

"I didn't think you were. I see your maid's apron." A pause. "I only wanted to escort you home. Or help you find accommodation for the night, if you have nowhere to go to."

"I have a room." I opened my eyes, looked at him closer. He was acting rather strange for a serial killer. But perhaps he wanted a cozier place to enjoy my body before he slashed my throat. Perhaps he'd even enjoy a cigarette later. "But I don't live alone."

"You have a roommate?"

"A husband." The lie didn't feel like a lie once it slipped off my lips. Alfred was more than a husband, despite the lack of a wedding ring or a marriage certificate. He was a comrade-in-arms, a fellow conspirator, a man I'd followed into the unknown without thinking twice... a man who'd follow me anywhere if I only asked. In sickness and health, tied with an oath more powerful than any meaningless papers—

"He must be worried sick for you then." The man's voice tore me out of my reveries. Before I could protest, he was on his feet, his hand in front of me, palm up, no razor. "Come. I'll walk you home."

"I'm fine right here."

"Mademoiselle, really, I must insist."

He leaned closer to pick my lifeless limbs off the bench. It was then that the lapel of his coat moved ever so slightly, revealing the dim shine of a shield so many of my kin had grown to fear.

I let him escort me to my hostel and all but cursed him and his solicitude as he tipped his hat before setting off back to the park he was guarding—the blasted undercover gendarme who wouldn't let me die in peace.

Such was my disappointment that, as soon as I opened the door to our room with my key, hot tears sprang to my eyes and I would have undoubtedly fallen in a heap right in the threshold if Alfred hadn't scooped me up and carried me to bed like the child I wished I was once again, an innocent child with not a care in the world, someone to be defended and protected.

But I was an orphan now. I realized it that night—the first night that I mourned my parents properly, with tears and anger and denial and so much guilt, I would have crumbled under it if it weren't for those warm hands that held me, cradled me and caressed me when all I felt I deserved was pain—self-inflicted or not, it mattered not.

"I promised to take care of them, Alfred."

I bit my trembling lips to blood and he kissed them instead.

"It's not your fault."

"They asked for my help and I did nothing."

"You did everything you could."

"I should have gone to Germany."

"And perished together with them?"

"Yes!"

My agonized scream rang through the room. The silence that followed was more terrible still.

"But that's precisely what they want, Dora. Those murderers, that's precisely what they want. For us all to die, either by their hand or by our own. It is because of that that we must live. Live out of sheer spite. Live just to make life difficult for them. Live to avenge those they've taken. Do you truly think if you went and offed yourself now it would make a difference to the Nazis? Or make your parents proud in any way?"

I couldn't tell if it was the harsh terms he'd put it into or whether it was his voice itself that was whipping me back into shape, like a lame horse on which its master refused to give up, but something shifted in me at that moment. My eyes still stung, but not with tears this time but with all-encompassing, annihilating fury.

Once again, Alfred had proven precisely why I'd chosen him as my husband-to-be, as my comrade-in-arms, as my soulmate and my closest friend. That night, he did what the Parisian Ripper couldn't: he killed the old Dora, the weak Dora, and out of her ashes, just like the phoenix, something formidable was rising. And just like the phoenix, this new creature would wield its fire to raze the enemy to the ground, until nothing but dust was left of them.

And on that dust, our victorious boots would trample.

EIGHTEEN

SEPTEMBER 1939

No one had believed that it would come, this dark day for all of
Europe. Even though everyone had realized that, despite his lies
and promises to the contrary, Hitler would never be satisfied
with just Sudetenland, just Rhineland, just Austria; everyone
had been aware of the German rhetoric growing progressively
more and more volatile, accusing Poland of harassing its local
German minority population, demanding Danzig back, issuing
one ultimatum after another. The smell of war had hung in the
charged air; the reports of troops amassing on the Polish border
had sounded the alarm in every newspaper, on each radio wave.
And yet, even when German Foreign Minister Ribbentrop, the
very same man who had been a guest of honor at Mademoiselle
Charlotte's wedding, had signed a non-aggression pact with his
Soviet counterpart Molotov, people still buried their heads in
the sand and went about their business, claiming that the war
wouldn't happen, that the last one was still too fresh in everyone's mind to purposely plunge Europe into a similar blood-
shedding atrocity, that some way, somehow, the whole affair
would resolve itself. The signs had been there all along, and yet,
when the first salvo of German artillery had lit up the night sky

over the Polish border, the news still punched like a fist to the gut.

I was one of those recovering from the blow, but for a slightly different reason.

A newspaper clenched in my hand, I walked past grocery stores all but mobbed by the restless public grabbing everything non-perishable in sight, past crowds with handwritten banners waving their fists in front of the elected officials' offices, past lines of young men in front of recruitment offices, smoking and exchanging bravados and spitting on the ground with great contempt whenever anyone mentioned the cursed Boche. Only, this time, the cursed Boche was me and no one cared whether I was Jewish or not; just that I spoke French with a strong German accent and was therefore a spy and a traitor of France.

The realization of it had dropped on me like an avalanche, when, shortly after France had declared war on Germany, I had made the mistake of joining a spontaneous antifascist demonstration driven, just like the rest of the protesters, by righteous anger at the Nazis, Italian fascists, Spanish nationalists and generally everyone who reveled in the idea of their country's exceptionalism and had sworn to destroy all who refused to swallow their hateful rhetoric. Bright flags of antifascist movements replaced the sky itself; the chants replaced the air; we breathed them in and out, one organism, propelled by righteous anger and incredible love for our brothers and sisters who had already perished and would soon perish in great numbers at the hands of the brutes if nothing was done and done now. But out of nowhere a hand had come, bigger than my face, and slapped me with such force, I had landed on my knees, tasting blood in my mouth, ears ringing, momentarily disoriented and still believing that it must have been a mistake, that the man didn't mean it; or course he didn't—

"What are you doing here, you Boche bitch? Spying on us, eh, Nazi whore?"

With my hand against my throbbing cheek, I had stared about me, dazed and confused to the utmost. There was no brotherly love in the faces of those who'd formed a circle around me. Their fists were clenched; eyes mad with fury.

"I'm Jewish," I had whispered, uncertain, but all they heard was my German accent.

Another kick had come, this time in the chin. I had yelped, more out of surprise than of pain, despite the fact that the boot was a worker's boot, heavy and made to last for years.

"I'm Jewish!" I had said louder, instinctively rising my hand in front of my face. "I'm a refugee."

"Refugee, my ass," one of them had spat. "Since when do refugees wear maid's dresses?"

"Refugees have no papers, you lying sack of Nazi scum!"

They were like a pack of mad dogs: baring their teeth, snapping, lunging for my neck as I crouched on the ground, now properly terrified. Someone had grabbed a fistful of my hair at the back and yanked hard, offering my face to the attackers. Their leader didn't have to be asked twice. Without listening to any of my pleas, he had landed another couple of hard blows on my cheek and lips, sending my head spinning. A cornered animal now, I had kicked and clawed and only stilled when I had recognized the unmistakable glistening of steel in one of the men's hands. A small folding knife, not one of the deadly SA daggers I'd seen more times than I cared to remember, but sharp enough to do the job if driven into someone's neck.

"I'm Jewish," I had repeated quietly but firmly, as though the Grim Reaper ever cared to listen to explanations before sending his victim to Hades. "I'm a communist myself, comrades; I can quote the entire manifesto to you; I work for Comintern—"

I still can't imagine how it would have ended for me if a whistle hadn't broken the spell and sent the entire crowd scrambling. For the first time in my life, I'd been thankful for the presence of the gendarmes.

And now, recalling how one of them had helped me to my feet and even dusted me off with a handkerchief he had kindly told me to keep, I was marching straight to their headquarters with my real papers in hand.

Alfred had told me that I was mad. Maxim, I hadn't even informed of my decision to try to legalize my refugee status. He'd cut my tongue out himself, simply for voicing such an idiotic idea.

The local prefecture was cool and almost silent after the madness of the street. Behind the glass of the reception desk, a gendarme on duty was having his afternoon sandwich with coffee, his eyes focused on the same newspaper I carried in my hand. On seeing me, he closed it promptly and even moved the plate with his lunch away, at attention all of a sudden.

"An assault?" he asked with visible concern, wetting his finger and pulling a form out of a stack in front of him.

Aware of what I looked like, with two-day-old bruises fading from ink-blue and black to deep purple, I smiled at him, but only enough that I wouldn't split my healing lips once again.

"No." I laid out the newspaper in front of him, pointing to page two. "It says here that now there's an expedited process for refugees to regularize their residency status. I'm a refugee. I would like to obtain some sort of paper confirming it. And, also, if I could acquire a work permit, that would be absolutely splendid. I don't need any assistance from the government. I won't apply for any aid or benefits. All I want is to work, legally, and to have at least some sort of status now that we're at war..."

My hand trembled slightly as I pushed my German passport through a narrow slit in the glass toward him. He regarded it for a moment as if it was some sort of explosive device, but then reached for it, even if with great reluctance.

"I'm Jewish," I rushed to explain. "I lived in Amsterdam before that. There's a visa in there—"

"Yes, I can see that," he said, flipping through the passport I had sworn to myself I'd burn as soon as my legal residency status in France was sorted out. "But I don't see any indication that you're Jewish."

"Whatever are you talking about?" I laughed in spite of myself. But the laughter rang out hollow and mirthless around the hall walls. All at once, I had a feeling they were closing on me. "Just look at my last name. Davidsohn! What other proof do you need?"

"All German refugees of Jewish origin have a J stamped in their passports," the gendarme explained coolly. "You don't." He gave me a pointed look.

"That must be some sort of new rule." Sweat suddenly broke out on my temples. My entire head was pounding once again, worse than after the beating I'd taken just two days ago. "I left Germany in 1933, almost right after Hitler came to power. There were no rules about stamping our passports with any Js back then."

"I see the exit visa from the Netherlands here and the entrance one for France. Dated 1934."

"That's correct."

"You've lived in France this entire time. Almost five years."

I didn't like the expression his face was taking one bit.

"That's right. It'll be five years in October."

"You have lived here illegally."

I opened my mouth and closed it. What was I supposed to tell him? About my work for the Comintern?

"I came here to escape prosecution in my own country. I truly am sorry for not applying for legal status, but surely you know that it's all but impossible. Those minuscule quotas for immigrants, they're unfairly skewed toward the wealthy ones, the people of means, preferably Catholics and Protestants, not someone Jewish and broke, like me. As soon as the quotas were lifted, as soon as the process was expedited, I came here right away. I want to have legal status. It was simply unobtainable for me before; or else, I would have come here on my very first day. I simply want to live without fear of being killed, and to work. Is it so much to ask?"

The gendarme regarded me for a long time, flipped through my passport some more and then picked up the black phone that stood on his desk.

Apparently, legal status and a permit to work *was* too much to ask for. In less than an hour, after a short interrogation and my fingerprints taken, I was arrested on charges of being an enemy alien. The next day, I was taken to La Petite Roquette prison. All throughout the first night in my new cell, I could hear the ringing of the prison lock after the door was slammed closed after me.

NINETEEN

A FEW WEEKS LATER

After the initial shock of incarceration, the injustice of the entire situation, came melancholy and it was worse than anything I could ever imagine. If I thought I'd known pain before, I'd known nothing. From the mildewed corners of my cell crept the darkness, and I drowned in its waves as they rolled over me, each more powerful than the one before. During the day, it was all right. We had chores to distract us from our unhappy musings. There were army uniforms to sew, our own laundry to sweat over, food to prepare for the entire prison population, interned just as unfairly as I'd been. But it was the night that I soon learned to dread the most; that dark hour just after lights out when sighs, sobs, and whispers wouldn't still and it felt as though the walls of the prison itself were groaning with unspeakable pain.

It was then, as I lay on my side with my knees pulled up to my chest and my arms wrapped around them, that I was overcome with such black despair, it constricted my very chest in its dreadful vise, squeezing the will to live out of me one breath at a time. Never in my life had I felt more helpless, more abandoned by the entire world, more alone and insignificant—useless flotsam tossed about by the ruthless tide of fate, hurled against the rocks and left to die on them, broken physically and mentally.

"It wouldn't be half as bad if there was something to look forward to," Marthe, my fellow prison mate, said.

Tall, with chestnut hair streaked with gray and piled in a thick bun atop her head, she was here on alien enemy charges as well—a German who'd been seeking refuge from her own country only to find herself imprisoned by the very people who were supposed to help her. Aside from the fact that she'd arrived here from Berlin, Marthe never shared much about her past. I didn't pry either. For many of us, picking that scab was still far too painful.

We were on laundry duty that day, inhaling the poisonous clouds of lye and chlorine for hours on end, locked in a purgatory with the temperatures so high, clouds hung over the room like some hellish mist; only, instead of the devils, it was us who dunked prison uniforms into cauldrons with boiling water.

"Angelique has just been sentenced to ten years," Marthe disclosed.

Angelique was a French prostitute who had turned herself in after killing her client in self-defense. He'd taken her to his house on the outskirts of Paris, locked her in his cellar, beaten her almost senseless and brutalized her in all ways possible for two days. Realizing that she wouldn't survive for much longer, Angelique had clawed at one of the planks covering the cellar's only window at ceiling level, torn her nails off but pried the plank off, together with its host of long, rusty nails, and taken the business end to her would-be-killer's face and skull. It if were up to me, if I happened to be the judge presiding over her case, I'd not only acquit her but shake her hand for ridding the world of that scum. But I wasn't the judge, and so, Angelique had been accused of bringing such behavior on herself for choosing her "shameful profession" and "more than deserved her sentence." Frankly, all of us in La Petite Roquette regarded her with great sympathy and respect and not one of us expressed the opinion that there was anything just about such a justice system.

"They may release her in five for good behavior," Marthe continued, breaking the chain of my thoughts. "But even if not, she can start counting the days now that they're transferring her. Lucky girl; regular jail for regular murderers and thieves, not this purgatory where we'll stew for years until we croak or someone remembers that we're actually incarcerated here and sets us free, a long time after the war is over."

Indeed, unlike in Angelique's case, there was no court date appointed and no attorney to defend us, and that helplessness, this uncertainty, chipped away at even the strongest psyche with the blunt teeth of an old rat.

We were called names and grew to believe them.

We were robbed of all hope and grew embittered.

We went through the daily motions but were so full of venom inside, it was slowly poisoning us, corroding our very selves.

I used to be so strong, but now the simplest task, such as washing my face in the morning in the communal latrine, had turned into a chore.

I used to be so defiant and full of fire, but now I was perpetually cold and indifferent to everything. Frankly, I welcomed that numbness with open arms, for in its place never came joy but only black, strangling despair, and I'd rather feel nothing at all than its claws slowly gutting me night after night.

After two weeks, I began to wish I could stay asleep all day just to make it pass faster. After three weeks, I began to dream of never waking up at all, just closing my eyes, drifting into nothingness and dissolving into it until not even a memory would be left of me.

However, when I approached Marthe and offered her my day's rations in exchange for a razor I knew she could procure from a male guard who liked her, she gave me a severe look that sobered me for a moment.

"Don't even think about it, girl. You don't want to end your life. You only want to end your pain. But it won't always be this way. You'll wake up one day with such joy in your heart, you'll feel like it could burst any moment, and remember me for refusing you today. It's a momentary weakness, love. It, too, will pass. You'll see. And besides, what shall become of your betrothed if you leave him in such a manner, without as much as a goodbye? There are others to be considered besides you, you know."

I knew but I was generally was too numb to feel even disappointment, so I shuffled off like the ghost I was becoming and went on about my day. As for my betrothed, I felt abandoned by him first. He'd dragged me into this country and this entire Comintern business; he'd contaminated me with this viral desire for universal justice and sacrificing myself in the name of nameless masses when I should have thought of my own family first and foremost. If I had done that, they would have been alive, they would have—

In periods of lucidity that were growing rarer and rarer, I tried to slap some sense into myself. I started realizing that the voices weren't real, that my blame was misplaced, that I loved Alfred more than life itself for showing me precisely that—the noble need to sacrifice oneself in the name of a universal good that would eventually win, for the world wasn't a dark place, only certain people were evil, but the majority were good, decent folk and the war would be won by our side and peace and love—

But then another wave of black melancholy would drown

the voice of reason and color the world in gray again, leaving nothing but agony in its wake.

And then one day, out of the blue, a familiar voice called my name from the other side of the courtyard we were raking.

"Hey, gorgeous! Come here often?"

For an instant, I stared at the heap of wet, musty leaves at my feet, too afraid to look up, too afraid to jinx it all. But then, in spite of myself, clutching at the rake for support, for I was certain I would faint had I not done so, I finally looked up and there he was, my Alfred—his hair shorn, stubble on his face so thick it would turn into a full beard in the course of a few more days, civilian clothes hanging on him two sizes too big, but his eyes glimmering with the same mischief I'd grown to know and love—the ghost of my past had materialized out of the ether when I needed him the most.

I blinked at him like an owl until Marthe prodded me in the back with the end of her rake—"Go to him, you silly cow!" —and I made the first uncertain step, then another, until I broke into a trot and then run and all but hurled myself against the barbed wire separating the women's part of the jail's courtyard from the men's, straight into Alfred's loving arms. They bled onto my own cuts sliced by the wire, but I couldn't have imagined a sweeter reunion in my most vivid dreams.

"Alf, Alfie... What are you doing here?" I whispered and laughed in between the kisses he was covering my wet face with.

"What do you mean, what am I doing here? You didn't come home."

"I got arrested."

"I gathered that much."

"What did you do? Oh, you silly, silly man, what did you do?"

"Turned myself in, of course. Brought some freshly printed

antifascist leaflets with me to rake up some additional charges as their author."

From nowhere, a guard smacked him on the ribs, without much force but to drive his point across, and I got a few slaps from my guard too. But all of a sudden, I felt as though the sound returned to the silent world. I heard birds once again. I smelled the rotting leaves underfoot and gathered into massive wet heaps. But, most importantly, I could breathe once again. Once again, I had a goal: to get us both out of here. Once again, my life had a purpose and it dawned on me that very first night of him sleeping just a few cellblocks away what exactly had brought us together, Alfred and I: our own lives didn't matter much. We lived to help others and as long as there was someone to fight for, we would fight with all we had.

That night, I felt giddy with anticipation of what was yet to come. It was impossibly good to be able to feel once again.

OCTOBER 18, 1939

The order for transfer came with the speed and brutality of the German blitzkrieg. We were just growing used to our routine when the uniformed men came and whisked us—alien enemies —into a new and terrifying unknown.

I scarcely remember the road itself: looking out of the train's windows could easily earn one the revocation of bathroom privileges and a smack on one's curious snout, so I didn't tempt fate. The only consolation was that Marthe was here, and so was Alfred—somewhere in the back of the train, together with the rest of the male inmates, but here nevertheless.

Restless from the road and general anxiety, we turned our misery into a guessing game to pass the time.

"I say, we're going south."

"South, my boot! The Riviera!"

"I said nothing about the Riviera, but there are prisons

there, just on the water. From centuries ago, back when the local aristocracy was squabbling among themselves."

"Rot."

"Not rot in the slightest!"

"You're from Bavaria; what do you know about French aristocracy at any rate?"

"I read books, you ignorant sow. Wouldn't hurt you either."

Guffaws; a guard's baton slammed against the train car's wall but half-heartedly. He, too, was tired from the mind-numbing, rhythmic clanking of the iron wheels and only wished to doze.

"No. I say, we're going east."

"Where, east? To Switzerland?"

"Why not? Perhaps, they'll just let us loose on the border and make us the Swiss's problem."

"Wouldn't that be nice?"

Another series of approving snorts, quieter this time, so as not to awaken the sleeping guard.

At long last we arrived and, as soon as we were herded out of the train, we saw at once that this was neither an old stone tower like the Bastille nor anything like the Swiss border. No; in front of us, as far as the eye could see, sprawled a complex of wooden huts and even tarpaulin-covered tents, all swarming with people enclosed behind rows and rows of barbed wire. The communal stench coming from the internment camp—now we saw clearly what precisely this was, just like the Nazis' Dachau—hit us with the force of an approaching train and all but knocked out whatever breath was left in us.

"Where the hell are we?" I whispered in spite of myself.

"Mende." Next to me, Marthe pointed to a painted sign over a makeshift unloading platform.

Mende. Rieucros Internment Camp.

I stared at it for a very long time before a chuckle escaped my lips. Another one followed, until it turned into a veritable attack I could neither prevent nor fight against. I was laughing like a madwoman while tears streamed down my face; hiccupping and laughing and shaking with my entire body as women around me looked on and nudged each other further and further away from me—the one who had finally lost it, as if madness was contagious.

Perhaps it was. Or else how had the world got to where it was now?

Only Marthe didn't step away. Instead, she slapped me hard on the face and regarded me with the concerned look of a Freudian scholar.

"You didn't have to slap me," I muttered, my brain gathering itself piece by piece into a semblance of normalcy.

"Yes, I did. Better me than the guards."

I rubbed my cheek. "If you're waiting for thanks, keep waiting."

"Daft bat."

"Should have given me that razor when I asked."

"And lose my only source of entertainment? Mad bats like you are hard to come by, you know."

"You're only two apples short of a picnic yourself with your psychoanalysis."

"What do you expect?" This time it was Marthe who laughed. "I used to work as a psychiatrist at the Charité. You may call it a professional habit."

I regarded her in stunned amazement and newfound respect. Marthe, the towering, sturdy Marthe who could always be counted on to break a fight among two inmates, who had done laundry with me without complaining once and with such contagious enthusiasm, as if it used to be her workplace instead of the most famous hospital in Berlin—Marthe had lost so much more than me and still took it all in her stride. And not only did she take it in her stride but sorted out mad bats like me on an almost daily basis.

All of a sudden, I was overcome with a profound feeling of shame and gratitude that choked me worse than the hysterical despair of just moments ago. I wrapped my arms around her and pressed my head against her shoulder—the mother I no longer had, the woman who still gave a damn about me even when I didn't give a damn about myself.

TWENTY

RIEUCROS INTERNMENT CAMP. WINTER
1939–1940

From behind the wall of frost-covered barbed wire, I watched the column of inmates depart through the gates, ropes coiled over their shoulders. A blunt ax in his hand, Alfred looked over his shoulder to give me a parting wink as was our morning routine. Only this time, a guard bringing up the column's rear whacked him with a wooden baton for upsetting his personal sense of order.

"Getting randy, Bolshevist scum? No lunch for you today and no shift changes either. You'll be chopping those trees until I get tired of watching you. That should calm you down a tad."

He was still muttering curses at Alfred's back until I could no longer discern individual words. Inside of me, anger bubbled and boiled, blackened and thicker than tar. One simple human gesture, one simple smile and a wink to see us both through yet another torturous day and the guard treated it as a personal offense.

"Why do they hate us so?" I cried to no one in particular.

In front of me, over two meters of barbed wire stretched into infinity, and behind, like a spike piercing the leaden winter sky, was an ancient forester's watchtower that had been here long before any of us had arrived—and, it was my utmost conviction, would survive us all yet.

"Because they're afraid of us Reds more than they're afraid of the Nazis; isn't that obvious?"

Startled momentarily by a husky voice that had answered my rhetorical question in the Catalonian dialect, I swung round on my heel. Looking not bothered in the slightest, an olive-skinned woman was rolling a cigarette with the skill of a true soldier who had spent far too long in the trenches. Around her mouth and nose, loose strands of her glossy black hair were white with frost; though, cold seemed to affect her much less than it affected me: the layers of her woolen shawl lay around her shoulders instead of covering her head. It was anyone's guess when the wind—there was always wind howling between the woodcutters' huts and barracks in this rocky land surrounded by pines as far as the eye could see—had blown it off. For some reason, that nonchalance of hers impressed me greatly.

"Are you from the International Brigades?" I asked.

She stopped rolling her cigarette and fixed me with her black eyes as if I'd just uttered something perfectly moronic. "I'm Spanish."

I had uttered something moronic indeed. The International Brigades consisted of foreign volunteers supporting the Republic. The Spanish, in contrast, fought with the nationalists for their own land, and not just for the idea, unlike their communist brethren.

"Of course you are," I said. "Forgive me, please. I don't know what I was thinking. The cold got my brain."

Instead of replying, the woman licked the edge of the rolling paper, placed the cigarette between her bluish lips, produced a match, and struck it on the side of the foresters' watchtower. As soon as the tip of her makeshift cigarette glowed red, she offered it to me. I took it that my apology was accepted.

"Thank you."

"*De nada.* Isabel."

I took her narrow palm in mine and shook it. "Dora."

She rolled another cigarette. For some time, we smoked in silence.

I stiffened when the wind brought the echo of the blunt axes cutting into hundred-year-old pines frozen stiff, remembering Alfred in his old boots with soles so weak, his feet got soaked after the first few minutes of the roll call, let alone trudging knee-deep in snow until the guard in charge would indicate the patch of forest that ought to be cut. Then, for the rest of the day, Alfred would swing his ax with his comrades, steam rising off their bodies despite the subzero temperatures, just to be sent—"Move your fat tails, you lazy scum, on the double!"—back to the camp. The run was for their own benefit, according to the same sadistic guard. He was only looking after their health. It wouldn't do anyone any good, strolling in their sweaty clothes in the middle of the night when the temperature in the mountains plummeted even further—

"Were you in the Brigades?"

Isabel's husky voice tore me out of my musings full of resentment.

I pulled on the cigarette I had all but forgotten. Even self-rolled ones were a luxury in the Rieucros Internment Camp. Wasting precious tobacco was a capital offense even in my eyes.

"You could say that."

"That's a fine way to answer the question without answering it."

"I didn't fight along with you in the streets, if that's what you're asking; no. But I did lose to Franco just the same." I felt my eyes glazing over with a film of memories. "We could, but we didn't stop him in time."

"Ah, you're with the Comintern then? The Foreign Intelligence section?"

"Foreign Intelligence, my foot." I spat on the ground—a disgusting habit I always detested, but which expressed just exactly what I felt at that moment. If only one could spit out one's bitter disappointment instead of walking around with its taste slowly poisoning you from the inside. "I don't know what the hell I am anymore."

"You're a communist and the enemy of the Nazi regime if I gathered that much correctly from your atrocious accent." Isabel grinned crookedly and, all at once, I felt lighter somehow; not as lonely as before. "Else, you wouldn't have been enjoying fresh mountain air in this fine resort and gaining strength through physical labor."

"I'm a Jew too, so add that to the list of my crimes."

She bared all of her teeth at me this time. Her laughter was perfectly soundless—the laughter of the fighter from the shadows. "Bah, you're a true recidivist then."

"At your service." I bowed theatrically.

"As for your question, they hate us because before the war, nationalism was on the rise everywhere, not only in Germany, Spain, and Italy; France was no better. And the Germans have such fine, sharp uniforms..."

"It can't possibly be about the uniforms. They kill people. Have been, for years now. One of the first things they did when Hitler came to power was to open a concentration camp for enemies of the regime. I was still in Germany when Dachau became the SA's favorite threat for everyone who dared to even insinuate something against the state."

"Once the Nazis come here, to France, they'll realize it, but it'll be too late." Isabel shrugged.

I froze for an instant after hearing such a frightful prophecy spoken with such enviable indifference. "Do you truly believe it'll come to that?"

"Surely it will. Have you heard how quickly they took Poland? Took them hardly a month."

Naturally, I had heard. We all did. It had been the talk of the barracks for several weeks. "But this is France."

"And?" She looked positively unimpressed. "Do you think the French army is somehow stronger than the Polish one?" She issued a snort of such a disdain, I felt my cheeks redden.

"Still, there is a reason they aren't attacking us yet."

"There is." Isabel yawned. "Winter. As soon as it gets nice and warm, they'll charge right through that waste of good capital called the Maginot Line and shall be drinking beer in Paris by summer; you take it from me. I've seen it happen in my own country."

"Even more reason for them to release us! Do they not understand that we're their natural allies, not enemies? We'd fight against the Nazis right alongside them without any hesitation—"

"As I said, my good Dora, the French won't see reason until it's too late. As of now, they're hoping the Germans shall leave them alone. As of now, an anti-refugee sentiment outweighs common sense far too much for them to make a connection. As of now, we—the Reds—are their threat. Because we're already here, ready to spread our propaganda and turn France into a socialist state, according to the local Goebbelses. And the Germans are still far away. They may invade and they may not. Until they do, we'll just have to—"

"Enjoy the fresh mountain air and gain strength through labor?" I finished for her.

Isabel grinned at the venom in my voice. "It appears you're beginning to grasp the idea, my good comrade."

SPRING–SUMMER 1940

Isabel's grim prediction was only off by a few weeks. May showers hadn't ceased flooding the earth floor of our wooden barrack when the first air-raid sirens began to howl somewhere in the northeast. Then, columns of refugees followed: we spied them crawling along the major roads, tiny and helpless as ants, from the height of our wooded vantage point. From time to time, German bombers dived at them with the atrocious scream of engines that sent the ground vibrating even under our feet despite the great distance.

"Here come Jericho Trumpets," Isabel announced through the cigarette in her teeth, perfectly unmoved among the general commotion the first German dive-bombers created among the inmates.

We had become fast friends in the course of the past few months—Isabel, Marthe, and I. Before long, the guards had begun to assign us to labor details together, knowing that we'd be much more productive if they "let us jaw until we were blue in the face" in their words. And besides, it fit in perfectly with their idea of separating certain groups of inmates so that they wouldn't start—God forbid—getting odd ideas into their muti-nous heads. One couldn't trust a bunch of Comintern witches any more than the female Spanish freedom fighters who smoked far too much, wore pants and used to shoot sharper than men. So, placing Jewish refugees with German enemy aliens and a sprinkle of communists and Spaniards among them made sense to our guards. They had assumed religious Jews would calm us down. Instead, we were slowly but surely teaching them our rebellious ways.

"The what?" Naomi asked from the ground on which she'd been crouching. A girl of fifteen, she had arrived with the most recent—and probably last—transport from the north. The Paris gendarmerie had long ago run out of communists and Spanish refugees to intern. Now, it was mostly foreign Jews they were shipping south.

"Stukas, German bombers," Isabel explained, her eyes narrowing. Her nostrils flared like those of a retired wolfhound who had suddenly caught the scent of the enemy she'd been bred to kill and she was at once in her stance, ready to pounce. "Junkers Ju 87, if you wish to be scientific about it."

"Why do they screech like that?"

Isabel only snorted, glancing at a trembling Naomi from the side of her eye. "Why do you think? To send poor little waifs like you scrambling."

I elbowed her with reproach.

Isabel huffed, drew her eyes to the gunpowder-gray sky and finally took mercy on our youngest crew member. It wasn't just men the guards chased through the gates each morning now. We women also were marched into the woods as soon as the sun rose, and made to bind the felled trees until our hands were bleeding from the coarse ropes as thick as our arms. *Contributing to the war effort*, as Isabel disdainfully called it.

"Someone in the Luftwaffe decided that just raining bombs on unsuspecting civilians wasn't terrifying enough," she went on to explain. "And so, they mounted special air-ram sirens to the bombers' legs to make that screeching noise as they dive. I used to wake up to that lovely alarm clock almost nightly in Spain. With time, one grows used to them, though. Closer to the end, in the cellars, we used to sleep right through them. It's the silence afterwards that one grows to fear..."

Just like the silence that had come right after the Stukas had departed, leaving a few torn bodies left scattered like broken dolls on the side of the roads. In the absence of any authorities in the vicinity, and only one policeman for the entire local village, camp inmates were deployed for clean-up duty.

As long as I live, I shall never forget the haunted look on Alfred's ashen face when he returned to Rieucros after such a deployment.

"There was a little girl there, Dora... both her legs were just... gone. And her mother, she was still clutching her in her arms. A piece of shrapnel shaved off the top of her head; her face all but gone, but she was still clutching—" was all he managed through the barbed wire to which I was clinging in my efforts to reach out, to hold him, to take at least a sliver of his pain away. And then, his entire face crumbled and he staggered away with his face in his hands. Only then did I see that they were covered in dried blood up to the elbows.

WINTER 1941

"Isabel Alvarez?"

Next to me, Isabel straightened, shielding her eyes from the blinding midday sun. It stood high and small in the winter sky, but the pale brilliance of its reflection on the pristine snow soon turned us all into moles with black spots dancing in front of our eyes as we groped for wood to be loaded onto yet another train north. The German war machine was gaining steam and, just our rotten luck, we were the ones feeding it fuel.

"Commandant Duplantier," Isabel said with a faint measure of disdain in her voice. "To what do I owe the honor?"

All around our loading work detail, inmates drew themselves up at the sight of the commandant and his four-guard armed escort.

From the top of the truck, I caught Alfred's questioning gaze. The honor indeed: it was not every day that the man in charge of the entire Rieucros camp deigned to visit our lice-infested quarters.

Commandant Duplantier was a squat man with beady, black eyes and heavy jowls that always seemed to work like those of some insect, with a net of burst blood vessels around his nose. Though, right now, the lower part of his face was all but hidden in the thick ermine collar of his overcoat. Isabel made a point of staring at his fur-lined gloves and flexed her own bare fingers—so bright-red they were one step away from frostbite. None of us, outside detail workers, could count on such luxuries as gloves.

"Maréchal Pétain, our esteemed head of state, is arriving with Minister Laval to visit and inspect Rieucros next week." Duplantier paused for effect.

Only, the new leader of the collaborationist regime that had sold France to the Nazis just a few months ago instilled just about the same amount of respect in Isabel—or any of us for that matter—as used latrine paper.

The commandant drew himself up when his announcement didn't produce the desired effect. There was nothing else but for him to continue. "It has come to my attention that you used to be an artist before..." He moved his jowls as he searched for the right word, grimacing as if he tasted something vile. "Before your involvement with the Popular Front."

Once again, Isabel made no reply; only kept staring at him in mild annoyance for distracting her from work.

"It is my opinion that it will please the *Maréchal* immensely if we present him with his portrait. Something stately and dignified, in his new uniform, with his new personal crest in the background perhaps and—"

Abruptly, Isabel broke into such loud, scornful laughter, it pierced the still afternoon air like shards of ice.

"What's so amusing?" Duplantier demanded, color rising in his cheeks. His voice trembled with anger as he repeated, louder this time, "I'm asking you, you insolent woman, what is so amusing?"

"Naturally, you're asking me. You wouldn't see the joke if it slapped you in the face," Isabel retorted. She broke into a fit of coughing and spat a wad of yellow mucus dangerously close to the commandant's polished boots.

"You... you..." Duplantier was visibly shaking now in his wrath. By his sides, his gloved hands clenched into fists. "You vile creature! You communist filth! You dirty Spaniard! You used to draw caricatures for your damned propaganda leaflets— that wasn't below your pride. You used to paint murals on walls with your blasted *no parasán* slogan—yes, I know all about it! *They shall not pass!*" He sneered in contempt, mocking the noble slogan of the Spanish freedom fighters. "But they did pass and they've won, and you, let me remind you, ungrateful bitch, are on General Franco's extradition list. It's only thanks to Maréchal Pétain that you're still in France and alive, instead of swinging from the gallows in Barcelona. And that's how you repay your protectors? You refuse to paint the *Maréchal*'s portrait when you drew your filthy Bolshevist leaders' portraits?!"

Isabel's laughter ceased just as abruptly as it started. The stillness that followed it filled my lungs with unbearable cold.

"Fine protection—slaving away in a holding camp so that you could supply your Nazi bosses with more wood for their armies and line your own pockets with cash. Extradite me then, because I'd rather swing from the gallows in the country I fought for than live like a slave in a country run by yellow-bellied cowards."

Duplantier's arm flew up to slap her for such unspeakable insolence, but Isabel, with her catlike instincts, grasped it midair. For a second that stretched for eternity as all of us looked on in stunned amazement, they locked eyes. In Duplantier's, there was a mixture of disbelief and hesitation. In Isabel's churned the ferocious, annihilating force of a hurricane ready to obliterate everything in its path.

She grinned the deathly grin of a skull—bared teeth and no emotion—and with lightning speed threw a punch square into the commandant's nose. Her fist connected with his face with a satisfying crunch. Duplantier released a surprised squeal and brought both hands to his nose, from which the blood was pouring freely, staining his rich ermine collar and the front of his tailored overcoat.

Behind his back, the guards recovered themselves at last and scrambled to draw their weapons. From his position on top of the truck, Alfred lurched forward in an attempt to prevent the inevitable. I made a move toward Isabel as well, but the commandant was already screaming, "Shoot that bitch!" at the guards as he clutched at his broken nose.

Tall and proud like a mountain that would cradle her body as her final resting place, Isabel raised her closed fist in the air— the freedom fighter, the martyr of Spain, the hero whose memory I would carry in my mind forever. "*No parasán*," she said in her clear, brilliant voice, and met the hail of bullets with her eyes wide open.

The snow opened its embrace to her body falling as if in slow motion and enveloped her silently. Under the cold stare of the indifferent sky, blood spread around her uncovered head, forming a perfectly round halo.

I was still gazing at it when the commandant's voice reached me from somewhere very far away, as if coming from purgatory itself.

"Alfred Benjamin."

Black grief still blurring my vision, I was instantly alerted to a new grave danger. Still cradling his bloodied nose with a handkerchief, Duplantier was now onto a new victim, and that victim was Alfred. My Alfred.

Moving with utmost care so as not to accidentally disturb Isabel's body, Alfred clambered from the truck and stood, grim and silent like an accusing specter, before the camp commandant.

"In your file, it says that you were in charge of the production of some propaganda leaflets in Paris."

"It was an antifascist newssheet," Alfred corrected him through gritted teeth. I could tell he was painfully aware of Isabel's body lying lifeless just behind him and the injustice of it all infuriated him to the utmost. I could only pray he wouldn't do something brave and stupid. "It was no propaganda by any means. Its aim was merely to inform the French population of the dangers of fascism."

Irritated and still in a great deal of pain, Duplantier waved the explanation off. "No matter the semantics. You're a writer then, so you shall sit down and write a greeting for the *Maréchal* and Minister Laval, expressing your inmates' infinite gratitude for not extraditing you back to your native countries where you all would be slaughtered as you should, and allowing you to live here, under Vichy government protection, and eat food that our own French people have to go without now that the war is going on and rationing has been installed."

"With all due respect, Commandant, we're all but starving here as we work ourselves to the bone in, let's face it, rather inhumane conditions."

Alfred wasn't as harsh as Isabel, but the message was there, loud and clear.

Duplantier took the soiled handkerchief away from his face. Smeared with blood, he was pale as death now and it frightened me much more than his previous rage. "Another antifascist martyr?" The commandant hissed like a snake. "Another hoping to die for the idea, eh?"

Behind his back, one of the guards shifted from one foot to another. His comrade inspected the gun in his hand, ready to put it to use on his master's orders. In the grip of ice-cold terror, I watched the French act like only Nazis would—or so I thought, a long time ago, in some dreamlike reality that was no longer my life.

Before he had a chance to reply, I leapt toward Alfred, placed myself between him and the guards' weapons and took his noble face into my hands.

"Alfred, no. Don't you dare," I whispered hoarsely into his ear. "Don't you dare do this to me; you hear? This is not the time and the place; not a worthy hill to die on. To Isabel, everything was lost, but for us there's still a chance. If we all die here, who shall avenge our fallen? Who shall ensure that freedom triumphs over this darkness?"

He finally met my eyes. With a measure of relief, I saw that something softened in him at the sight of my tears. "But, Dora, to live like slaves..."

"But we won't!" My hand was on the back of his neck. I was whispering to him, pulling him close, for the first time in my life unashamed of my pleading. "We'll escape. I swear to you on everything that is dear to me, I'll make it happen. I'll work something out. We'll be out of here before long. You just believe in me, Alfred; please? Don't leave me alone. Because if you do..." I shook my head. His tragic expression began to swim in my eyes as my eyes filled with tears anew. "If you do, I'd rather die right here with you now than face it all alone."

He pulled me away and regarded me sternly. "What nonsense is this?"

"Not nonsense in the slightest." *It's just, without you, life won't amount to much, is all.*

He must have seen it in my eyes; felt it in the unmovable resolve of my body that he couldn't pull out of the guards' line of fire no matter how much he tried. At long last, he released a breath of surrender and met the commandant's eyes over the top of my head.

"I'll write such a manifesto, *Maréchal* shall fall over with pleasure," he announced to Duplantier. "But on one condition."

Duplantier's expression changed from murderous to one of mild curiosity.

"You shall allow us to marry. And you shall issue a marriage certificate that will be valid in France."

I regarded Alfred in stunned amazement, not quite believing my ears.

"You shall have it," Duplantier said, brightening even further as he heard the condition. His authority was being restored. He would have his welcoming speech written by a communist, no less, which Laval's people could use as splendid propaganda in newspapers all over Vichy and maybe even in occupied territories. "I have nothing against weddings taking place in Rieucros. Why, I imagine even *Maréchal* himself shall approve of it greatly!"

He had long since departed with a new spring in his step, but we still stood in each other's embrace, madly in love for each other and filled with incinerating fury for the world in which a newly engaged couple had to stand by a corpse instead of an altar.

Duplantier kept his word. Shortly after *Maréchal's* visit, we were summoned to the officers' quarters for our marriage ceremony. Bundled in scarves but barefoot—the sentry on duty had forced us to remove out pitiful footwear, lest we tracked melted snow and mud onto their thick rugs—we stood in front of one of the adjutants' desks as he filled in our marriage certificate in between taking sips of coffee and gossiping with his comrade lounging in the visitor's chair across the room.

"Sign here."

The fountain pen passed between our frostbitten hands with never-healing cracks on our fingertips.

The adjutant pulled away as we leaned over the certificate. "*Putain,* you people stink!"

A snort of scornful laughter from his colleague.

"All right, no need for any flourishes." He all but yanked the paper from under my pen before I could complete my signature. "The certificate shall be kept here together with your passports. And now, about-face and get out of here before all of your lice decide that they like our officers' quarters better and change their residence."

Romantic as all hell.

And yet, Alfred and I were giggling in sheer delight as we

pulled our footwear on, lacing our boots in between kisses—husband and wife, till death do us part. At least this much France afforded us. We'd take it, too; we didn't need much. We never asked for much. Just returning to one another at the end of the day was enough. Stolen moments in an empty barrack were more precious than food even; we traded our rations easily for ten minutes of pure bliss of tangled limbs and teeth sinking into soft flesh on our shoulders to silence our love so that the world wouldn't explode with the sheer power of it.

But there was no need to give away our stale bread and hard-as-rock cheese to our fellow barrack mates that night. With Marthe in charge, they surprised us with a real feast they had managed to put together to celebrate something finally worth of celebrating in our tiny world that had long since lost all hope of hearing good news from beyond.

Touched to the marrow, we kissed and drank well into the night, for no one wanted the makeshift camp wedding to end. For a few precious hours, they had forgotten the Nazis plundering their lands and local yellow-bellied *collabos* and drank to the new couple until they couldn't stand or see or sing in time with the half-torn accordion. And in the middle of this wonderful madness, Alfred and I drank and danced and kissed each other shamelessly, open-mouthed, to the explosion of applause and deafening cheers that even the guards didn't care to break.

"Till death do us part, Frau Benjamin?"

"Till death do us part, Herr Davidsohn," I responded cheekily, making Alfred howl drunkenly with laughter and joy.

Yes, we were lice-ridden, and yes, we stank to high heaven, and instead of a white dress I wore rags and so did my new husband, and yet...

Yet, frankly, I couldn't have wished for a better wedding.

SUMMER 1942

With grim eyes, we watched the inmates carry Antonio's body back into the camp from which he'd been so desperately trying to escape. Both sections of the camp—men and women—had been ordered to stand for roll call until the escapee was recaptured. We had braced ourselves for hours in soul-crushing heat with mosquitos sucking our blood and the sun burning our scalps to a crisp, but it only took the guards and their Alsatian a little over two hours to return with their victim in tow.

I couldn't tell if my eyes stung from sweat or tears of bitter disappointment as I watched his lifeless arm streaked with blood swing in the air in time with the inmates' steps. Behind the macabre procession, two guards were strolling with rifles slung over their shoulders, smoking and exchanging jests as though congratulating themselves on the success of some twisted hunting party.

"Well," Alfred said later as he dropped to the earth floor of our barrack. He'd been sent here to fix the leaking roof, but instead he dropped the wooden case with used instruments next to him, not caring one whit if anyone reported him for shirking his duty, and sat with his arms resting on his bent knees, looking suddenly much older than thirty-one. "Another comrade is dead. It looks like there won't be any honeymoon trips for us anytime soon, dear wife. And to think of it, he almost talked me into running with him." A pause, graver than a grave Antonio would never have. "Almost..."

Grateful for the privacy the other inmates allowed us— everyone had suddenly remembered that they had urgent business to attend to outside the barrack—I lowered myself to the swept ground next to him and wormed myself into his lap.

"Don't give up hope yet, Alfred. It was bad timing is all."

His laughter was mirthless and hollow. "Bad timing? He ran at night, right after the roll call. It should have given him several hours' head start. And they still got him as if he was right there, just outside the wire."

"He must have gotten lost in the woods. It was a moonless night. And that damned fog always hangs in the firs... He must have been wandering around in circles until the dog sniffed him out."

Alfred only looked at me with tender reproach. "He was an experienced partisan, Dora. He could find his way around with his eyes closed."

"In familiar Spanish villages, perhaps." I stubbornly refused to admit the truth. "Here, it's French forest. And the timing. The timing was bad."

"Whatever you say." Alfred kissed the top of my obstinate head, too exhausted to argue.

For a year and a half, we'd been desperately trying to poke and prod holes in the Rieucros' defense, only to confirm to ourselves once again that there were none. Despite the illusion of a seemingly lax perimeter control and the number of guards, our little camp in the woods turned out to be an impenetrable fortress. Even being conscripted to an outside work detail didn't provide any more hope than being restricted to the inside of the camp. We were working in the woods, yes, and weren't guarded all that zealously, but soon we realized the reason for that: Rieucros sat right atop the mountain. There were firs for as far down as the eye could see, with the nearest road so miserably far and the nearest villages even farther, they might have been on another planet. Running in winter was entirely out of the question unless one wished to die of exposure within hours. In early spring and late fall, the conditions were no better, with hungry wolves stalking the forest for prey and the ground turning to mud, all but impossible to navigate. That left us with only a few months' window to try our luck, but Antonio had just done so and look how well that had turned out.

"Our anniversary is in a few months," Alfred said out of the blue.

I regarded him in surprise, to find him looking at me with infinite affection. My chest swelled with a love for him that was so overpowering, it pained me to even breathe.

"Nine years in the fall that we have known each other," he continued.

"Feels like we've always been together."

"It does; doesn't it?"

"That's some life we've lived."

"To be sure. Not every husband takes his wife to Paris before he even marries her."

With great relief, I noticed the familiar playful spark return to his eye. He'd worried me for some time with that haunted look of his that mirrored my own far too much—back when I'd just been arrested and wished to end it all, end all the pain at once before it became impossible to bear it any longer.

"You're just a damned romantic, aren't you?" I replied, and joined him in his laughter. It was only an echo of his old one, but I was grateful to hear it all the same.

Eight years. It seemed more like eighty after everything we'd been through. Gone was the mad, hungry passion of our Amsterdam nights together and our very first Paris ones, but in their place had come something much more profound, something that had set roots in both of us and fused us together. Before we had a chance to realize it, we had become one, not really thinking of one another like we used to in the beginning of our time together but sensing each other's thoughts no matter the distance between us. Alfred would approach the wire and I would instinctively know what he was about to say; discern what was in his soul before he uttered a single word.

I wasn't lost in daydreams about him like I used to be, but instead he had become such a familiar, irreplaceable part of me that if he were—God forbid—to be gone, I would stumble about like an amputee with a severed limb, not quite knowing how to navigate life without such a vital part of myself. Looking deep into his eyes now, I saw that he felt exactly the same. It had suddenly dawned on me, the reason why he'd refused to run with Antonio: he couldn't bear the thought of being apart from me, even for such a short period of time; couldn't bear the idea of leaving me behind by accident... or even worse, of losing me altogether.

Both of us leapt to our feet as the barrack's door flew open after a kick from a guard's tall boot.

"Canoodling, doves?" He issued a chuckle but didn't reach for his baton. "Keep your hair on. I won't report you if you organize a few bottles of that Spanish stuff they make. You know, for the Bastille Day celebrations." He even winked at Alfred.

Alfred nodded, quickly making the connection. With the rationing and Rieucros being virtually buried in wilderness, it was all but impossible for the guards to procure enough alcohol to get thoroughly drunk. And the Spanish internees knew just how to distill fuel in such a way that produced an incredibly strong grappa, or whatever the devil it was—one shot of it had knocked me off my feet the single time that I'd tried it. Needless to say, they kept the secret to themselves and positively refused to make any for the guards, no matter how much the latter tried to bribe them with rolls of cheese and smoked venison.

The guard had already left, satisfied with the arrangement, when an idea suddenly occurred to me.

"Alfred! This just might be our chance!"

Before I could finish, I saw the light igniting in his own eyes as well. "Are you thinking what I'm thinking?"

"They'll be drinking themselves silly on Bastille Day."

"And will be nursing the mother of all hangovers the next day."

"The timing—"

"Couldn't be more perfect."

For a moment, we grinned at each other like idiots, before breaking into a fit of conspiratorial giggles. It was nerves as much as actual exhilaration at the renewed hope, but we didn't care any longer. Bastille Day was only two weeks away.

"And if we play it smart, we can just make it to the Swiss border," Alfred whispered, sending shivers of excitement through my entire body.

Swiss border. Endless green pastures. Silvery lakes surrounded by small wooden huts. Freedom. Together...

I dreamed of it that night—the first night devoid of nightmares—and traded my day's rations for a bottle of Spanish grappa the following evening. It was the first of many to come. I would see to it that the guards would drink themselves into oblivion even if it meant starving myself to half-death. I could live on hope for the next fourteen days. Sometimes, it sustained one better than any food could.

BASTILLE DAY

The morning of Bastille Day dawned muggy, with the promise of a storm in the still air. Not a single fir branch stirred. The woods stood watchful against the expanse of the cobalt blue sky. Only in the south, the clouds were beginning to churn, coloring the horizon in purple hues.

By the time I had reached the camp infirmary, my hair was plastered to my temples and my shirt was thoroughly soaked with sweat. Marthe was in no better condition as she hustled between her patients, making use of whatever scarce supply she had to alleviate their suffering. Despite not seeing much of each other in the past years—Marthe had been assigned to the infirmary, whereas I'd volunteered to join the woodcutting detail to be closer to Alfred—she had embraced me with extraordinary warmth when I'd slipped in to whisper my goodbyes to her the day before.

Embraced me, and asked me to stop by to see her before I left.

"I'll have something for you. For the road," she had added with a meaningful look and a gentle press of the hand.

Now, as I watched her agonize over the uneasy choice—set the moaning woman's broken arm using whatever little ether she had left or save it for the other woman clutching the right lower side of her stomach (I suspected appendicitis in its last stages, judging by the woman's burning skin)—I had all but walked out of there. However, Marthe caught me by the wrist, her gaze stern and maternal over the edge of her medical mask.

She removed it as soon as she pulled me after herself into a small cubicle that served both as her personal quarters and a medicine storage room.

"Don't even start shaking your head at me," Marthe said before I had a chance to open my mouth. "It's a long trip to the Swiss border. It'll be a shame if you make it just to die of sepsis because you cut yourself on a thorn in the middle of a forest and got a blood infection."

With tears of gratitude welling in my eyes, I watched the former Charité psychiatrist fill a small pouch with rubbing alcohol, bandages, iodine, sulfa drugs and whatever little aspirin she had left. Lastly, she removed the watch from her wrist and placed it on mine, refusing to listen to any of my protests.

"Get out of here, Dora," she said as she closed my trembling fingers over the pouch. "Get out of here, stay alive, and have as many children with Alfred as you can so that we can avenge the ones who perished and keep perishing daily. Get out and stay as far away from Germany as possible; you hear me?"

The gravity of her request stunned me momentarily.

Seeing my confusion, Marthe hesitated for a few moments, and then stepped so close to me I felt her warm breath on my cheek as she whispered by my ear. "There are different kinds of camps in Germany now, Dora. In Germany and in Poland and in most of the occupied territories. But the ones in Poland, they..." She threw a quick glance over her shoulder—one could never know when an overzealous guard could pop up for an unexpected inspection. "They kill people there, Dora. Outright kill them upon arrival. They're not concentration camps any longer, but extermination ones. Places built with one purpose only—to kill everyone who steps through their gates."

"Whatever are you saying now?" I pulled back, a nervous giggle escaping my parched lips. I'd known what the Nazis were capable of, but this sounded like too much of a mad fantasy, something too atrocious even for them.

"One hears a lot in the infirmary." Marthe tried to smile, but only grimaced instead. "I treated Jewish women who told me all about it. They were fortunate to escape while they still could, but not before they heard of entire communities being wiped out. Word gets out, you know. You can't just slaughter hundreds of thousands of people without any witnesses."

I stared at her in quiet terror.

"We're safe here for now, under Vichy government protection, but mark my words, Dora: it won't be long before the Nazis in the occupied zone begin making their demands. I want you gone before they start shipping us east. Run to Switzerland, girl; run as fast as you can as if the devil himself is chasing you."

And so, I did—first out of the infirmary and away from Marthe's words that would haunt me for eternity, and then towards Alfred's and mine meeting place we'd agreed upon the day before: a small tool shed that stood right on the border of the men's and women's camps. He was hoeing at a patch of dirt next to it as I approached him from my side of the barbed wire.

The guard in his watchtower threw a glance in our direction but only in passing. Still, we only had a few moments together before we would arouse his suspicion.

"Marthe gave us medicine. You take it." I quickly produced the pouch from under my shirt and threw it to Alfred's side.

With the skill of a thief, he caught it midair and concealed it under his shirt.

"It looks like it's going to storm," he said, eyeing the horizon.

"Good. The rain will wash out our tracks. Dogs won't be able to sniff us out."

Alfred nodded, his brow creased with determination. He suddenly reminded me of the old Alfred, the émigré doctor with his medical case and the same sharp wrinkles knitting his dark brows together. It was the Alfred I'd fallen in love with. All at once, such a desire to reach out and touch his face came upon me, I felt I would suffocate with my affection for him.

"I hate it that we have to run separately," I said softly, biting into my lip so as not to break down.

In my chest, my heart was pounding with a dull ache of some premonition I couldn't quite explain. Perhaps it was Antonio all along. Seeing him being brought back, riddled with bullets and bloodied like some buck carcass, did nothing to inspire my confidence in our success. But we had thought everything through. Today was indeed the best possible day. Even nature itself seemed to be on our side. As though in confirmation of my feelings, something grumbled in the distance—the first echo of the approaching storm.

"Dora, we spoke about this. It's much easier this way. One person has a much better chance to slip away unnoticed than two. And we'll meet by that tree we'd just felled at midnight and run together from there. Like we agreed."

Yes, like we agreed. Yet, I hesitated to walk away from him.

"What if one of us doesn't show up?" I asked in a hoarse whisper, voicing the biggest fear of mine. "What if—"

"Then the other one runs all the same," Alfred interrupted me sharply. "We agreed on this also."

"But—"

"Dora, if I don't make it by midnight, just go. Like we agreed. And I'll follow whenever the next chance presents itself. I'll follow and I'll find you. And the same goes for you. If you can't find a way to escape without risking your life, don't even attempt it. Stay put, wait for the next time and then go."

"And what if I don't find you?"

He grinned at me, that side grin of his that I'd grown to love more than anything in the world. "Remember what our good comrade Spider said? *You don't find me. I find you,*" he said in a deep voice with a pronounced Russian accent and for the first time that day, I laughed, genuinely laughed, together with him —my husband—so close and yet so out of my reach. "Tonight, Dora," he said, reading my thoughts as always.

"Tonight," I repeated and, having already stepped away from the fence, turned around, suddenly overcome with a powerful need to see him one last time. "I love you, Alfred."

"I love you too, Dora. More than life."

It took me all my willpower to tear my gaze away from him. He stood, hands resting atop his hoe, still grinning at me as I was walking away. With each glance I threw over my shoulder, his image was fading in the muggy afternoon like an old sepia photograph, until I couldn't make out his features anymore.

I'd waited for him in the torrential downpour, my feet sinking into the ground next to the trunk of the tree that served as my natural hideout.

I'd waited for him, measuring minutes in sobs that kept escaping my heaving chest, already knowing the truth deep inside me as the hand of Marthe's watch on my wrist inched threateningly closer and closer to midnight.

I'd waited for him even after it passed the one o'clock notch, soaked to the bone and trembling from unspeakable grief and terror.

I'd waited for him like a dog waiting by its master's grave...

Only when I saw, in the momentarily blinding flash of lightning, that the small hand had moved past two did I draw myself up, make the first unsteady step back, skidding in the mud and slippery carpet of fir needles underfoot, and break into a run. Slowly at first, stumbling and still weeping, but then faster and faster until I felt the ground underfoot no longer—away from Rieucros and away from my love, my heart tearing itself in two.

TWENTY-ONE

LYON, FRANCE. JULY 1942

The Frenchman's skeptical look softened somewhat as I recounted my incarceration story. Deep in his eyes, I saw the reflection of my own suffering. He, too, had gone through gates that had been locked fast after him. Perhaps he, too, had lost someone important.

The cellar was damp and smelled faintly of wine gone sour. I had not the faintest idea how big the estate was and neither could I make out much inside the cellar itself after the man, who'd brought me here, had taken the blindfold off my eyes. All I could see in the dim light of the candle was the sturdy wooden table with names and dates carved into it, the Frenchman's stern face, his deep-set, black eyes and thick mustache, and the shadow hovering just over his shoulder—my first contact with the Resistance.

I'd been lying on the side of the road, delirious from hunger and thirst after wandering around the wilderness for weeks, when a young man smelling faintly of camphor and gunpowder brought a flask with brandy to my lips. In my half-mad state of mind, I'd blurted out my entire story to him and asked him, with frankness that had sent him snorting softly, if he knew anyone from the Resistance because I had a few scores to settle. He'd introduced himself as Claude seconds before he'd blindfolded me and tucked me under sacks on the back of a truck heading to Lyon. I was in the city itself, according to him—that was all I knew about my present situation.

"How long have you been incarcerated in Rieucros?" the Frenchman asked. He was the one in charge here; that much was obvious.

"Long enough." I looked at his cigarette pack. This time, he moved it toward me. I took one out and lit up. I was about to tell him the story that would rip my very heart out and yet, here I was, striking this match at the first attempt and holding it with hands steadier than those of a Buddhist monk. "It's difficult to trace time when one has no calendar."

He nodded. He understood.

"Let's see." I focused on the glowing tip of my cigarette, watching the thin paper slowly turning to gray ash. "Alfred and I were still at Rieucros when we learned that France was lost. So, that makes it June 1940. We were still there when Germany attacked the Soviets. We were married by then."

"Married?"

I mentally cursed myself for even mentioning it, but, since I'd promised him the truth and only the truth and he would surely see through any such omissions, there was nothing else for it but to nod and try to ignore the dull pain throbbing where my heart used to be. Now, a heavy stone seemed to lie there, unmovable and cold.

"Married, yes. That was February twenty-second, 1941. Local authorities issued us a marriage certificate. That's how I know the date."

I went silent once again, my memory flooded with the images of the camp aide officiating our wedding with one hand while holding his nose with the other, of Alfred's wonderfully beautiful hands taking mine in his, of the bootleg liquor we shared with our bunkmates and the rebellious songs we sang well into the night until the guards came in and told us to shut it, but gently somehow, with half-grins on their faces. The happiest day of my life, now also reduced to gray ash, just like the cigarette slowly dying in my lifeless hand.

"Next January—wait, no; it must have been February—we began to plot our escape."

"I see that you made it," the Frenchman noted.

"I made it, yes... It was Bastille Day. The guards were too busy being pissed on its account to pay any heed to the inmates, so... yes. I made it." I pulled hard on my cigarette, enjoying the burning sensation of hot, bitter smoke filling my lungs. "I don't know what happened to Alfred."

"Was he supposed to follow?"

"Yes. We had a rendezvous spot at the forest nearby. I waited for him for as long as I could, but it was either waiting for him or setting off east before the guards sobered up and realized that they had an inmate missing."

I went silent, guilt dripping off my lips instead of words.

"And you chose east."

I was supposed to head to the Swiss border, but I couldn't manage to put even more distance between myself and Alfred. He'd promised he would find me. It would be easier for him to find me in Lyon than in Switzerland, but I didn't share my reasons with the Frenchman; not just yet.

"I am here, aren't I?" I met his gaze. Whatever he saw in my eyes just then made him regard me with something akin to respect for the first time. "Now, I would really appreciate if you stopped wasting my time and told me straight: do you need my services or not?"

"What if I say not?"

"Then I'll walk all the way to the Soviets and offer it to them. They could more than use a German-speaking Comintern agent just about now."

The Frenchman's impenetrable expression cracked for the first time, stretched into a grin. "All right." He raised both hands into the air, chuckling openly now. "All right. I may have to give Claude that. You are Resistance material. Welcome to Lyon's cell, Renée Gilbert."

Renée Gilbert. I shook his hand, sealing the deal.

I had a name now.

I finally had a purpose.

TWENTY-TWO

LYON. NOVEMBER 1942

It was early afternoon when the first military truck rolled through the streets of Lyon. Soon, soldiers on foot followed as we looked on, Claude and I, our faces clouded over just like the heavy November skies above our heads. As they trudged on, their uniforms no longer sharp and elegant but visibly worn and faded, the city itself seemed to have come to a halt, paralyzed with apprehension and brewing anger. Fear, too, for the soldiers, no matter the state of their uniforms, still had their guns slung over their shoulders and no one in the crowd had any doubts that they'd use them given half a chance.

There hadn't been too much for me to do in the past three months, while the unoccupied zone was still precisely that—unoccupied. Free. Just little coffins to make and inscribe with the names of collaborators: businessmen mostly who supported the German war machine. I had been leaving the coffins in their mailboxes on my morning route while familiarizing myself with the city: its peculiar streets so different from Parisian ones, its *bouchons* (not quite cafés, but bistros typical only of Lyon, where tables were uncovered, and the *soup du jour* and cheese was to die for), the route of its *ficelle* (the funicular going from the Croix-Rousse to Caluire) and the numbers of the streetcars that would take me to the addresses provided by Claude.

After that, if the collaborators hadn't taken the Resistance's warning seriously, Claude's turn came. Making use of the gasoline stolen from the same *collabos*, he sent their entire businesses up in flames by the following morning, both as a punishment for collaboration and as a warning to others.

But now, as we watched tall German boots marching on our formerly free streets, the realization that the real work, the life-risking work, was about to begin dawned on us both.

"Here they are," Claude said and spat on the ground. "Your compatriots."

I glared at him but made no response. I was still a damned Boche to them, Jewish or not. I was yet to gain their trust with action, not just mere words, which, let's be frank, cost little in the time of war. So far, I'd been a mere messenger, trusted only with dropping coffins to *collabos* and sealed notes to people who knew the password and passing their notes back to Claude—the only man, apart from the Frenchman, who I'd been trusted to work directly with. They were still watching me closely—a German girl who had conveniently escaped from the holding camp for the enemy aliens and whose story conveniently couldn't be verified. I took no offense. If I were them, I wouldn't trust me either.

"Here's to the Free Zone, may she rest in peace," a man, already half drunk on Beaujolais, declared from the depth of our small crowd, pouring some of the wine on the ground and gulping the rest of it like someone going to the gallows. At his feet, a small red puddle was slowly spreading like a bloodstain from a gunshot wound.

It was an odd feeling, watching my "compatriots" passing so closely to me I could reach out and touch the sleeves of their uniforms. I could smell the wet wool of their winter overcoats and the old sweat and tobacco and gunpowder that had seeped so deeply into their creases that no amount of washing would ever be enough to erase it. Here they were, my fellow Germans, familiar and yet so very alien, and, all at once, my very heart was at war with itself, not quite knowing whether to feel violated and soiled by their invasion in the only safe haven I had left, or to skip a beat of its own volition at the familiar sound of the German language that caressed me like a mother's loving hand despite the absurdity of such a comparison. In my head, I loathed them with all my being. But there was still a part of me that yearned for something long lost.

Fatherland.

Not Hitler's cursed Reich, but the country in which I'd been born before he'd turned it inside out and feasted on its disemboweled carcass until only bones were left of it.

Claude's arm around my waist and his warm breath in my ear brought me out of my unhappy reverie.

"We ought to change your papers, sister," he whispered, kissing my ear like a lover would.

"Why?"

Instead of a reply, he pinched me playfully on the waist and motioned his head toward the unit following the soldiers on foot. An unsettling chill set deep in my bones when I recognized the double lightning bolts of the SS.

"Because you're going into the maw of the beast, love."

On top of the building of the former medical school at 14 Avenue Berthelot, a swastika flag was now hoisted instead of the French tricolor. Someone had already drawn a Resistance cross on its doors with white paint, overnight most likely, while the soldiers were still settling in. Now, one of them was hastily painting it over with green paint not even closely matching the door's original shade.

I excused my way past the soldier and his paintbrush—"Terribly sorry to bother you, they're expecting me inside, I'm here to inquire about the secretarial position"—but he didn't even give me a second look, this unbelievably young boy of barely eighteen, with the face of a child who didn't even need to shave yet.

The soldier at the hastily set-up reception was only a few years older. He sat at his desk surrounded by mounds of papers, with medical school posters still glued to the wall behind his back, preoccupied and visibly irritated at everyone around and the constantly ringing phones—I could see three of them on his desk, one of them already half-buried under the bundles of letters tied with rope. Yet, his expression of annoyance instantly changed into one of surprise and then delight at the sound of the familiar language coming from what he'd expected to be yet another French broad.

"Good morning, Herr Offizier. My name is Renée Fabre. I heard you're hiring bilingual secretaries and even though, I'll be frank, my French isn't half as good as my German—my family is from Alsace, but a very German village and we only spoke German at home, I'm afraid—I was hoping you could use at least some of my services." I beamed at him as I pushed my new passport—Renée Fabre, not Gilbert anymore—under the glass partition toward him.

Claude had assured me that this one was good, that it would hold up under even the closest inspection, for it wasn't something manufactured for the French gendarmes who didn't bother checking our identities. No, this one was the real deal that would withstand even SS scrutiny, for it was obtained from an actual corpse, who had a birth certificate in Alsace, Claude had assured me with an unsettling amount of enthusiasm given the subject matter, who'd attended school in Alsace, who'd had dental records and such. A perfect cover for a *résistante* sent to pump the information straight from the very vein of the German military postal office.

He would have been very disappointed to learn that he needn't have gone to such pains: the German at the front desk scarcely gave my new papers a second look before returning them to me, smiles chasing one another across his face.

"Don't bother yourself with French," he rushed to assure me. "This is a German military postal service. You'll only need German here. We called for bilingual secretaries because we figured we wouldn't have such luck as to find any German ones here. But here you are."

"Yes. Here I am." I bared all of my teeth at him. "I can type very fast and I can—"

He was already waving me off—"No need for any formal interviews; you're already hired!"—and gesturing for someone uniformed and just as harassed-looking to escort me to my new office, which I would share with the rest of the local staff.

All around me were German uniforms only. I was indeed in the maw of the beast, but somehow, I felt oddly calm as I settled at my new desk, which I would share with a Wehrmacht orderly, Schwartz. The regular army was no SS. Regular army fought wars instead of exterminating innocent civilians for the idea.

"Otto," he said in an undertone as soon as his superior, Hauptmann Brandt, had gone out of the room. "Don't mind my last name. I'm not Jewish."

"Renée," I replied and shook his hand. "Don't mind my last name either. I'm not French."

He snorted in amusement and lowered his head at once at the wrathful shout of our superior from behind the partially opened door.

"You're here to teach Fräulein Fabre to sort the mail, Schwartz, not jest around with her! If you can't manage that duty, I shall assign you to the night patrol."

All at once, Otto straightened in his seat and began digging in the papers furiously. With the growing number of maquis—

partisans who lived in the forest and attacked the Nazis when they least expected it—and lone German patrolmen attacked, no one wished to be assigned to that duty.

"Where is the blasted order for the latest troop movement?"

As the rest of our secretarial staff looked on, Hauptmann Brandt was in the middle of virtually turning the contents of our desks upside down. Immaculately organized papers were flying in every direction like a flock of frightened birds; pencils and pens ricocheted off the walls and floor like shrapnel. Even the drawers where we kept our personal belongings, such as purses and paper bags with lunches, weren't spared Brandt's assault. He flipped them upside down and shook them furiously like a Gestapo agent trying to shake information out of a stubborn suspect.

In the corner by the barred window, Gabrielle, a Catalonian girl who had the misfortune to know German and had been commandeered from her position of a local schoolteacher by the new authorities, broke into silent sobs. As I watched her entire body being racked by bouts of violent trembling, I felt a pang of guilt. It wasn't the first time that I had put someone innocent in harm's way to keep spinning my web of deceit. But just like it had been with Madame Charlotte's maid, the stakes were simply too high—this time, for us, the Resistance. No matter how revolting it was thinking about it in such terms, Gabrielle was collateral damage.

And Brandt, black eyes blazing, neck muscles straining under the collar of his uniform, was already hanging over her like a cobra. "Do you understand what it means, losing a document of such paramount importance?"

Otto, with the innocence of a puppy who wasn't all that bright but wished for nothing else but to serve his master the best he could, stepped over the mound of papers and picked up the receiver of the service phone. "Herr Hauptmann, it's no big loss. I can call the regional OKW headquarters and inquire—"

"Put that damned phone down before I shoot you where you stand!"

Otto dropped the receiver back into the cradle. Its faint, plaintive ringing hung over the office, together with the cloud of Brandt's anger.

"You wish to call them, you feebleminded donkey?" Brandt asked in a menacingly low voice. His breathing was deep and labored. "You wish to call them and admit that the Lyon office has lost the order for the troop movement? That it could be anywhere by now? In the hands of those damned Resistance terrorists, for all we know? Do you wish to admit to it, you brainless dung-beetle? So we can all get court-martialed and shipped off to the Eastern Front for our negligence? Is that what you're suggesting?"

I stepped in between the two men before Brandt smacked Otto on his poor mouth. "Herr Hauptmann, why don't I make you coffee and sort all this out? I'm certain it's somewhere here. Give me twenty minutes and I'll find it. You have my word."

"You will sort *all this* out"—Brandt suggested mockingly, gesturing to the mess around us with his hand—"*and* find the order in twenty minutes?"

"*Jawohl*, Herr Hauptmann. But first, I shall make you coffee."

He was about to drop another sardonic remark, but surrendered at last; waved his arm at me—*do as you please*—and stalked out of the office.

As though some invisible string holding her together had been cut, Gabrielle fell into a heap by her desk, sobbing openly now as she shifted through the useless papers with shaking hands.

"Leave it." I pulled her away by the shoulders. "Leave it to me. Go to the kitchen and make him coffee. I shall take it to him later myself. Otto, could you please go with her and give her something to drink? Some cognac perhaps?"

Relieved to have something to focus on, Otto left the room with Gabrielle in tow, saying something comforting to her in his school-level French. I listened to their steps receding in the distance and, satisfied with being left well alone, stepped onto the second shelf of a tall bookcase riveted to the wall that held rows of green binders, patted the dust on the very top and bit back a satisfied grin as I stepped down with a troop movement order in my hand.

One thing Hauptmann Brandt was wrong about: the Resistance "terrorists" like myself weren't stupid enough to steal these sorts of things. I had memorized them, certainly, but stealing them would have just been idiotic. Much too obvious. Much too suspicious for everyone involved. Instead, I neatly placed it under Gabrielle's typewriter, which had miraculously survived Hauptmann Brandt's wrath, and began picking up and reassembling the papers into neat stacks. By the time Otto returned with the tray—alone—I had cleared the entire area around Gabrielle's desk.

"Is she all right?" I asked, genuinely concerned. After all, I was the reason for the poor girl's breakdown.

"She will be. I gave her some brandy. She's in the ladies' room, putting herself back in order."

"Thank you, Otto. You're such a fine gentleman."

He blushed furiously at the compliment.

"Put the tray right here," I said, gesturing to Gabrielle's desk I was presently organizing.

"There's not enough space."

"Yes, there is. Let me just move—" I pushed the typewriter to the side, revealing the document I'd neatly placed under it just minutes ago.

"Is it—" Otto's eyes lit up.

I flipped it and waved it in the air triumphantly. "It is, Otto, my dear! We're saved! This entire time, it was under her typewriter!"

Otto all but dropped the silver tray on the desk and began to reach for the paper, but I slapped his hand playfully away.

"Oh no, you don't. You'll just lose it again."

"I wasn't the one who lost it," he protested.

"You weren't the one who found it, either," I countered with a wink, picked up the tray and sashayed out of the staffroom and into Hauptmann Brandt's office. "Here it is, Herr Hauptmann. Your coffee and the order."

He was instantly on his feet, groping for the paper in my hand. "Wherever did you find it?"

"Under Gabrielle's typewriter, believe it or not." I gave him a silvery laugh.

"Renée, what would we do without you?" Brandt asked, examining the paper almost reverently as if it were some long-lost artifact.

"You would be freezing somewhere in Stalingrad is my guess," I answered, all playfulness now.

He laughed too, visibly relieved, and patted his forehead dry with a handkerchief. "Stalingrad is right, Renée, angel."

I wish I could say that I stopped myself there with sabotaging everyone else's work just to come to their aid at the last moment, but I had to make myself truly indispensable to Brandt; someone whom he could trust better than himself, and it just so happened that I was the only German among the secretarial staff. The more I sabotaged their work, the more suspicious Brandt was growing. Soon, he only trusted me and Otto to sort out the most important documents—troop movement orders, firearms shipments—leaving ordinary field mail from soldiers to their homes in the hands of the local French girls.

I felt like a swine, but Claude assured me that feelings

didn't matter much in war and the Frenchman himself gobbled up my reports with the appetite of a savage, just to feed them later to his other cells, the ones working in the field. And the next day Brandt would be stomping around the office, cursing the blasted maquis who had planted the bomb and derailed yet another train with troops just as it was heading off to the east. I would keep my eyes low and sorrowful, just so he wouldn't recognize the victorious light in them.

I was a savage too. They'd made me into one and so, on their blood I would feast until there was not a drop of it left to spill.

TWENTY-THREE

LYON. DECEMBER 1942

The man was young and positively unremarkable, resembling a bank clerk or a lawyer at the very beginning of his career— perhaps, not even a lawyer, but an accountant, someone with an absolutely unexciting position. Yet, as soon as he strolled into our little office and leaned casually against the wall, hands in the pockets of his dark navy suit, a bland smile on his face, all the German clerks, including Brandt himself, froze like rabbits under the hypnotic gaze of a king cobra.

Brandt was the first one to snap to attention, saluting this young fellow as though he was the Führer himself and breaking into a stumbling welcome.

"Please, be perfectly at ease, gentlemen," the young man purred, issuing Brandt a smile of an extraordinary charm. "Forgive me for barging in in such a shameless manner and interrupting your preparation for the upcoming Yuletide festivities."

This time, the same wonderfully kind, apologetic smile was directed at me. I was still balancing on top of the window desk in my stockinged feet like a right idiot with a whole garland of dainty swastika flags in my hands, unsure of whether to climb down and put my shoes back on or stay where I was.

"Apologies are all mine, Herr Hauptsturmführer," Brandt mumbled, white as chalk for some reason. "We weren't prepared for your arrival so soon. The Dijon office informed us that you would be arriving on January twelve..." He chewed on some words silently, second-guessing himself. "Or was it me who misunderstood something—"

"No, no!" The newcomer stopped Brandt in his tracks with his hand raised in the air, all benevolence and courtesy. "You haven't misunderstood anything, Hauptmann. The fault is all mine." Another smile followed; only, this time, something predatory gleamed behind those blue eyes. "I simply couldn't wait to start."

For some reason I couldn't quite grasp, the words hung like a menace in the air.

"In fact, I should like to start right this instant and with a matter that, I'm certain, everyone present shall greatly appreciate."

The young man roved his gaze around the room, taking in each Wehrmacht clerk with an attention that unsettled me in spite of myself. It was as if he was already familiar with them, their ranks and entire service dossiers, and was now simply matching the faces from the photographs he'd studied in great detail to actual people. Once again, the penetrating gaze of those glacial eyes settled on me. After a short inner battle, I decided to stay on top of the desk—the further away from him, the better. Despite his magnificently charming mask, there was something about this man that made my hackles rise.

"I'm preparing the list of the servicemen that have distinguished themselves since the occupation of Lyon," the man said, finally pushing himself off the wall with the lazy grace of a panther, and moved to Julie's, our third secretary's, desk. From the stack near her typewriter, he plucked a blank sheet of paper and handed it to Hauptmann Brandt.

Our immediate superior regarded it for a moment, dumbfounded. "Herr Hauptsturmführer, we've only been here a short while—"

Even I, a civilian, understood the absurdity of such a request. The occupation of Lyon was nothing like the occupation of Warsaw, for instance. It was perfectly bloodless and uneventful; the Wehrmacht troops had only been stationed here for a little over a month, sorting field mail. What distinguishing feats could he possibly be talking about?

"Herr Hauptmann," the young man said, taking the button of Brandt's uniform in his fingers in a purposely intimate manner. "My good fellow. A soldier to a soldier: those pencil-pushers in Berlin are none the wiser, and surely your men could use a Christmas raise and a few bonuses, a promotion perhaps, that would greatly help them and their families back home. It is my profound conviction you can come up with something."

Brandt nodded; still a bit unsure, but nodded nevertheless. He understood.

"And while we're at it, don't forget your marvelous secretaries. Even though they're French citizens, it doesn't mean that they shouldn't be rewarded for helping the German war effort."

"Renée here is a German," Otto blabbered in his usual uninhibited manner, and all at once I cursed him and his boneless tongue inwardly for attracting such unwanted attention to me.

The fact that the newcomer's eyes landed on me without any hesitation proved my previous theory correct. He did know us all; had studied us all like some specimen long before meeting us in person.

"Is she now?" The young man pressed the paper to Hauptmann Brandt's chest and walked around him to approach my desk, having already lost all interest in the Wehrmacht official. "Where in Germany, Fräulein...?"

He let the question hang between us, all playfulness now.

But there was nothing innocent about his teasing. It was the playfulness of a cat toying with a mouse.

"Fabre. Renée Fabre," I supplied. The flags in my hands were getting damper by the moment. "I'm from—"

"Wait, don't tell me. Let me guess." He pressed his index finger to his mouth, curved in an enigmatic smile. Up close, I saw that his hair was dark brown and not black as I'd originally thought, and it was naturally wavy. I could see it curling lightly near his ears and neck, even though the rest of it was smoothed with pomade. "You're not from the east. Not from the south, either; I would recognize the accent right away. I want to say... west. Northwest. Somewhere... Please, oblige me and say, 'the weather is lovely today'."

"The weather is lovely today," I repeated, feeling a tiny trickle of sweat slide down my back.

"Somewhere near Essen?"

My heart dropped, together with my stomach. For a short instant, I couldn't get my breath. Blood rushed to my ears, drumming its dread-instilling tattoo: *he knows, he knows everything about me, my real name, my entire life story; he can see inside of me, into every dark corner of my soul—*

I could have crumbled there and then, admitted to everything and pleaded for mercy, but instead, with an inhuman effort, I nipped the panic at the bud and held the gaze that was more intrusive than an X-ray machine.

"I wish I was so fortunate as to have been born in the Reich, Herr Hauptsturmführer. But I'm afraid I'm rather local, from Alsace."

"Alsace," he drawled, a trifle mockingly, it seemed. Not to lose it completely, I tried my utmost to persuade myself that this was paranoia speaking. "I could have sworn you were from Germany. Your lack of that obnoxious French half-a-droll tripped me."

"We lived in a tight community. Mostly everyone spoke

German. In fact, my French is rather frightful." I let out a chuckle, hoping that it sounded embarrassed enough for him to swallow it.

"Your family are still in Alsace?"

Real Renée's family was. It was them, who'd sold Claude the papers. Besides that I knew virtually nothing of them.

"They are." The only option was to volunteer as little information as possible, as per Claude's instructions. *Less is more. Let them make their own conclusions. Don't go venturing into any details, because this is how you are sure to trip.* My cheeks were aching from the forced effort to smile as widely as possible.

"Any siblings?" he pressed.

How am I supposed to know?

"Died at a young age. I'm the only survivor." The trickle of sweat was turning into a river. "It was right after the war..." I lowered my eyes to look appropriately mournful, just so he wouldn't recognize panic in them. "Times were hard for us under the French governance."

"I can well imagine. Your mother and father are still alive though, correct?"

They must have been, at least at the time when Claude purchased my passport from them.

"They are, yes."

"That's great. I'm certain they'll appreciate special food rations. My office shall send them for the holidays and, naturally, it's up to you if you wish to send any bonus money to them as well."

"Thank you, Herr Hauptsturmführer. They will appreciate it greatly."

"Are you the only German among the secretarial staff?"

"I am yes. But we all speak German and French—"

But he was already waving me off, much like he'd done with Brandt. And much like he'd lost interest in our superior, he now lost interest in me, turning his attention to Brandt once again.

"The Lyon Gestapo office needs only the most reliable personnel, so I'll be taking Fräulein Fabre with me. Have her transfer paper ready by noon. Heil Hitler."

With that, he was gone.

As soon as the echo of his steps turned to silence, Brandt exhaled loudly, his shoulders sagging with visible relief.

"Who was that, Herr Hauptmann?" I whispered the question that was on everyone's mind.

"Klaus Barbie, head of the Dijon Gestapo. Sent here with the sole purpose of hunting down every single member of the Resistance." Brandt regarded me with a frankly sorrowful look. "I suppose this is a goodbye. Good luck, Renée."

I climbed gingerly down from the desk, feeling my way with shaking hands. If I had not done so, it was my profound conviction that I would faint right where I stood.

TWENTY-FOUR

"Klaus Barbie?" the Frenchman asked for the second time in apparent disbelief. Something in the manner in which he stared at me unnerved me even further. "From Dijon's Gestapo?"

"That's what he said."

Claude, who was sitting perched on the table in the wine cellar where the Frenchman had first interrogated me and where our emergency meetings were now taking place, jumped down and began pacing the floor, raking his hands through his hair.

"And he made Brandt transfer you under his command?" the Frenchman probed.

"We need to pull her out of there," Claude said, coming to an abrupt halt. "It's too dangerous. He'll uncover her in no time."

The Frenchman held his hand up, silencing him. "Why you, out of all secretaries available?" His eyes slightly narrowed.

I shrugged. "Because I'm the only German among them."

He still didn't trust me; I could almost feel his suspicion in my very skin. He still didn't trust me enough to even offer me his name, his false name. After all these months working together, I didn't know the first thing about the man. He was still just a Frenchman to me, a phantom without a past or present; an anonymous puppeteer pulling my strings.

Not that I blamed him. I wouldn't trust a Boche broad appearing out of nowhere just in time for the Nazi occupation either.

Claude, in the meantime, resumed his pacing, shaking his head furiously. "You ought to listen to me," he addressed his comrade-in-arms. "Her story may have held for the Wehrmacht. They're soldiers, not trained policemen. But Barbie, that"— another frantic splash of his hands—"he'll sniff her out in a matter of days."

"Her passport is real," the Frenchman said without taking his eyes off me.

"Yes, real enough for the Wehrmacht!" Claude was losing patience. "Not for the Gestapo. Do you not think it'll occur to them to dig into Renée Fabre's biography? Pull her family records? Her death certificate, for Christ's sake?"

"I thought there was no death certificate." It was my turn to stare at Claude.

"The Fabres told me they destroyed it. But who knows if there's a record at church? At one mortuary or the other? I paid cash for it and came back to Lyon; I didn't stay there to investigate all the details."

The Frenchman was chewing on the inside of his cheek, pondering, calculating. I could all but hear his thoughts churning: on the one hand, all the information they could procure through me, all the Resistance members my clandestine work could save by warning them in advance, all the planned Gestapo operations subverted because of my timely tips. But on the other, the possibility of my capture, or, even worse, of my being the enemy agent in the Resistance's midst.

"What do you say, Renée?" he asked me at last. "Do you want to stay or do you want me to pull you out of there, get you a new identity and transfer you someplace... away from Lyon?"

I didn't need time to go over my options. "I want to stay."

I want to find my husband.

"You heard Claude. It's very risky."

"I understand the risks." I nodded.

He cocked his head slightly. "And you don't mind dying for France?" Under the seemingly innocent question was a much darker undertone. "I don't have enough Frenchmen who would want to go anywhere near the Gestapo, let alone infiltrate its chief's office. Particularly if that chief is Barbie."

"What's so special about him?" I asked.

For some time, the cellar was shrouded in deathly silence. Somewhere in the distance, water dropped rhythmically from the leak in the ceiling.

"There was a man in our cell in Dijon, his name was Mark." The Frenchman's eyes were half-closed as he began recounting the story. "A brilliant man, sharp like a whip. Used to be a scientific mastermind before the war. At any rate, one day he came up with an idea to tap into the Gestapo phones. The plan was genius in its simplicity: he sent a couple of fellows to cut the Gestapo office's phone line. Naturally, they called the French servicemen to repair them, cursing those blasted Resistance terrorists right and left, and even promising to pay the fellows for their troubles, even though it's never their habit to pay for anything."

He reached into his pocket and produced a pack of cigarettes; lit up.

"Mark and his comrade say that it's no trouble; immediately go to survey the damage, begin their work. Mark thought it would be tricky, installing a second wire that would allow the cell to listen in to any incoming and outgoing calls from the office, but the SS man who had called them wandered off almost immediately, leaving only some fellow dressed in civvies to watch over them. A male secretary or some pencil-pusher, Mark decided, and set to work, whistling to himself, not even bothering to cover what it was precisely that he was doing because, really, would you expect some civilian worker to understand anything about phone wires?"

He chuckled wistfully to himself, wreathed in grayish smoke.

"As soon as they finish, the secretary is all delighted, so very grateful for such excellent swift work. Invites them inside to receive their payment. But Mark is afraid that someone will commandeer their bicycles while they're both inside and, despite the German's insistence, leaves his comrade outside to guard them. The comrade waits with the bicycles, allows himself a cigarette break as he waits for Mark with their payment, picturing all the accolades they will receive for tricking those Gestapo morons. All of a sudden, he hears the glass breaking in one of the barred windows above and, as he looks up, he sees Mark, his bloody hands clutching at the bars, screaming at him to get the hell out of there before a shot rings out and Mark's head explodes right in front of his eyes. As he stands there with his jaw hanging open, unable to process the horror that he's just witnessed, the familiar face and civilian suit appear where Mark has just stood. The fellow, whom they'd mistaken for a harmless pencil-pusher, sticks his hand out through the bars, smiles like a devil himself and discharges the rest of the rounds at Mark's comrade. That woke that idiot up some and he pedaled away as fast as he could before the SS poured out of the building. By sheer chance, all three bullets that hit him didn't do any serious damage."

He put the cigarette out as though cauterizing the old wound, reached for his collar and pulled it down to reveal two pale pink circles—one in his shoulder and another, just above his heart.

"Mark was my brother. I don't think I need to name the man who killed him."

He didn't. I recognized him well enough from the description. An inconspicuous office worker, perfectly harmless, with a smile of an extraordinary charm.

Klaus Barbie.

"I'll ask you the second and last time, Renée. Do you want me to pull you out before it's too late?"

"No."

Behind the Frenchman's back, Claude sucked his breath in sharply.

"You're not afraid?" the Frenchman asked.

"I am," I admitted honestly. "But the SS are in charge of all the holding camps and my husband is still in one of them."

"Ah, so that's what it is."

"Yes, that's what it is."

That's what it always was—Alfred, leading me like the North Star through the impenetrable forest full of dangers and beasts; my Polaris that was the only constant, on whose guiding light I could rely in the darkest of days. Without him, I'd be long lost. Seeking him was in my very nature now.

Something in the Frenchman's softened gaze told me that he understood.

The room was immersed in the tender, melancholy notes of Chopin. They poured from under Barbie's graceful hands as he moved his head in time with the music, eyes closed, dark brows drawn together by a profound emotion. In the opposite corner of the room, a man sat tied to a chair, not with ropes but with thin piano wires that were cutting into his skin like razors. One of his eyes was swollen shut. From his nose, broken so badly that it was almost flat and misshapen, moved at an unnatural angle to the left side of his face, blood was running in long, ghastly strings.

It was my second day at work.

In the corner, by the window, a Gestapo man smoked. Just like Barbie, he had removed his military jacket and hung it neatly over the back of my chair before he had set to work on the man on Barbie's orders.

I was supposed to type the man's answers, only, so far, they hadn't succeeded in beating them out of this proud Brit.

They knew he was no *résistant*; they knew he was a downed airman; they knew he'd been aided by the locals, but that was all they could deduce solely by the fact that he spoke virtually no French and sheer logic.

Downed RAF pilots themselves were of no particular interest to the Gestapo. They were effectively prisoners of war, useless without their powerful fighters and bombers and therefore presenting no threat to the Germans whatsoever. The only reason the poor fellow had found himself on the receiving end of the new Gestapo chief's wrath was because Klaus Barbie was interested in unearthing the Resistance people aiding these pilots.

The music came to an abrupt halt. Suddenly annoyed, Barbie swiveled in his chair.

"I don't understand what you're being so obstinate for." Much like his French, Barbie's English was fluent. It was the SS man who was translating their conversation so I could type it down. "You don't know the names—fine, I believe you. They never use their real names and even the members of their own cells don't know their real identities. That's of no importance to me. But surely you can't claim that you don't remember their faces or where precisely they picked you up and where they took you to shelter you."

"I had a hood on my head," the RAF pilot rasped, ungluing his swollen, broken lips with visible difficulty. "They only took it off once I was inside. It was some kind of barn... I don't know. They left milk and food for me outside and knocked so I could take it."

"See?" Barbie was suddenly on his feet, positively delighted. "Now we're getting somewhere, my good fellow!" He approached the Brit and smiled at him almost tenderly as the man tried to pull away, his entire body shaking with uncontrollable waves of terror. "You have no reason to fear me. I wish for nothing more than to release you right this instant, process your POW papers as I should and send you on your merry way to one of the Stalags, where you'll sit out the rest of this war together with your jolly comrades, playing cards and consuming generous Red Cross rations. Right now, it's you who stands in your own way. Now, there is one thing you should know about me: I don't get tired and I don't stop until I get what I want. I shall get those *résistants'* identities and addresses from you sooner or later. And the only difference between sooner and later is the number of bones I'll have to break in your body or the number of nails I shall pull out of their beds. Or the number of times I will submerge your head in the vat filled with water until you're gasping for air."

The monotone manner in which the SS man translated Barbie's words presented a truly chilling contrast with the almost tender tone Barbie himself was using to describe all of the atrocities he was about to inflict on the poor RAF devil. With every word of his, my own head was growing lighter and lighter with nausea and nerves, as though it was me tied to that chair in place of the British pilot.

Barbie, meanwhile, having produced a monogrammed silk handkerchief from his pocket, was wiping the Brit's bloodied face, purring a mixture of threats and reassurances into his ear.

At long last, the man, utterly petrified by such obviously irrational behavior and the gentleness with which the hands that had been beating him senseless not twenty minutes ago were now tending to his wounds, broke into sobs. In a strangled voice, he promised to show his tormentor everything he could recognize from the farm over which he'd bailed out and the train station to which the Resistance members had taken him to ship him to Lyon.

"And the barn?" Barbie gently wiped the bloody saliva off the RAF pilot's chin.

"If I see it again, I'll recognize it."

"And the people? You did see at least one face before they put the hood on you."

"They might have been just regular farmers, who had called the Resistance to aid me later."

"But you did see the farmers?"

"The farmer and his son, yes."

"Good, good." Suddenly on his feet, Barbie snapped his fingers at his orderly. "Untie him, have him cleaned up and have someone tend to his wounds. Get him food—our food; some coffee with brandy, a pack of smokes and a cell that isn't too cold."

"*Jawohl*, Herr Hauptsturmführer."

As the SS man began working on the piano wires with the same pliers with which he'd been working on the man's nails, Barbie positioned himself in front of the window, his gaze almost dreamy with anticipation.

"Yes, you rest today, my good fellow," he murmured, in German this time. "We have a big day tomorrow."

Later that afternoon, as I was handing a transcribed and typewritten interrogation to one of the SS men working under Barbie's charge, I quickly scanned the cabinets into which all such reports disappeared.

"Anything else?" the SS man asked as he noticed my lingering near his desk.

He was a young man, dreadfully bored judging by the look of him. No wedding ring on his right hand.

I stole a glance over my shoulder and, ensuring that no one was paying us any heed, dropped my elbows on top of his desk, revealing just enough of my décolletage for him to notice. "Just curious. Herr Hauptsturmführer said the Brit will be going to one of the Stalags."

"Yes?"

I leaned closer, whispering like an excited teenager, "Is it true? The way Herr Hauptsturmführer described it? Like it's a veritable resort?"

"For the British and American POWs, yes." The SS man was grinning now, hands atop the paper, playing with his mechanical pencil. "They have it better than us here."

"You're full of it." I play-swatted him with a familiarity that I'd never allow myself, had it not been for an almost reckless desire to locate Alfred. "They don't have it better than us."

"They do, too!" he protested, the color creeping into his cheeks, chuckling in spite of himself. "When I was in *Hitlerjugend* before the war, we had the same cabins in which they live now. Nice double bunkbeds, warm blankets, pillows, mattresses —all business as it should be. They have their own little stove in each barrack, a communal kitchen for the entire Stalag. Exercise grounds; mail privileges. They don't even take away their uniforms after admission. And pilots are a different class altogether; they live like princes there!"

"Burgess!"

With my back turned to the exit, I hadn't noticed Barbie; only recognized his voice instantly and straightened at once. The SS man—Burgess, I committed the name to my memory—leapt to his feet as well and froze to attention.

But rather to our joint relief, Barbie was in too good a mood for scolding. "Quit your jawing and assemble a team for me for tomorrow. Two cars, five fully armed men in each should do it."

Passing Burgess's desk, he winked at me playfully before stopping in front of the detailed map of Lyon and its surrounding areas pinned to the back wall of the office, stroking the waxed paper like a farmer stroking a sheep he was about to slaughter. "We're going hunting."

TWENTY-FIVE

"Can you procure a box of pastries for me?"

Claude regarded me as if I'd lost the last of my marbles.

We were sitting in the *bouchon* that offered onion soup of the day every day and where the bartender, with his off-white sleeves rolled up and a towel thrown over his shoulder, reminded me painfully of Alfred. He served us Pernod with water. His fingers brushed my hand by accident when I reached for the glass he was setting down and I had to bite the inside of my cheek to remind myself that this was Lyon and not a Parisian hotel room and the man was not my missing husband, no matter how much I had been searching for him in the features of his countless doppelgangers. He had promised to find me but, if he didn't, I would just have to find him instead. No matter the price.

"Or two, better yet." I downed my aperitif in one go.

"I realize the work is stressful, Renée, but that's some hazard pay in war times."

"Ha-ha." I signaled the bartender, who was not my husband, for another drink. "And leave the bottle. Now, Claude, my love, can you or can you not?"

"It's going to cost a lot of money on the black market."

"It'll pay off. I promise."

"Just whom are you bribing?"

He'd finally realized the confections weren't for my Sunday afternoon pleasure.

I smiled sweetly, baring all of my teeth in a savage grin. "The entire second floor of the Lyon Gestapo, of course. So, make sure the cream is fresh and the confectioner is generous with sugar powder."

Claude sucked the air through his teeth, mentally calculating the astronomical cost of such an indulgence. "It'd better be worth my troubles."

"Oh, it will be. You have my word."

For a few weeks now, I'd been watching them closely—the enemy I was rubbing shoulders with on a daily basis. No matter the effort it took, I went out of my way to flatter and flirt my way into their good graces, those uniformed butchers who tortured people for a living; who would have, undoubtedly, strung me up on the same piano wire if they had only learned who I truly was. But, miraculously, my papers held and Barbie was in the best of dispositions, all the recent success going to his head and, hopefully, clouding his judgment for long enough for me to do some damage... or it was all a ruse, and he knew perfectly well who I was and had me followed just to strike when I least expected it—that was very much a possibility. One could never know with him. He was cunning like a fox and vicious like a vulture.

Every day that I walked into the stone bowels of the Gestapo office, I remembered Mark, the Frenchman's brother, and wondered if today was the day that I'd meet his fate.

"One must have nerves of steel to do what you're doing," Claude admitted to me on the day he handed me three boxes filled with pastries, reserved respect in his voice. "Frankly, I cannot fathom how you descend into that pit of snakes day after day."

"Like an Indian fakir, Claude, my friend." I winked at him with easiness masking all the angst inside. "Like an Indian fakir."

And like the good little snakes that they were, the Gestapo craned their necks at the sight of the stacked boxes as soon as I poked my head inside their office, whispering theatrically, "Is the boss here?"

"In his office." The same conspiratorial whisper and a finger pointed at the ceiling, to Barbie's lair just two flights of stairs up.

It was a familiar game by now. I snuck inside when Barbie wasn't present and shared sweets and gossip with them, pulling state secrets out of them "like no man ever could"—the Frenchman's own words, spoken with a measure of uncharacteristic admiration in them at our next meeting.

"Of course, a man never could," I replied, passing a paper with written details of the latest planned operation into his eager hands. "Because he's a man. And I'm a woman, and, when they aren't butchering anyone, they're men too and they're hungry for a woman's attention. They're lonely here. Even local whores don't want anything to do with them. They aren't harmless Wehrmacht; they're the Gestapo."

"I don't blame the local whores."

Neither did I. It was difficult to watch the hands delicately pick up the meringue and forget all about the same hands beating the life out of my fellow *résistants*. They were permanently stained with blood that no amount of washing would ever erase.

But, much like when I'd worked together with Alfred, back in Amsterdam, tending to gangrenous wounds and resetting broken bones, I had to put my disgust and revulsion aside and do the job I'd signed up for. So, I shared the pastries with these beasts and toasted coffee with them and asked them seemingly innocent questions, each answer to which was bringing me closer and closer to my most coveted treasure: "So, where do all the French Jews go?"

"East, mostly. Poland. To farm the lands."

Communal laughter, behind which hung the menacing implication: there were no farms where those condemned souls were going. Death only.

"And the communists?"

"Depends on the communist."

"A French communist?"

"He may stay in France. Or go to Germany to work on farms or factories there."

No laughter this time. So, there was hope for the gentile French—slave labor only, not immediate extermination.

"Are there camps in France?"

"Former prisons mostly. Some old holding camps, too."

"What do they do there?"

"Be productive members of society, for a change."

Another burst of laughter.

"And what happens if they get tired of being productive and try to escape?"

A shrug from Burgess. "They get shot." He was more interested in refilling my cup with coffee than speaking of communists.

Something sank inside of me. "Not recaptured? Just shot on the spot?"

"Why, yes." Stahl, the SS man who had assisted Barbie with the British pilot, yawned, reaching for another caramelized apple. "If they tried it once, they'll do it again. And besides, why encourage the others with such antics?"

Inside, my very soul was bleeding, but outwardly I just opened my eyes wider, appearing hungry for juicy details, and

leaned closer to the murderer sinking his teeth into the brutalized treat. "Has anyone tried to escape recently?"

Stahl stopped chewing for a moment; considered
something.

"Wenzel, grab me a couple of local holding camps binders,"
he called to the youngest one of the crew, a strawberry-blond
fellow with wire-rimmed glasses, for which they teased him
unmercifully.

For his bad eyes and low rank, he was their personal gofer
and the butt of their jokes. I'd feel almost sorry for him, had he
not tried to compensate for it with inventing the most sadistic
methods of extracting information out of Barbie's victims, in
which Barbie himself took great delight. Just two days ago,
when one particularly obstinate *résistant* refused to utter a
single word while Barbie's men sent electric currents through
the wires attached to his genitals, it was Wenzel who'd come up
with the "brilliant" idea of bringing the *résistant*'s ten-year-old
daughter into the interrogation room. At first, when Wenzel
held heavy-duty wire cutters to the hysterical girl's little finger,
the man had tensed visibly but called the man's bluff. Surely
the SS man wouldn't go through with the threat. This was just
an innocent child, after all; no one was as vile and merciless—

The harsh snap of the wire cutters and the girl's bloodcur-
dling scream had proved the father wrong. His inhuman half-
scream, half-wail, like that of a wounded animal, still echoed in
my mind, just like the near-silent sobs of the cleaning woman
who had to pick up the severed child's finger off the floor under
Wenzel's self-satisfied direction.

Now, the wildly beating drum of my heart in my ears
drowned out all other sounds as Stahl leafed lazily through the
files.

"Here's one. Josef Mendel, a foreign Jew and a communist.
Attempted escape, October eighteen, 1942; captured and
executed by hanging."

"Good riddance to bad garbage," someone muttered from behind his back, eliciting chuckles from everyone present.

My eyes riveted to the files, I didn't dare to look away and see who it was.

Wishing to impress me, Burgess grabbed the second binder from Stahl's desk. "There's another one. Gustav Fielding, an alien and a communist. Attempted escape, August twenty-third, 1942. Shot while resisting the guards."

"A feisty one!" someone commented, surprised.

"Fat lot of good it did him," Stahl murmured and, once again, the men guffawed.

"Oh, there's a successful escape!" Burgess's eyes widened in spite of himself. "Dora Davidsohn, an enemy alien and a communist."

It took me all my strength to remember how to breathe.

"Escaped, July fourteen, 1942. Presumed dead."

"Why presumed dead?" I asked, keeping the tremor out of my voice by sheer willpower.

"The holding camp from which she ran is in the middle of wilderness. When she hadn't turned up in one of the nearby villages and towns, they presumed she hadn't survived the forest."

"Maybe the wolves got her," Wenzel suggested.

I glared at him. *You'd like that, wouldn't you?*

"The heat, probably. The heat and the absence of water. It gets awful hot here in July," I murmured, thanking all the higher powers there were for the absence of prisoners' photos in the SS binders.

"And there's another one. Same day, but this fellow didn't make it," Stahl said gleefully, licking his finger and turning the page. "Alfred Benjamin, an enemy alien, a Jew and a communist. Shot multiple times as he was attempting escape."

"Rotten luck, son of Israel. Looks like you're not so God-chosen after all, eh?"

"This is getting too morbid." Burgess snapped the binder shut and reached for Stahl's as well. "Let's talk about something more pleasant. Renée, you promised to tell us how that story ended, when your neighbor back in Alsace discovered that his wife was seeing the milkman behind his back?"

"Yes, Renée, tell us! The boss walked in at the most interesting moment last time and we didn't get to hear it."

My heart dead as a stone, I swallowed the tears and jammed them deep into my throat; yanked the strings of my smile until it hurt and began my story, entertaining the SS who'd mocked my husband's death just moments ago, trading pastries for lives and my own soul for nothing.

TWENTY-SIX

I mourned Alfred alone, in the solitude of my rented room. At first, there was only disbelief. There must have been a mistake. He hadn't been shot but *shot at*, to stop him from running; reinterned perhaps; punished, beaten—yes, but not dead. Alfred, my brilliant, kind, unbreakable Alfred couldn't have been reduced to a dead body hurled away by a couple of inmates, thrown and forgotten in some ditch without as much as a grave marker to dignify his death with.

Then, came numbness. Overwhelming, tingling numbness, heavy like a sack of rocks, pressing me down closer and closer to the ground, where I was sitting, right there on the ice-cold floor with my knees pulled up close to my chest, thinking that this was where I belonged now—in the ground, together with him.

After that, came tears. At long last, they broke through the dam, utterly prohibiting any emotion from showing, and choked me with such force, I was left gasping for air, clawing at my throat and wailing like a wounded animal. I wept until my eyes stung with salt, until my chest was aching, until there were no more tears left to cry.

After that, came silence. Silence, and the sound of my own breathing that was somehow louder than sobs.

And as the night descended, along with it descended fury, the blinding power of which I hadn't experienced before. I was craving revenge with the same primeval hunger a wild beast craves blood. Rage was washing over me, wave after wave, and I allowed myself to revel in it, to drink it in until it filled me up; to drown in it until nothing was left in me from the old Dora, from the kind Dora—the Dora whom they had killed along with Alfred that night.

I mourned Alfred alone and for one night only, for when the morning dawned, I was ready to obliterate the entire world that had tried to obliterate me.

"You don't seem yourself, Renée, my love."

I looked up from my shorthand pad to discover Klaus Barbie gazing at me intently. He had seemingly lost all interest in the Resistance member he had captured not a day ago, seizing him on the train station after another *résistant*, beaten within a breath of his life, pointed him out to the chief of the Lyon Gestapo.

The man's name was Hardy. I didn't know him, but knew enough of him—from Claude and the Frenchman—to realize the danger in which his capture had put not only Hardy's own cell, but the few cells in Paris. Unlike the strictly local opera-tors, Hardy presented a lifeline between the Lyon and Paris Resistance, with a direct line to de Gaulle himself—the leader of Free France presently directing the Resistance actions from London.

"I'm fine, Herr Hauptsturmführer." I forced a smile, appeasing those glacial, inquisitive eyes. "Just a headache."

"You aren't getting sick on me, are you?" Leaving his deathly pale victim alone, Barbie approached my desk and, his brow creased with a concern that would make any physician proud, touched my forehead with the back of his hand. It took me all my effort not to recoil from his touch. "You're a tad warm."

"I'm fine, Herr Hauptsturmführer, really."

"I can let you go home, if you aren't feeling well. Wenzel knows shorthand and can finish for you."

Behind his back, Wenzel glared at his boss for burdening him with such an unmanly task when he was itching to put his fists to Hardy's face instead. However, he caught himself swiftly and looked at his polished boots. Not even the SS wished to incur Barbie's infamous wrath. They'd seen too well what he was capable of—the Butcher of Lyon with a body count going into the hundreds now, the only man whom the Resistance truly feared, for he broke bones first and asked questions later.

And yet, the one man who hadn't suffered at his hands was Alfred. Like a fever sending tremors through my limbs, a thought that it was the French who'd killed my husband and not the Germans kept coursing through my veins, plaguing my mind, driving me madder and madder by the minute.

"It's nothing serious, Herr Hauptsturmführer. Just a headache, I promise."

He regarded me for an infinitely long moment, during which I was wondering whether he saw the puffiness around my eyes, the burst blood vessels around my nose from all that weeping the night before, and had somehow, with his animal-istic sixth sense, put two and two together. Who knew if he was aware of all of the secret shenanigans happening in the SS quarters in his absence? Who knew if the same Wenzel reported everything I said and asked on a regular basis? But I held Barbie's gaze all the same and smiled brighter until my jaw ached.

Barbie nodded to some thoughts of his, reached into his pocket and produced a small roll of pills with SS lightning bolts on the wrapper. "Here. Best aspirin in Germany. Will cure your headache in no time." He watched me dry-swallow them and nodded once again, satisfied.

I wished to hate him with all my being, but for the life of me I couldn't see the enemy in him at that moment. It was the French who had mistrusted me, who had incarcerated me, who had murdered the man I loved and who were still using me without much regard for my safety. It suddenly occurred to me that neither Claude nor the Frenchman would bat an eye were I uncovered. Perhaps, would only shrug it off with an "oh well, I guess she wasn't a Nazi infiltrator after all," and toast to my memory.

Or not even that.

All at once, out of nowhere, a wave of such black hatred washed over me, I thought I would howl with grief and the maddening desire to inflict the same pain I was feeling on the nation that had wronged me so after everything I'd given it. The trouble was, the man in front of me wasn't my friend either. He only cared for me for the same reason the French treated me with such suspicion: I was a German. It was my blessing and my curse and only I could decide which side to choose now that I neither had anything else to lose nor much to fight for.

"As for my headache," Barbie said, turning back to Hardy and pinning him down with his impish stare, "no aspirin in the world is enough to cure it. Now, Monsieur Hardy, you have two choices: first, you continue your work for the Resistance with the only change being you'll report everything to me. Names, cells, organization, supply routes, maquis hideouts, dropout zones—everything."

"I'll take the second choice."

In spite of the fear written plainly on his pallid brow covered with beads of sweat, Hardy hadn't been defeated yet. He was still trying to bargain, to persuade himself that he could withstand what the others couldn't.

"My good fellow, you haven't heard it yet."

"I assume you'll try to torture me into submission. It won't do you any good. And any *résistant* knows to grow suspicious once one of us goes off the grid for more than three days. You only have two left to release me. If you try to beat me into cooperation with you, they'll see the injuries and will avoid me like the plague. So, the other only option you have is to kill me. So, get it over with, because I won't reveal any names to you and you shall be only wasting your precious time."

Barbie smiled at him as one would at a child. "But, Monsieur Hardy, that was not my second choice at all."

Hardy blinked at him, suddenly on guard.

"You're quite right. I can't hold you here for long, so the sooner we come to an agreement, the better. You're also right that I can't physically hurt you, for it shall betray me—and you —to our now common enemy at once. Neither shall I kill you. It is rather counterproductive. No, my friend." Barbie's grin turned outright devilish. "The second choice is you continue working for the Resistance and still report everything to me, but without your lovely lady friend to go home to at night. In fact, I have one of my men with her right now, waiting for my signal to kill her. A robbery gone wrong. Times are tough for people, with war and rationing; you understand? And she has such nice silver, her grandmother's. And that beautiful ring you gave her as a promise to marry her once all this war business was over."

Hardy's face turned ashen. In his lap, his hands began to tremble faintly. He clasped them together.

His terror struck a chord with me; opened the wound that was still much too fresh and sliced into it even deeper.

"I don't promise he won't violate her in the process. To make it look more realistic," Barbie continued, suddenly interested in his nails. "Wenzel was begging me to go, but I gathered it would be safer to send a French fellow instead of a German. You know him, by the way. He used to man the secure mailbox you people used to exchange messages. It hasn't been secure in about two months now"—in spite of himself, Barbie burst into laughter, positively delighted with the joke—"and Gaston the Fisherman had been turned even before that and you all were none the wiser, but that's irrelevant."

Hardy's face fell at such a brutal announcement of this betrayal. He didn't wish to believe a single word; I could see it written clear in his eyes, but Barbie knew their cell inside out— there was no avoiding the fact. He even knew what ring Hardy had bought for his beloved. He had been following the man for months now.

I straightened in my seat, peering into Hardy's tortured eyes, pleading with him silently to make the right choice. Naturally, he was unaware of the silent war inside of me, of the invisible knot tightening around my stomach—*choose wisely, my good fellow, for if you decide wrong, if you don't redeem your entire nation through this one action, I'll lose the last faith in humanity and drown myself in the Rhône this very evening.*

"Yes, Gaston works for me now and I pay him very well. Just like Caesar, the proprietor of that *bouchon* you all loved to favor. He'd been reporting all conversations to me, the little weasel! Just like Marianne. She's ours too now. Everyone sooner or later chooses our side, Monsieur Hardy. It's only logical." Barbie spread his arms in a disarming gesture, grinning ear to ear, and, all of a sudden, it became easy to hate him and his cunning, manipulative ways, his whole rotten, sadistic nature.

For a short instant, I expected Hardy to lunge at him; to make a grab for a gun bulging in his civilian jacket's pocket; to reach for the crowbar resting on the floor by Wenzel's chair; to grab that chair and bash them both over their heads before shooting them—anything really. But all he did in the end was drop his head on his chest and agree to everything without Barbie touching a single hair on his head.

Everyone eventually did. No one could outwit the Butcher and live to tell the tale.

"Hardy is turned."

I was still out of breath, leaning against the counter of a pharmacy where Claude worked when he wasn't busy with the Resistance business. It was early evening, a busy time of day, when the trams rang their bells incessantly at the commuters and their bikes, and lines outside the stores began to form with truly astonishing speed.

At the end of the narrow glass counter, another pharmacist was serving an elderly gentleman. Throwing a glance at his colleague, his customer and another woman browsing the shelves with a five-year-old child in tow, Claude grasped me by the elbow and, flipping the wooden partition separating the counter into two sections open, maneuvered me towards the window.

"Have you completely lost your mind?" he hissed at me, staring over my shoulder at the street outside. "Coming in here —" An expletive bitten back, more huffing and puffing. "Have I not told you, this is for emergencies only!"

"This is an emergency, Claude. In case you missed it the first time, Hardy is turned. You ought to warn Paris before he goes there and does any damage."

"How do you know you haven't been followed here?"

"Are you listening at all to what I'm saying?"

"Are you?"

For a few increasingly tense moments, it was a staring contest between us.

With a resigned sigh, Claude threw his hands up. "All right. You're already here. May as well report."

"Someone sold out Hardy. And Barbie threatened his lady friend with death in case he doesn't comply."

Hardy had had tears in his eyes as they'd been leading him away and I couldn't help smiling. Not out of some perverse triumph as Barbie must have suspected, but because Hardy had chosen right, because he'd made me see light when I was drowning in black waters of despair. Hardy was the reason I'd ran all the way here. Hardy was the reason I still cared enough to risk my life, just so men like him could live and fight for the women they loved. The feeling of witnessing such fierce love and loyalty exist in times of such darkness warmed me once again.

"Barbie has already released Hardy, a few hours before I could leave work and warn you. You must do something to warn Paris, but try to be subtle if you can. Tell them to turn him back so, instead of reporting to Barbie, he can supply him with misinformation without knowing it. This way, neither Hardy nor his lady friend suffer and Barbie will be none the wiser."

Claude nodded. "We'll take care of it. Don't fret. I understand that you're afraid that the SS will suspect you—"

"I'm not afraid of anything," I countered calmly. "It's just, if they realize it's me, they'll kill me and then who will help you with all the inside work?"

"Well, thank you kindly for your concern." His tone was meant to be mocking, but there was an undertone of respect and, for some reason, melancholy to it. "Anything else?"

"Yes." *My husband is dead, but the only good German is a dead German and so I'll just carry his death in my heart and to hell with your sympathies I won't believe in anyway.* "Someone named Gaston the Fisherman is now working for Barbie as well. And some fellow named Caesar?"

Claude wiped his hands down his face, muttering more curses under his breath. He knew the names. And, apparently, was now aware of two more traitors in our midst.

"Also, Marianne."

This time, Claude blinked. "Who's that?"

I shrugged. "I have just as much idea as you."

"Did Barbie give any indication as to what she was doing, who she was connected with?"

"No. Not a hint. I'll try to pry it out of my Gestapo colleagues—"

"Don't. Too suspicious. We'll sort it out ourselves."

"As you wish."

From the corner of my eye, I noticed Claude's colleague throwing yet another dirty glance in his direction. While we were standing by the window, the small silver bell over the door rang almost incessantly. The pharmacy was getting busy with commuters in search of cold medicine on their way home—or morphine, if they could afford it—and Claude's fellow pharmacist was growing impatient serving them all alone.

"I'm leaving, I promise!" I cried cheerfully for his benefit and threw my arms around Claude's neck, thinking just how strange it felt, hugging this man who was not my husband. Same strong shoulders under my arms, a similar scent of aftershave and something masculine and faintly familiar, and yet all alien and wrong at the same time. He stiffened even further in my embrace. "It's only for show. I won't molest you, don't fret."

"I don't." He was gazing somewhere past my shoulder, suddenly misty-eyed and infinitely miserable. "I have lost someone... recently and this"—another shuddering breath—"feels too much like a betrayal."

I let my arms fall by my sides. "Was she in the Resistance?"

A shake of the head full of some desolate finality. "No. Jewish. They put her on the train and that was that."

I rubbed my chest that was suddenly swollen with emotion, feeling like a right swine for hating his entire nation solely because one drunk guard was much too trigger-happy. A decision came to me that had been brewing for some time and it was clear as the sound of the bell ringing yet another customer in.

I squeezed Claude's hand by means of goodbye. "Meet me

at Place Bellecour, under the statue's horse's tail, after you finish work tomorrow. It's on your way home."

He narrowed his eyes at me.

"I'll make it worth your while, I promise."

With that, I pecked him on his cheek for the audience's benefit and disappeared into the swiftly falling night, blending with the shadows, a shadow myself.

TWENTY-SEVEN

It was almost curfew time. In the diffusive light of the lamps, people hurrying home turned into mere silhouettes, washed-out ghosts with pallid faces, haunting the streets of Lyon and haunted themselves. In the growing silence of the streets being rapidly emptied of life, the echo of women's wooden heels resembled the sound of nails being driven into a coffin, one sharp rap after another.

Somewhere in the distance, like great bumblebees, heavy bombers buzzed on their way to destruction. Directly over my head, the searchlights probed the skies for the enemy flyers. The tide of the war was turning for Germany. From all fronts, the Allies were creeping closer and closer, severing retreat routes and supply lanes; liberating Italian cities in which just yesterday the Germans were drinking famous red wine and enjoying their promenades along the ancient cobbled streets; sweeping aside the last German resistance in Africa like an unforgiving sandstorm; pushing them out of Soviet Russia with every salvo of the famous Stalin's organ—the dreaded Katyusha rocket launchers. Even here, in still-German Lyon, the air was beginning to take on a tinge of gunpowder. The distant winds carried it from faraway coasts and I inhaled lungfuls until I grew dizzy with the promise of freedom.

Punctual to the second, Claude materialized out of the darkness, flowers in hand to appear inconspicuous—a simple lover on the way to meet his beloved; *résistant* to the marrow of his bones.

"You shouldn't have," I said, planting a kiss on his cheek.

"They're geraniums," he said in the same low tone. "Stole them from someone's windowsill on the way here."

I bit back a chuckle and threaded my hand through the crook of his arm. "Walk with me a bit."

For some time, as we measured the plaza with our unhurried steps, there was only the sound of our breathing mixing together and the hushed whispers of our clothes touching each other.

As if sensing the gravity of the moment, Claude stayed perfectly silent to give me all the time I needed to gather myself for whatever unsavory business I had summoned him here for. He'd been in the Resistance long enough. He had long grown to know these subtleties.

"I found out about my husband." My voice sounded cold and alien in this cold and alien night.

"Oh, yes?" There was no excitement in his voice. Only infinite sadness, as if he'd already known where this was going.

"He was shot while attempting escape. On the same night when I succeeded in mine."

"I'm sorry, Renée." He pulled his hand out of his pocket and wrapped his arm tightly around me, placing all of his sympathy into one comradely gesture. "I truly am."

"I know you are. Thank you."

"Damned rotten business, losing someone you love."

I nodded, feeling the rough tweed of his coat against my cheek. There was nothing romantic about our nocturnal stroll, even with our arms wrapped around one another. No; we were merely holding on to each other, like two drowning people just keeping one another afloat in this shipwreck of a life caused by this damned war. "I know the curfew's soon. I won't hold you any longer. Just wanted to give you something."

"Curfews are for cowards and collaborators. I have all the time in the world."

I grinned in gratitude for the jest, dug into my pocket and produced a small black notebook.

Claude's expression clouded over when, after revealing it to him for a moment, I dropped it into his pocket. "Whatever this is, I already don't like it."

"Oh, but you will. As soon as you open it once you get home. I know that the Frenchman will like it even better."

"Renée—"

"It's a complete list of all the Lyon Gestapo's SS staff—names, ranks, physical descriptions, crimes committed, along with the names of their victims. I've been assembling it for some time. Finished it a few weeks ago but..." A ragged breath tore from my chest. "I was going to hand it over to you at the end of the war, but then I thought, why wait?"

I laughed, but Claude didn't buy either my bravado or the laughter itself. It came out too strangled and hollow to lend it any credibility.

"One thing you have to promise to me. Get the list to London and make sure they blast their names all over the BBC. I want the entire world to know them and to hunt them down once this is all over."

"Renée, don't do this. Barbie will realize at once who is behind all this."

"I know. It makes no difference."

"This is assisted suicide if ever I've seen one and I will have no part of it," he announced and tried to give me a stare that was meant to instill some sense into me, only I'd long since grown immune to such stares.

"But, my dear Claude," I said, smiling at him with a tender smile full of wistful melancholy, "in that case, I shall simply give it to the Frenchman."

He stopped abruptly, took me by the shoulders as though to give me a thorough shake; had already opened his mouth for one lecture or another... but then saw something in my eyes and dropped his arms by his sides in utter helplessness.

"So I see you have decided everything for yourself. My brave Renée."

"My name is Dora. Dora Benjamin, née Davidsohn. Make sure they know it once..."

"They will. I'll see to it personally that they will."

The bell on the old church chimed a quarter to eight. Claude grasped me briskly, planted the tenderest kiss on my forehead and swung on his heel to march back into the night, as though it was unbearable to him, just standing next to me another moment. And I remained standing alone in the darkness, feeling oddly at home with my decision, finally at peace.

The morning of Wednesday dawned misty and late. Thick waves of fog rolled along the Rhône, seeping into the streets of the city, soaking it to the bone. Inside the Gestapo quarters, though, there was none of the translucent serenity of the streets of Lyon. There were only grim faces, bristling remarks and a general air of mistrust hanging like a cloud over the corridors and offices, creating no difference between high-ranking officers and their lowest underlings. All of them had heard the news by now and whoever hadn't heard the BBC translation blasting their names all around the world had learned about it from their colleagues the very next day. Suddenly, everyone was looking over their shoulder, scanning their own ranks for the traitor in their midst.

Everyone, except for Klaus Barbie.

Exceptionally calm, he strolled through the carpeted hallways whistling a classical tune to himself and jested with the secretaries and even inmates as if he hadn't been officially declared to be one of the most wanted war criminals among the Nazis; as if the whole of Europe didn't whisper his name with loathing and an equal amount of fear—the Butcher of Lyon.

For seven days now he had made no effort to address the situation. Among themselves, his agents began to question if it bothered him at all, the fact that there was a Resistance insider among their very staff. Only the grave fear he instilled in them prevented them from voicing their concerns openly.

All these days I came to work awaiting the ax to drop on my neck. My nerves had been frayed; I jumped at every sound, torn between resignation and an almost instinctual, animalistic fear of death... or, what was even worse, what would precede it. I'd seen far too many of my fellow Resistance fighters being broken—both physically and emotionally—by the Butcher to believe otherwise. And yet, he smiled at me just as charmingly as before and even complimented me on my new hairstyle that very Wednesday morning. There was no hairstyle; I had simply chopped it all off the night before out of sheer nerves and accumulating madness.

"You should have cut your hair a long time ago, Renée. It was a shame, hiding that gorgeous swan neck of yours."

For an instant, the palm of his hand landed on my bare skin just above my collar and I froze as though he held a blade to my throat.

"Thank you, Herr Hauptsturmführer."

"Are you very busy now, Renée?"

The hand was gone but the sensation of being branded with those graceful, cruel fingers remained.

"Not too busy, Herr Hauptsturmführer."

"Could you help me type out yet another idiotic report for Berlin? I'd ask Burgess, but he'll just make twenty typos per fifteen words. They're all out of sorts after that BBC affair, as if it matters all that much."

"Doesn't it?"

Barbie only raised his brows and grinned at me, amused with the suggestion that something of that kind should bother him in the slightest.

I followed him out of the staff office and into his personal one. It was beautifully paneled in oak, with a grand piano in the corner and plenty of Aubusson rugs muffling our steps—the cozy living room of someone who likes to entertain; certainly not an office from which orders to arrest, execute, and mutilate were being dispatched on a daily basis.

"Sit, sit," Barbie said, gesturing toward his own chair behind his exquisitely carved desk. "Make yourself comfortable. We ought to invent something plausible for those feebleminded Berlin donkeys to swallow, so it'll take some time."

I moved the typewriter toward myself and adjusted the paper.

"Well, don't just look at me for instruction." Barbie laughed his silvery laugh. "You know how it goes. Top corner: Office of the Reichsführer SS Heinrich Himmler. Then, greeting: Reichsführer, exclamation point. You know the drill."

I quickly typed the formulaic greeting and looked up at him again with my hands poised over the keys. He ceased his leisurely pacing for a moment and was watching me closely, the same enigmatic grin on his face.

"And now comes the difficult part, Renée. How do we explain what happened to the Reichsführer?"

With tremendous effort, I forced myself to hold his gaze. On the opposite wall, the tall clock was ticking loudly, though much slower than my heart. It was thrashing inside my chest like a bird battering its wings against the glass, trapped, petrified to the utmost. The room was suddenly devoid of air. Time itself stood still.

At last, Barbie resumed his stroll in front of the desk, back and forth, back and forth, hands clasped behind his back. "I don't know where the leak came from. Do you?" Stopping abruptly, he arched a playful brow at me.

Painfully aware of cold sweat breaking on my temples, I forced something akin to an amused snort—*naturally I don't; what a silly question, ha-ha!*

Barbie nodded slowly, deliberately. "And since neither of us knows the truth, we'll just have to improvise. Correct?"

"I don't see any other option, Herr Hauptsturmführer." How my voice managed to remain so calm and steady was utterly beyond my understanding.

"Good. Improvise, it is. I suggest telling him that the leak came from the outside. The Resistance people were watching us for a few months, learned our names, and released them to the general public. What do you say?"

I should have feigned enthusiasm, nodded eagerly—*yes, yes, sounds absolutely splendid, let's write just that!*—but it was too idiotic a suggestion and he'd made it on purpose just to see my reaction, knowing perfectly well that I was smarter than that.

"I don't think he'll believe it, Herr Hauptsturmführer."

"No?" He appeared almost upset.

"There were too many personal details revealed about the SS staff for him to believe that it came from an outside source."

"Oh no, Renée, not you too!" Barbie cried, making a theatrically desperate gesture with his hands. "You don't honestly believe that we have a traitor among our ranks, do you? Among the staff that I selected personally, down to the last cleaning woman." He suddenly gasped, widening his eyes. "Was it the cleaning woman? What do you think? She's here often enough. Perhaps she's been a Resistance agent all this time. Shall I summon her here and interrogate her? I bet she'll confess."

I bet she would too, after he'd held her hand over a gas burner until the entire inside of her palm turned black.

"I don't think it was the cleaning lady, Herr Hauptsturmführer."

"Oh no?" He threw me a curious look from under his lowered eyelashes. "And why not?"

"To begin with, she only speaks rudimentary German."

"That can be a ruse."

I acknowledged such a possibility with a nod. "There was too much information in that leak that she would be unfamiliar with."

"Such as?"

I regarded him with accusation. Did he truly want me to spell it out for him? "Such as the victims' names."

"*Ach*, yes, yes; stupid me!" He slapped himself on his forehead. The act would be almost hilarious, had it not been so sinister. "The victims' names and the supposed crimes committed against them by specific officers. See? That's why I need you here. I would have entirely forgotten about it and made a complete fool of myself in front of the Reichsführer."

His smile of gratitude was almost sincere. Only the eyes remained glacial, watchful.

"So, who then, Renée? One of our own? An SS man whose conscience suddenly turned him against his own brethren in favor of those pitiful creatures fighting for their sorry freedom?"

I made no reply.

"Come now, Renée, don't hold back. Tell me your theory. You're the savviest secretary here. You were Brandt's favorite back when you worked at his military post office. He didn't want to part with you and was devastated when I stole you from him. And you're not only my favorite; you're my officers' favorite as well. Always bringing them treats, always inquiring about their families back home, talking them through their cases. No, no, no need to look so alarmed, my dear Renée." He held up his hand. "It was never my intention to embarrass you, or my men. I love all of those bastards, but I'll be damned, sometimes they aren't the sharpest tools in the box and they need help. There's no shame in helping them look good in front of their superior by asking them about their cases. It only goes to show how much you care. Doesn't it, Renée?"

I nodded, my neck stiff as a board.

"Yes, you care. I care too, and that's why I hate to even entertain the idea of one of my loyal men being the traitor. But there is no other option. Is there, Renée?"

He pinned me down with his razor-sharp gaze like a live butterfly to a board. With the best will in the world, I couldn't stop my hands from trembling faintly over the typewriter.

"The secretaries," I croaked, my throat suddenly dry and scratchy. I cleared it to Barbie's inquisitive look—*The what?*— and repeated in my normal voice, louder this time, "The secretaries, Herr Hauptsturmführer. There are also secretaries to be considered."

His eyes sparkled with inexplicable mirth. "*Ach*, that's right. The secretaries. How silly of me to forget. Naturally, the secretaries! Now, that's much more plausible."

He'd known it was me all along, it occurred to me just then. He'd known this entire time, from the very beginning, and, as was his habit, had been toying with me like a cat with a mouse waiting for the perfect opportunity to strike.

"So, one of those French bitches then, eh? Who do you think it was? Or shall I just arrest them all and interrogate them myself until one of them confesses? Yes, I think I'll do just that. You write that to the Reichsführer. That we have detected the perpetrators and they shall be liquidated shortly. And their family members punished in retribution accordingly. To set an example for all other so-called freedom fighters who wish to go against us."

The milky-white morning was slowly turning into the darkest of nightmares. He wasn't threatening me with just one cleaning lady any longer; he was threatening me with the lives of not only eight innocent women, but all of their closest family members, who would undoubtedly be shot or hanged in retribution for the crimes they didn't commit. No one would be spared the Butcher's wrath—neither elderly grandmothers nor the youngest of children. And he kept staring at me, grinning like a serpent, asking the silent question that hung between us like a sword ready to drop: *Is that what you want, Renée? All of these lives on your unclean conscience? All you have to do is to say nothing and I'll make you the reason all of those people are dead. I'll make you a killer, one of us. Will you be able to live with yourself then?*

"I don't think it's wise arresting all of them, Herr Hauptsturmführer."

"Why not?"

"First, it won't be such a good look for you in the Reichsführer's eyes, the fact that you could have so many Resistance agents working here under your nose."

"Agreed. What's second?"

"Second, it's easy to deduct which one of them is the spy. You only have to put together the names of the victims that were leaked and the person who typed reports or files related to them."

I hated that I had to explain just how he was to go about proving that it was me all along; hated having to play this game with him, but there was really nothing else for it but to follow his demented lead until he grew tired of this charade.

But Barbie was nowhere near finished. Perching on the edge of his desk within arm's reach of me, he tapped his chin a few times, suddenly very interested in the plasterwork surrounding the ceiling. "Sometimes Wenzel typed them."

"So, it can be Wenzel then." I had no qualms about Wenzel. Wenzel could go to the devil for all I cared.

"But why would Wenzel help the Resistance? He's a more rabid nationalist than I am and, frankly, he hates the French."

I shrugged. "We have no insight into those men's hearts, Herr Hauptsturmführer. He may have fallen in love with a French woman and—"

"Wenzel? In love?" Barbie burst into laughter. "Renée, you're being ridiculous now. Come, don't make me doubt your deductive abilities. We both know it wasn't Wenzel."

"Who then?" I asked him, suddenly very tired of this blasted charade.

Barbie leaned so close to me, I could feel the warmth of his breath on my cheek as he said, very softly, "You tell me."

For a few interminably long moments, it felt as though it was just me and him in the entire universe. This was what hell must be like: the person you loathe and fear the most and you, locked in the same purgatory for eternity. This was what the devil must have looked like: young, handsome, impossibly charming, but with hellish fire in his eyes, a mouth watering with the desire to submit you to such tortures you would plead with him to end, but there is no end to suffering in hell and that's the reason why he waits, why he has all the time in the world to play with you before the hellish work begins.

I was about to spit my own name out at him in my last act of defiance when the door to the office flew open and Burgess, disheveled and wild-eyed, broke into it against all regulations.

"Herr Hauptsturmführer, forgive me for the interruption, but there has been a terrorist act in the SS café, Moulin à Vent. A bomb went off," he rattled off, still trying to catch his breath after his marathon up several flights of stairs. "Several officers wounded. We don't know how many are dead. We have the car ready for you downstairs. I've already dispatched an armed team there; we're only waiting for you now."

Throwing a last hateful look at me, Barbie was instantly on his feet, snapping his fingers at Burgess as he passed him by at the door. "You stay here with her and make sure she doesn't leave this room; you understand? Guard her with your sorry life, if you know what's good for you!"

With that, he was gone, not forgetting to slam the door after himself.

Completely at a loss, Burgess stared blankly at the door, then at me; blinked a few times before recognition changed his expression from one of utter bewilderment to disappointment and embarrassment.

Disappointment, I could still understand, but the fact that he wouldn't meet my eyes after Barbie's explicit order was more than odd. I had expected anger, hissed curses under his breath, but not that mute studying of the carpet.

"Burgess, I—"

"You don't have to say anything," he interrupted me in the same mild voice. "I completely understand. It's my mistake, I didn't know."

I scowled in spite of myself, confused even further.

Burgess continued. "He's certainly very protective of you. It's... nice."

"The—" I stumbled over my own words, the realization of the extent of Burgess' mistake dawning on me just then.

The poor sod, he had assumed Barbie had ordered him to guard me with his life because I was his mistress whom he didn't wish to fall into "those terrorists' hands"; not a suspect he couldn't possibly let out of his sight, not now that he had me, finally had me right here in the palm of his hand, with all the information that could be squeezed out of me with the last drop of my blood.

"Yes, he is very..." I swallowed; passed the hand over my

damp forehead; laughed at such impossible coincidence. "I have to go wash my face. Do you mind?"

"No, of course not." At the door, which he gallantly held open for me, Burgess paused momentarily, seized by a sudden doubt. "You aren't going outside to look at the damage, are you?"

I couldn't help myself; reached out and took his face into my hands. "I swear on my life, I wouldn't go anywhere near it."

Aware of his eyes still on me, I walked along the corridor and turned toward the wing where the restrooms neighbored the narrow side staircase; pushed the staircase door open and, unnoticed by anyone in the general commotion, descended to the ground floor and walked out of the lair of the beast, unharmed.

As a natural curtain, the folds of mist enveloped me as soon as I stepped into the street. For an instant, I couldn't get my breath. The air suddenly refused to enter my lungs, leaving me gasping for it, lightheaded, on the verge of fainting. I tasted metal on my tongue. Inside my ears, the blood pulsed so violently, I could scarcely get my bearings. It took all my effort to slow my steps when my entire body screamed at me to burst into a run—*run, run, and run even further, even faster, little rabbit, before the hounds recover your scent.*

The fog distorted the sounds and angles of the familiar streets and I could no longer tell whether I had truly caught a faint scent of cordite in the air or whether it was my imagination, overexcited by my nerves, playing tricks on me. All around, uniforms and civilians emerged from the milky ether and disappeared back into it almost at once as they passed me. Along the river, the barge issued a foghorn full of mournful, desolate finality. Haunted land all around me, a night terror in which one was doomed to roam for eternity. And somewhere in this maze of streets, the Grim Reaper himself was riding his black Citroën with his hell hounds in tow and it was anyone's guess if I walked right into them as I turned the next corner.

But instead of Barbie and his henchmen, a small corner motel's charwoman got to me first. A thin scream issued from my lips as the dirty water from her bucket splashed my feet, instantly soaking them. For a few seconds, we stared at one another like two idiots. She hesitated before cursing and apologizing; had just opened her mouth but closed it again and retreated slowly back into the motel's entrance holding a bucket in front of herself like a shield. I didn't blame her: somewhere in this mist, someone was cackling like mad. The howling laughter echoing around the narrow street sent ice needles down my spine as well...

An entire minute must have passed before I realized that it was me who was laughing. The thought was so unexpectedly sobering, I drew myself up at once; turned my head this way and that to orient myself; located the street leading in the direction of Moulin à Vent and set off in the opposite one.

Before long, I reached Claude's pharmacy. He took one look at me, instantly understood, and told his colleague to go hang himself when he demanded just where Monsieur Claude thought he was going in the middle of the workday.

In the street, he pulled his white medical gown off and draped it over my shoulders. And just like that, we were no longer two suspicious *résistants*, but medics on official business. Our haste had purpose about it now. No passerby spared us a second glance as we hurried onto the tram and hopped off on some nondescript narrow street—surely to attend to a bedridden patient. Even if questioned by the Gestapo later, they would only recall a white smock and Claude's clean-shaven, trustworthy face.

"Two medics, yes," they would agree on their shared illusion and fill the gaps of their memory with what their imagination would find suitable.

"A medical bag in her hand."

"A stethoscope around his neck."

"Two white gowns, yes."

"Masks hanging under their chins. Spoke of a tubercular patient they were about to see."

"A case of a burst appendix."

"Why, they were on their way to help you fellows after that attack. They were heading straight to Moulin à Vent."

And even if my former chief Barbie sniffed out my trail eventually—he was a bloodhound of the highest order after all—I would be long gone by then. Of that Claude assured me as he pressed the passport into my hand that he had stashed for me a week ago.

"Had a feeling you would need it soon enough," he grinned.

I had already changed into factory worker attire my thoughtful comrade had squirreled away as well: oil-stained overalls, a sweater of an unidentifiable color and a kerchief over my hair, tied in such a way it covered most of it, concealing its shape and color. I was a chameleon once again, blending perfectly with the environment and all but dissolving in it with each new skin shed. Years of living in hiding did that to a person. I could no longer recall what real Dora looked like.

"Don't talk too much on the train," Claude mumbled by way of goodbye as we stood in the doors of his rented apartment. "Your damned Boche accent..."

I smiled through the tears of gratitude. One more friend lost. Hopefully, not forever. "I'll fall asleep as soon as I board. Not even a maquis attack shall wake me, I promise."

He nodded, reluctant to let go of my hand. "Good. Don't 'wake up' till you reach Marseille."

"I heard our troops shall be there soon."

Ordinarily, he would make a joke about *my* troops being there for months now and overstaying their welcome quite a bit, but the moment was much too sorrowful and tender for such jests. He knew precisely what I meant. *Our* troops. The Allied troops. Liberators.

"Welcome them on our behalf, will you, Dora?"

The lump in my throat made it impossible to form any words, so I just nodded and, instead of shaking his hand, wrapped my arms around him and squeezed him as tightly as I could.

"It was an honor serving with you, Dora."

"It was an honor serving with you too, Claude."

EPILOGUE

BERLIN, SOVIET OCCUPATION ZONE. 1946

"And it was. My greatest honor. In no time, I was on my way out of Lyon. And that's how I escaped the Butcher of Lyon himself. A feat not too many are alive today to brag about, I suppose."

Hans Schaul, the journalist who was interviewing me for the first Soviet-German newspaper, placed his shorthand pad on top of the coffee table and removed his steel-rimmed glasses. He was my age but, just like everyone who'd gone through what we'd gone through, looked older than his years, his intelligent, handsome face lined with suffering and memories that still haunted us at nights—sleepless for the most part or filled with nightmares of the past.

"That's... quite a story," he said softly. "And I've heard quite a few of them by now."

"You have quite a few of your own, from what you've told me."

He waved my comment off as if such an unworthy comparison with the "Resistance heroine" he was planning to paint me as embarrassed him somehow. "Have you found out what happened to your family?"

I nodded and reached for a crumpled cigarette pack, discovering that it was nearly empty. We'd been talking for several hours now and I'd smoked a great deal. So did he, until we'd clouded my small, rented apartment with a gray, swirling haze. As a former Comintern agent and an antifascist, I was one of the few fortunate ones to receive my own quarters from the new occupying Soviet forces in the capital that had been all but leveled to the ground just a year ago. Widows and mothers who'd lost their sons to the war still climbed mounds of ruins daily, digging out their bloodstained pasts and assembling the memories, along with broken bricks in neat piles to be used for the construction of the new Germany, fresh Germany, free of its fascist past and nationalistic filth.

"All killed in Majdanek in 1942. Gassed upon arrival, after suffering for three years in Buchenwald." I pulled on the cigarette, inhaling bitter smoke that matched my mood just perfectly. "I knew they were dead—or as good as dead—back in 1939, when my fellow Comintern agents failed to locate and extract them. But I only found out how exactly they perished when I returned to Germany. The Red Cross had the lists from every single camp... It didn't take me long to locate their names. First internment—November 1939... Second one, which didn't even last a day—March 1942. The infamous German bureaucracy and the habit of keeping lists and tabs finally came in handy." I grinned crookedly, tasting ash in the back of my throat.

"I'm sorry."

"Me, too."

Hans Schaul lowered his head and was silent for a few moments, honoring their memory.

"I was trying to find my former roommates, Amory and Ashley, once I returned to Berlin."

He glanced up at me with his quick hazel eyes, a spark of hope igniting in them. For some reason, he desperately wished for me to have at least something to return to, someone to share these stories with.

However, I only had him—a journalist with a law degree no one had use for in the immediate postwar months and his shorthand notepad.

"They were both arrested as antisocials and killed in Dachau." I regarded the glowing tip of my cigarette pensively. "The men who taught me how to be anybody. How to switch personas and playact like the best of the Hollywood elite. It was thanks to them that I survived Barbie. And Hitler's thugs went and killed them just because they were different. Because they liked being women when they didn't want to be men. Because they liked silk kimonos and expensive creams for their beautiful faces. God, for as long as I live, I'll never forget their beautiful faces!"

Those last words tore out of my aching chest in a strangled sob, and all of a sudden, I felt Hans Schaul's hand on my back, rubbing it gently in small circles between my shoulder blades; heard his soothing words that I couldn't quite discern but somehow felt comforted by—because he'd lived through persecution too. Because he understood. It was only because of his own past that I had agreed to grant his newspaper this interview.

"I truly am sorry for your friends. And for your family, Frau Benjamin. And for your husband, of course. Frankly, I don't think I would have found enough strength in myself to survive everything you've been through."

I grinned wistfully at the sincere admiration in his voice. "If you had told me, back in 1933, that this would be my path, I would have told you the same thing. That I was not strong enough. That I was not brave enough. That I would never survive it because the pain would be too great. But once you hit the very bottom and you're still somehow alive, there's nowhere else to fall. And so, you collect your broken bones, assemble yourself back into something faintly resembling a person, and begin climbing back up again."

For some time, we sat next to each other in companionable silence. I finished my cigarette and stole a glance at him while stubbing it out in the coffee cup with the broken handle that I'd found in a heap of rubble in the street and had been using as an ashtray ever since. I discovered that I was hoping that he had more questions for me. He looked like he was desperately trying to come up with something as well, but I had told him every-thing and there was nothing else to discuss.

"Well, I suppose this is it." He fidgeted with his notepad and pencil but made no motion to rise from the sofa. "It's been a true pleasure and honor talking to you, Frau Benjamin."

"Please, call me Dora. You know me too well now for such formalities."

"Dora," he repeated with a certain emotion in his voice. Suddenly, his expression brightened a bit. "Oh, just one more thing before I go. If you still have time, of course?" He cocked his head to one side questioningly, almost pleadingly.

"I have all the time in the world, Herr Schaul."

"Please, just Hans."

"Hans." His name rolled off my tongue so easily, as if I'd been saying it my entire life.

"Now that the war is over, what are your plans?"

Now, this was an easy one. "To make sure a new one doesn't happen."

"You'll re-join the antifascists then?"

"I never left."

His grin was growing wider. "And Barbie? He's still missing."

"We'll find him," I said confidently. "I'm still very much in touch with Claude and Hugo. Hugo the Frenchman, the man without the name..." The man who'd mistrusted me so but who'd been the first one to shake my hand and declare me a hero right after France's liberation.

Hans was outright beaming now, baring all of his brilliant teeth at me as he inched nearer. "It's such a fascinating coincidence you've mentioned it! My former colleagues—lawyers, that is, not journalists—are in the middle of organizing their own group of prosecutors under the antifascist movement umbrella. We're planning to join forces with Nazi hunters and help them track down and prosecute escaped war criminals to the full extent of the law. We have the complete backing of the Soviets as well, so if you would ever consider coming to a meeting—"

"Hans, I would love to."

He released a breath and smiled at me with such extraordinary warmth, I felt a small fragment chip off the block of ice into which my heart had turned in the past few years.

"We're gathering this Friday."

"Sounds splendid."

"Would it be all right with you if I come to pick you up? Getting there can be a bit confusing with all of those roads still half-cleared and the street names all changed..."

"Perfectly all right, Hans."

"All right then." He finally rose to his feet, even if with visible reluctance.

"All right." I got up too, smoothing my skirt over my knees.

"I'll be going now."

"Your glasses."

"Oh!" He slapped his forehead and laughed in embarrassment. "Would be difficult to navigate the streets without them."

"I bet." In spite of myself, I was laughing too as I held out his glasses for him—genuinely, for the first time in what felt like years.

At the door, he held my hand for much longer than etiquette required and gazed into my eyes with his frank, hazel ones. In his, also for the first time in years, I saw my own hope for the future reflect with immense intensity—a future worth fighting for, a new dawn, a new world purged of darkness once and for all. Until my dying breath I'd make sure of it, and, after I'm gone, some other young girl shall pick up my banner and carry it proudly upon her shoulder alongside her comrades, alongside her lover, until the evil is purged and banished for good.

A LETTER FROM ELLIE

Dear reader,

I want to say a huge thank you for choosing to read *The Undercover Secretary*. If you did enjoy it, and want to keep up to date with all my latest releases, just sign up at the following link. Your email address will never be shared and you can unsubscribe at any time.

www.bookouture.com/ellie-midwood

Thank you so much for reading the novel inspired by the incredible life story of a very real Resistance heroine, Dora Schaul. While writing it, I tried to stick as close to historical fact as possible, only using creative license to fill the necessary gaps. In my research, I mostly relied on Dora's own recounting of events (she has her own chapter in *Resistance: Erinnerungen deutscher Antifaschisten*) and expanded on whatever was omitted by piecing together accounts of other Resistance fighters operating in the same area at the same time.

Dora's entire life story, beginning with her life in Berlin and immigration to Amsterdam and later Paris, is based on true fact. She indeed met her future husband, Alfred Benjamin, and ended up traveling to Paris along with him not just as his girlfriend but as a fellow Comintern member. After several difficult years as an undocumented immigrant in Paris, Dora tried to apply for a permit to reside in France once the war broke out in

1939 but was instead arrested and incarcerated together with Alfred as an enemy alien and spent a few grueling years in different holding camps. She managed to escape in July 1942, making use of the Bastille Day celebrations; Alfred, however, wasn't as fortunate and was killed during his escape attempt.

As described in the novel, Dora eventually made a connection with a Resistance cell in Lyon and soon became one of its most irreplaceable members due to her position first in the Wehrmacht post office and, later, in the Gestapo quarters with Klaus Barbie as her boss. Countless times she risked her life by gathering and delivering information to the Resistance concerning troop movements, planned operations, the names of the SS men serving under Barbie's charge, their crimes and the names of their victims. It was thanks to her that all of their identities were uncovered and aired all over Europe via the BBC—a feat that could easily have cost Dora her life, but which she still undertook bravely and selflessly.

As you can probably conclude from the epilogue, Dora ended up marrying Hans Schaul, another German antifascist, a lawyer and a journalist, after the war and together they continued their fight to bring to justice whatever Nazi war criminals were still in hiding, including the infamous Butcher of Lyon, Klaus Barbie.

It was thanks to Dora's heroic actions that the heinous crimes of Lyon Gestapo agents, along with their names, were uncovered, resulting in their prosecution (Klaus Barbie was extradited to France in 1983, where he was convicted of crimes against humanity and sentenced to life in prison), and I felt it was incredibly important to bring her story to light, so she could get the recognition she deserved. Huge thanks for reading her story and for spreading the word about this truly remarkable woman.

I hope you loved *The Undercover Secretary* and if you did, I would be very grateful if you could write a review. I'd love to hear what you think, and it makes such a difference helping new readers to discover one of my books for the first time.

Thanks,

Ellie

www.elliemidwood.com

 facebook.com/EllieMidwood

ACKNOWLEDGMENTS

I owe a lot of thanks to so many people for helping me shape Dora's story into the novel you're holding in your hands right now.

My wonderful, incredibly talented editor Christina—huge thanks for all your invaluable input and all the motivational Cavalier pics! Nothing inspires me more than your encouraging words in moments when I doubt even myself. I wouldn't be able to do what I do without you.

To everyone in my lovely publishing family at Bookouture for working relentlessly to help my book babies reach the world. Richard and Peta, you made it possible to have my babies translated into eighteen (!) languages. I know I'm an author, but I honestly have no words to fully express my gratitude to you.

Huge thanks to Jess and Noelle for organizing the best blog tours ever and securing the most interesting interviews for each new release. Even for an introvert like me, you make the publicity aspect a breeze. Working with you is sheer delight!

Ronnie—thank you for all your support and for being the best partner ever! And for keeping all three dogs quiet when I work. I know it's not easy given how crazy they are. I love being on this journey with you.

Vlada and Ana—my sisters from other misters—thank you for all the adventures and the best memories we've already created and keep creating. I don't know how I got so lucky to have you in my life.

Pupper, Joannie and Camille—thank you for all the doggie

kisses and for not spilling coffee on Mommy's laptop even during your countless zoomies. You'll always be my best four-legged muses.

And, of course, the hugest thanks, from the bottom of my heart, to all of you, my wonderful readers. I can never explain how much it means to me, that not only have you taken time out of your busy schedules but that you chose one of my books to read out of millions of others. I write for you. Thank you so much for reading my stories. I love you all.